CON Artist

A Sweet Romantic Comedy By

TIFFANY ANDREA

Paperback ISBN: 978-1-990724-35-0
eBook ISBN: 978-1-990724-34-3

Cover Design by: Burden of Proofreading Publishing featuring Graphics by Kudryashka via DepositPhotos.

Interior Graphics by Marco Livolsi and Mykola Lytvynenko via Canva

www.boppublishing.com

To anyone whose head and heart have been at war with each other.

Table of Contents

Preface

I want to make a quick note here to say that this book is a work of fiction. It is meant to be a feel-good romance with some laughs along the way. It is by no means an FBI procedural drama and is not meant to be a reflection of any present or past FBI agents and their conduct. I'm Canadian, and everything I've learned about the FBI was from Miss Congeniality. Take a second to forget everything you know about federal law enforcement and their protocols. Just go along for the ride.

Also, if you have any potential triggers, please read the warning below.

 DO NOT CROSS 

● JUST KIDDING ● KEEP GOING, YOU REBEL ●

This story has a brief mention of suicidal thoughts and depression, though it is just glanced over in conversation. If this is something that could be troubling for you, please proceed with caution.

Archie

1

L-EVADED

How can someone so beautiful be such a ruthless criminal?

My years in the FBI White-Collar Crime Division should have drilled into my head that you can't assess a threat based on appearance. It's always the smallest guys who are the most dangerous in an altercation. It's always the sweetest-looking old ladies who have the harshest tongues. And it's the gorgeous blondes with piercing blue eyes who roam the streets like a goddess, but secretly operate an art-theft ring from their studio apartments in the South Loop.

Though, that may be specific to this case.

I have yet to make contact with my number one suspect, Miss Georgia Dewan. Age: 26. Height: 5'4". Address: 351 East 14th Street, apartment 502. Occupation: freelance artist. Graduate of *The School of The Art Institute of Chicago*. Relationship status: single.

On paper, she's a law-abiding citizen with no reason to resort to a life of crime. Her parents are still married after thirty years, living in her childhood home in North Utica. They both have successful careers and don't appear to have any criminal contacts. Georgia achieved good grades through college and, based on her online presence, is remarkably talented and well liked. Somewhere along the line, like so many others, she decided a life of crime was easier. At least, that's what my criminal informant has assured me.

For four months, I've been tirelessly working this case, scouring the city for a lead. Until last week, nothing had materialized and my supervisory agent was pushing me to scrap the investigation and take on one with a more promising outcome. But I wasn't about to give up. I negotiated with her to give me seven days to come up with something useful, and with a stroke of luck—and promise of a hefty sum of cash should it pay off—my CI, Bobby, presented me with a name: Georgia Dewan.

She approaches my passenger-side mirror, striding down the sidewalk in her hot pink mini dress, white sneakers, and denim jacket, carrying a large canvas tote bag. Her toned legs eat up the distance in my mirror until she's in my blind spot. She passes by my unmarked SUV without glancing my way. Good. Her wavy hair sways rhythmically, brushing her shoulders and giving brief glimpses of her silver hoop earrings. If I'm not careful, it could land me in a hypnotic trance; it's mesmerizing.

Once she is a few yards past the front bumper, it's time to trail her on foot.

I climb out of the driver's seat of my Bureau-issued SUV and walk around the rear so I can follow my target from a distance. The warm early autumn air is a stark contrast to my comfortably air-conditioned vehicle.

"SA Prewitt, in pursuit of target. White female. Blonde hair. Traveling north on South Wabash between East Fourteenth and Roosevelt," I relay through my comms.

"SA Prewitt, copy," the operator replies.

Georgia may not look like a criminal, but I'm not about to leave myself exposed if she leads me somewhere she could be meeting with other criminals. This heist crew has proven themselves to be merciless and tenacious. Two qualities I don't want to come face to face with without reporting my whereabouts.

She continues northbound, talking on her phone. I'm too far away to hear what she's saying, but it's possible she's scheduling a meetup. I don't have enough evidence to tap her phone or request a warrant, so I'll have to stick close and find out where she's going. As she ascends the stairs to Roosevelt Subway Station, I text an update to SSA Lancaster rather than keying my radio. If Georgia is meeting someone in her crew here, I can't risk being heard.

We reach the open area of the elevated station and stop thirty feet apart. She positions herself, leaning on one of the concrete pillars, still fiddling with her phone. I mimic the gesture, watching her out of the corner of my eye.

I pull up the "L" schedule to see what time the train should be arriving. Six minutes. It doesn't look like she's meeting anyone here, so I guess I'm going for a ride.

A throat clears to my left.

"Are you following me?"

My eyes travel up the shapely form of Miss Georgia Dewan. She's wearing sunglasses, so I can't read her eyes, but judging by her crossed arms, she's not happy about my presence.

I slide my phone into my pocket, trying to act casual. "No. Why would I be following you?"

"Usually when a strange man follows a single woman on the streets of Chicago, it's not for noble reasons. So if you're planning to kidnap me, know that I have a black belt in jiu-jitsu, and I will not go quietly." Now she pairs her crossed arms with raised eyebrows that peek over her thick-framed sunglasses.

My research never turned up anything on jiu-jitsu, so I'm pretty sure she's making that up, but I make a mental note to look into it. Maybe that's where she met the people she's working with.

"I'm not going to kidnap you... or anyone, for that matter. I'm just waiting for the 'L'."

"Where are you going?"

I stare down at the feisty blonde, analyzing her body language. Based on her confrontational manner, I doubt she realizes I'm an FBI agent. I can use this to my advantage. "*The Museum of Contemporary Art.*"

Her eyes don't relax at all as she asks, "Why?"

"Listen, I'm just waiting to get on the train. Same as you and everyone else here. I don't know what's with the twenty questions." I release a deep sigh, trying to sell my irritated reply. "If you must know, I've been waiting to see Calder's exhibit for months, and I finally have a few hours off to do it." In reality, I couldn't care less, but based on the rash of thefts, I've familiarized myself with the more popular art exhibits in the city, so I attempt to use that as common ground.

"You're going in a suit?"

I look down at my crisp white shirt and navy two-button jacket. "I had a meeting this morning."

Finally, her arms fall to her sides and the twin lines between her brows disappear. "I'm sorry." She chuckles and flashes a tense, toothy grin. "A girl in the city can never be too careful, you know? It's just, I saw you walk all this way behind me, and it set me a little on edge."

I silently berate myself for being spotted, but try to maintain a neutral expression so I don't look like a guilty wannabe kidnapper.

The squealing brakes of the train interrupt our conversation and draw her attention to the tracks. "Well, this is me. Take care of yourself..." She pauses and glances around at the other pedestrians on the platform corralling themselves into the train. "Sorry. I didn't get your name."

My plan was not to interact with her, so I don't have a cover identity in place. But now that my covert operation is blown, I go off script to work with the new parameters of the case. "Usually kidnappers don't share their real name. It's bad for business."

"Right. I really am sorry." She shrugs and steps closer to the door that won't remain open much longer. "Small-town girl. Big city. Some habits die hard."

"It's a good habit." I give her a reassuring smile. If she wasn't a criminal, I'd appreciate her self-awareness to keep herself safe. "I'm Archie."

She steps forward to the stopped train alongside me, thrusting out her hand in offer to shake mine. I oblige.

"Georgia."

Yeah, I know.

We enter the crowded railcar, her in front, and she turns right, dropping into a seat on the left side, crossing one leg over the other. She sets her bag on the floor in front of her since the train isn't too busy on a Tuesday afternoon. I park myself opposite her so I can study her non-verbal cues. Though, much of that relies on a person's eyes, which are currently covered.

There's a reason an extensive part of Quantico training revolves around reading body language—most criminals don't outright admit they're guilty. I only have a few moments to read as much of hers as I can.

"So, Georgia, the jiu-jitsu master, where are you headed?"

She snaps her head from her focus at the front of the train car back to me. Direct eye contact from behind her glasses. "Why do you want to know?"

"You asked me. Only seems fair."

She grips her left hand with her right. "So you can call your kidnapper friends to pick me up where I'm going and get off on a technicality that you weren't the one to do it?"

The right side of my lips tilts upward as I do my best to keep a straight face. "You have a very active imagination."

"Combination of too many true crime documentaries and life as an artist. We're notoriously eccentric."

This is exactly the window of opportunity I was hoping for. "You're an artist? Are you going to the museum too?"

"No." She doesn't elaborate, nor offer any insight about where she *is* going.

Our conversation has stalled, and the clock is ticking as we speed toward Chicago Station.

"If I guess, will you tell me?"

"I'd be really impressed if you guessed correctly, but it wouldn't do much to convince me you're not stalking me. So, no."

With that, we squeal into my stop, and since I opened my big mouth and admitted I need to get off here, I stand, holding onto the horizontal rail above my head. I am able to peek inside her bag from this vantage point. Art supplies. A pair of small canvases, a sketchbook, a few flat boxes of paints, miscellaneous brushes, and a variety of pencils. Bingo.

To my surprise, Georgia stands, grabbing the bar on the opposite side of the aisle. The movement causes her dress to expose more of her legs. I look away before she has any more reason to suspect my intentions are less than noble.

The game has changed, but the goal remains the same. I'm not a kidnapper, but if I have it my way, she'll be locked up somewhere soon enough.

Georgia

2

SHADY CHARACTER

I consider myself an excellent judge of character. After years of studying the intricacies of the human form, I'm trained to spot the miniscule details that would slip most people's notice. The subtle shift of lips or raise of an eyebrow. Dilation of pupils or flushing of cheeks. All things I'm proficient in noticing. But this guy's face is as expressive as The Mona Lisa and is cloaked in an equal level of mystery.

As soon as the train comes to a stop, I nod goodbye to Archie and beeline through the underground station, up the escalator, to street level. Once I emerge onto North State Street, I head east toward my destination. Again, I feel a palpable presence. I whip around to find Archie only a few steps behind.

"Are you following me now?"

"You knew I was going to the museum. It's not my fault you're headed the same way."

I keep my pace brisk, assuming he'll give up and fall back, but his tall frame traverses the pavement a lot faster than mine can. Within seconds, he's in stride with me and slows his pace to match. It irritates me for no good reason that I'm walking as fast as physically possible, and he's out for a casual stroll, yet we're going the same speed.

While I am a trusting person by nature, my instincts are still geared toward self-preservation. I don't *think* Archie has ill intentions, but I'm not going to present my itinerary on a silver platter, either. Instead, I go straight for the topic of conversation within my comfort zone. "What is it about Calder?"

"Huh?" Archie's dark eyebrows show the slightest hint of movement, but otherwise, his face is neutral. His hair, on the other hand, the most uniform shade of espresso, possesses all the animation his face lacks. Its slicked back length at the top moves with each step, but the neatly trimmed sides maintain an air of seriousness.

"You said you've wanted to go to Calder's exhibit for a while. What is it about his work that made you want to experience it?"

"You mean see it?"

I huff a sigh. If I'm being honest, I didn't peg him for the artist type from the get go. His response confirms it.

"No, I mean experience it. A full exhibit like that isn't one you go 'see'. You immerse yourself in it. Feel the emotions. Question the logic. If you do it right, you walk out a new person because you grow from it. It's not just something pretty to look at."

He remains silent for several paces before replying. "It sounds like I need a guide." Not only does his face not give anything away, his tone doesn't fluctuate, either. "Can you spare an hour to make sure I do it right?"

We approach the gardens in front of *The Water Tower*, and I see it as my opportunity to cut ties. "Sorry. This is where we part ways."

For the first time, Archie's countenance expresses something other than indifference. Maybe it's presumptuous of me, but judging by the downturn of his lips, I'm guessing he's disappointed. At least, if I was drawing a disappointed person, that's the expression I'd give them.

"Oh, sure. Don't let me keep you from whatever you've got planned."

The way he makes that statement, laced with a hint of contempt, makes me relieved I've got a legitimate reason to end this interaction. It's been a wild ride, start to finish.

"Right. Enjoy your experience, Archie." I turn to head down Michigan Avenue toward my destination.

Archie calls from behind me, "See ya, 'round, Georgia."

I almost laugh. In a city of 2.7 million people, the chances of ever running into him again are slim. There's a certain level of freedom offered in the anonymity of the city. You're surrounded by more people, but you're practically invisible amongst the crowds.

After growing up in a village of just over a thousand people, it's refreshing. That is, until you're trying to make it as an artist and you *need* people to know your name. The only way to do that is to keep creating and hope someone takes notice. So that's what I'm doing.

Oak Street Beach has always been one of those places where I can really soak in the city's beauty. I love sitting along Lakefront Trail, listening to the waves pound the shore in a steady rhythm as if set to a metronome, watching the tourists and locals enjoy their own anonymity, and studying the ever-changing skyline. The entire landscape varies so much through the seasons and even at different times of the day. Shadows shift, casting different buildings in darkness, illuminating others. Crowds of people appear and disperse. Leaves change color, shed, and return. Every single scenario is uniquely beautiful if you pay close enough attention.

I take a seat on my favorite bench and pull out my art supplies. The fall is such a great time of year to draw the waterfront. The beach is deserted because the waters of Lake Michigan have dropped to temperatures no reasonable person wants to be submerged in, and the hordes of summer tourists have returned home. There are still the odd groups of people who scream "small town" from a hundred feet away. They're my favorite to draw because their faces are always lit up with wonder at the sights, sounds, and smells of the city. It's as if you experience the magic of Chicago for the first time all over again, each time you see it from their perspectives.

The perfect family to feature in today's work saunters along the trail. Mom and Dad each hold their daughter's hands and swing her as they walk. Their knit sweaters and floral dresses are a stark contrast to the monochrome attire of most city dwellers. The little girl giggles, and I automatically smile. Once a moment makes me feel—regardless of what that feeling is—I know that's the one I need to capture.

For over two hours, I sketch, shade, erase, and re-shape my drawing, paying special attention to the expressions on my subjects' faces. They're long gone, but the moment is etched into my brain, so I work at transferring it to the thick ivory paper. The little blonde girl reminds me of myself. Me from a simpler time. When life was more about pursuing things that brought me joy and piqued my interest than finding ways to pay bills and keep food in the fridge. A time when I didn't have to sacrifice what I wanted to keep up with adult responsibilities.

I stare at the completed picture, questioning whether to change a few minor details. But that smile—the joy in this little girl's eyes—is perfection. There's not a single person with a soul who could look at her face and not feel her happiness.

I close my sketchbook, careful not to crease the drawing, and tuck my supplies back in my bag. I brought a few canvases and some paints with me, but I'm not inspired to dive into that medium today. Instead of staying here and trying to force creativity, I start walking back toward Chicago Station.

As I pass *The Sports Museum*, I glance up to see a happy family bounding down the stairs.

The lanky brunette man is beaming, wearing a vibrant new *Chicago Bears* hat and gushing to his wife. "That was awesome. I can't believe Michael Jordan's hands were that big!"

The sweet little girl tugs at her father's arm. "Daddy, can we go to the zoo now?"

He doesn't just reply to her. He stops walking, bends down to meet her at eye level, and tells her they'll go to the zoo tomorrow so they can spend the entire day. Mom watches the interaction with so much adoration and pride in her eyes, I wish I could capture that too.

I approach them, pulling my latest drawing from my bag. "Excuse me."

The man straightens and all three of them study me as I walk closer.

Mom replies, "I hope you're not asking for directions because we're hopeless." She has a distinct Midwest twang that her husband and daughter don't seem to have.

"No, but if you need directions, I'm happy to help. I actually..." I pause, holding out the drawing to show them. "I saw you guys walking along the trail earlier and... well, I'd like you to have this."

The mom reaches her hands out to take my offering. As soon as she sees the image, she claps one dainty hand over her mouth, which causes the paper to droop. With tears in her eyes, she passes it to her husband. He has a similar reaction, but both hands stay on the edges of the paper.

"This is amazing. You just drew this?" the man asks.

"Well, it took a couple of hours, but yes. I've never drawn anyone and then run into them again, so I'm happy I can pass this one along."

The woman starts digging through her purse. "Let me pay you. We can't just take it for free. How much does something like this cost?"

I offer the little girl a smile, who is trying to sneak a peek at the drawing, then address the mom. "No, really. It's my pleasure. Save your money to buy this sweet little one a souvenir at the zoo." I wink at her, which makes her giggle again.

"Wow. Thank you, Miss..." Mom juts out her hand to shake mine, giving me a sweet nostalgic feeling. People in the city don't often shake hands unless it's a business deal, but my manners deem it a necessity when introducing myself to someone.

"Georgia Dewan."

"Thank you, Georgia. I'm Caroline; this is Molly and Steve. You've absolutely made my day." She leans closer to me, shielding her mouth with her hand, but speaks at a volume her husband can still hear. "I don't know much about the bear cubs or the white hawks, so the sports museum wasn't my first choice."

Caroline and Steve chuckle in tandem, while Molly beams at them both. Their family makes me a little homesick. I miss these moments so much—the ones when my parent's love felt like a strong enough force to solve every problem in the world. When I felt like their love for *me* was strong enough to combat any sadness or discouragement.

Before I get too emotional in front of these amiable strangers, I wish them well on their visit, wave at Molly, and carry on my way.

One day, I hope someone looks at me with that level of love and adoration. For now, I'll keep capturing it with graphite pencils.

Archie

3

STING OPERATION

"**M**a'am, I'm telling you. She's good for it. My instincts say she's the one creating the forgeries. She's got the means, talent, motive, and opportunity. Based on her tax returns, she's barely earning enough to afford her rent each month, so she has to be supplementing her income somehow."

Special Supervisory Agent Arlene Lancaster, longtime employee of the *Federal Bureau of Investigation*, runs her White-Collar Crime Division with an iron fist. She also has great instincts, which landed her the best conviction record in the Midwest and was the catalyst for her ending up in her current rank. She's the type of person, if you pay attention to what she's doing, you'll never stop learning. I respect her as an agent and as a person, so I will not make a fool of myself with this case. Her personal reference carries a lot of weight.

"I have to say, I'm pleased you have a lead. But based on what you're showing me here, you still have nothing. This evidence barely qualifies as circumstantial. You need more."

She closes the file folder I've presented her with, containing photos of Georgia, tax returns, copies of paintings she created in college, and social media posts, including a photo of her with her degree from *SAIC*. Some of this was gathered by the original team of fourteen agents tasked with this case, but after months of no progress, that team has dwindled to one. Me.

"Give me time and I'll get it. I made contact with her yesterday, so I can work on infiltrating her circle and dismantling their entire organization. This is way bigger than one person."

"It always is, Prewitt. But I don't love the idea of you playing undercover agent. Maybe it's time to hand this off to the PD and they can surveil her for a while. There are other cases you can be work—"

"No!" I shout, but immediately backpedal. "Sorry. I don't want to hand it off now. I can do this. If you sign off on an operation budget, I'll get to the bottom of it."

Lancaster glares at me as she taps her pen on the manilla folder. The longer she stays silent, the more nervous she makes me. "Fine. You have two months. Not one day longer. I'll get you set up with a cover job and apartment. You need to check in twice a day and submit progress reports weekly. Don't contact her without reporting in first."

I consider myself a level-headed guy, but a small part of me wants to fist pump in celebration. My determination to solve the case got this lead, and now I'm going to bust it wide open. "Thank you, Ma'am. I won't let you down."

"Not every case is winnable. So just don't do anything stupid and you won't let me down." She flicks the file folder at me and waves me away with her opposite hand. "Don't get yourself killed."

"Wouldn't dream of it." I walk out of her office so light on my feet, I could pass for a boxing champion. I'm about to sting this art fraud operation like a murder hornet.

DO NOT CROSS

● JUST KIDDING ● KEEP GOING, YOU REBEL ●

Twenty-four hours later, I walk into the furnished studio apartment I'll call home for the next two months or less. It's not even five hundred square feet, so it's about a third the size of my house. It's just temporary, though; I can deal. The view also leaves a lot to be desired. The one wall of windows looks out over a rooftop terrace above the third floor, straight across at another fifth-floor apartment on the other side. Rows of concrete planters look very metropolitan surrounded by wider strips of paving stones and withering deciduous trees. The odd evergreen sprinkled in maintains a bit of green, but I still wouldn't consider it "outdoor" space.

After taking in the view, or lack thereof, I do the first thing that comes to mind: check the fridge. No surprise, it's empty. Lancaster arranged a short-term rental, but food is up to me. My only option for tonight is takeout and a trip home to grab some essentials.

My house is ten miles away, but like most law enforcement professionals in the city, I made it a point not to work in the same area I live. I've encountered a lot of unsavory people in this job, so I bought a house in Oak Park four years ago in order to keep some distance between work and home. It makes for a twenty-five minute commute to the office most days, but at least I'm not running into people I've indicted at the grocery store. Or worse. The angry girlfriend of someone I've testified against.

I pull into my driveway, admiring the curb appeal my home now has. When I bought it, I was looking for a bargain and wasn't afraid of hard work. It had boarded-up windows, an overgrown lawn, and two large spruce trees with roots invading the foundation. You'd never know looking at it now. Just like in all areas of my life, I'm not afraid to dive in and do whatever needs to be done.

This case is no different. If Georgia Dewan thinks she can weasel her way out of criminal charges with her ethereal face and innocent doe eyes, she's in for a real surprise.

Once I pack up a few kitchen essentials in a box, some clothes and toiletries in a suitcase, and grab two of my more temperamental houseplants, I ensure my security cameras are on and active, then lock the front door on my way out.

SSA Lancaster assigned me a gray Jeep Cherokee as my undercover vehicle, so I open the tailgate and set everything inside. It was impounded from another white-collar crime involving insurance fraud. Spoils of war.

My neighbor, Bruce, hollers at me from his porch, wearing a tattered terry robe that doesn't quite have the overlap needed to protect his modesty. Though, based on the number of times I've seen him parade around naked, he has no desire to protect it, anyway. "Going on vacation, kid?"

I will not admit where I'm actually going, nor that my house will be empty for a while. I don't care how innocent a person appears; he's not getting the inside scoop on my plans. "Just taking some stuff for the office. You know I don't take days off."

Bruce grunts, which makes his protruding middle bounce and his robe gape even more. "You need to take some time off, Archie boy. Don't give your whole life to a job that doesn't give it back."

We have had this same conversation at least once a week since I moved in. He's constantly reminding me to take a step back, and that only catapults me further. My job is my life, and as it stands, I don't feel the least bit unfulfilled doing it. I'm determined to make a difference in this city and days off don't help accomplish that.

So I wave at Bruce in silent acknowledgement, climb in the driver's side of the Jeep, and speed off toward my temporary home by way of the grocery store.

With sustenance, clothing, plants, and kitchen equipment in tow, I strategically maneuver into the elevator so I can carry everything up from the underground parking in one trip. The plants are perched on top of the kitchen box I'm shuffling along the ground with my feet, and I looped the grocery bags around my forearms and the suitcase handle. When the elevator dings, announcing my arrival on the fifth floor, I push the box out with my foot and struggle to get the suitcase moving with its unbalanced load. I don't get it all the way through the door before the elevator closes, crushing one of my bags.

"Ugh. I hope I'll have a craving for cracker powder later."

"Cracker powder doesn't sound very appetizing."

I glance up to see a beautiful, deceptive blonde holding the elevator door open. She takes a second, but recognition sparks in her blue eyes.

"You! What are you doing here?" She makes the same angry face she did at Roosevelt Station yesterday, only this time my view is unobstructed with regular glasses perched on her delicate button nose. I'm pretty sure if she knew jiu-jitsu, she would use it.

"Me? I'm moving into 508. What are you doing here?" I throw my question back at her with an equal amount of accusation.

"I live here." She eyes my belongings and seems to realize I'm telling the truth. "Well, isn't this convenient? Yet you claim you're not following me." She rolls her eyes, but her subtle smile betrays her words.

The elevator door dings shut and takes off to its next location. The distraction gives me enough time to come up with an answer. "I could just as easily say you're following me. You're the only one who threatened violence. My plants and I are just trying to get settled in our new place."

She stares at me for a few more seconds, then drops her hands to slap her denim-clad thighs. "Fine. I'm not going in your apartment, but I can stand watch over your stuff so you don't have to take it all at once."

"Such a warm, neighborly welcome." I smirk at her, knowing I'm more likely to get in her good graces if I act friendly. Even if she is a criminal, I'll take this over Bruce's hairy bread basket escaping its fabric confines.

"Take it or leave it. But don't complain to me if your blender and fern get hijacked."

My arms are losing feeling from the bags cutting off circulation, so despite there not being anyone else in the hallway and the fact I suspect Georgia to be part of a heist crew, I leave my precious Boston fern and zebra plant in her care while I hustle to my door. Unlocking it proves to be another challenge with numb hands, but after a few seconds, I get it open.

The bright side of living in under five hundred square feet is that the trek from the front door to the fridge isn't a long one. I drop everything on the floor in the kitchen/bedroom/living room/home office area and rush back out to where I left Georgia with the rest of my belongings. She's still there, and none of my stuff appears disturbed, so it doesn't look like she's searched through it. Not that she'd find anything. Undercover 101: don't bring anything personal.

"I'm charging you by the minute for my security services, Archie. Chop chop." She raises her blonde eyebrows and nods toward my door.

I don't answer to this woman. I didn't ask her to stay and watch my belongings. Yet, I still find myself speeding to drag my suitcase and remaining groceries thirty feet down the hall. In the safety of my apartment, I give my head a shake. *Man up, Archibald. This woman cannot get in your head.* Every time I chastise myself, it sounds like my mother's voice, and she always insists on using my full name.

Georgia is leaning against the wall beside the elevator doors when I return, checking her phone. I bend down to pick up my last box and temperamental plants.

"Final tally is fourteen dollars, twenty-two cents, but I'm willing to round down if you pay cash."

I study her for a few seconds, trying to determine if she's being serious, but she clarifies when she starts laughing. She has a sweet, melodic laugh that would be pleasant if it wasn't coming from a con. I know, I know. Innocent until proven guilty. But I have a gut feeling this bust is going to change the trajectory of my career.

Nothing—not even a gorgeous smile and captivating laugh—will derail this case.

Georgia

4

LEFT-TENANT

This man was a complete stranger two days ago. It was weird enough that we walked the same way to the subway station. It was an understandable coincidence that we got off at the same stop. But this? Having him move in three doors to my left? That's astronomical odds.

Unless the meeting he claimed to have was viewing the apartment. That must be it. I'm just being paranoid. He hasn't given me the impression he's set on harming me or anyone else. He actually gives off a real protector vibe. Like a broody alpha male who would wrestle a Komodo dragon to save someone else.

"You better get your plants situated. I guess… welcome to the building, Archie."

"Thank you for your services, Georgia. Christofern and Vincent Van Grow thank you too."

I watch his facial expression closely, but it never wavers. Not even a twitch of his lips. "Did you really name your plants?"

He chuckles for the first time in the twenty minutes we've ever interacted. "Plants thrive when you speak to them. It's scientifically proven." He adjusts the box in his grip, causing the fern to wobble.

I lunge forward and reach out to steady it. "Woah."

Once the plant is secure, Archie's piercing brown eyes lock on mine. If I were drawing them, I'd choose sepia as the main shade, then I'd add in flecks of copper and dashes of coffee. His eyes have a lot of dimension and so much vibrancy, I don't notice I'm completely lost in them until he clears his throat.

"Thank you. I'd be gutted if anything happened to Christofern." He smirks again, which makes his eyes even more radiant. "Listen, uh… I'm new in the neighborhood, and since I owe you for your security services, would you let me take you out for a coffee or something?"

I snort-laugh, which is an embarrassing habit of mine. He wouldn't be the first guy to ask me out, then change his mind after discovering that little gem. Either that or my penchant for terrible puns. But he doesn't do anything except smile wider.

Why am I not running through a thousand excuses to say no? That's what I always do. My habit of disappearing for days on end when I lock myself away to create isn't conducive to dating. But you can never have too many friends. It's just coffee. Right?

"Okay. I'm easy, so I'm available whenever." That came out wrong. "I mean, I'm flexible." No, that gives the wrong impression. "I mean… just knock on my door whenever you want to go." Stop. Talking.

"Which door is yours?" He isn't the least bit put off by my babbling.

"502." I point at my door and suddenly remember I'm supposed to meet my friends at a paint studio for a wine and paint night. "I have to go. Welcome… again."

The elevator doors open a few seconds later—my incessant pressing of the button paid off for the first time in my life—so I step in beside a portly older gentleman with a friendly smile. Archie watches me as the door closes, his face back in its default setting. His multifaceted gaze seems to scrutinize everything as much as I do. I'm not sure what to think of him, but I guess we're having coffee together, so I'll figure that out another day.

Twenty minutes later, I run into the modern high-rise with the art studio hosting tonight's event and find Rene and Michelle waiting in the lobby.

"We thought you forgot." Michelle pulls me in for a hug first. She's a year older than me and Rene, so she's taken on the motherly role. It helps that she's married to her high school sweetheart and has a three-year-old daughter, Savannah.

"No, I got tied up because someone was moving onto my floor." I hug Rene, even though she's as warm and fuzzy as a cactus. I bet if Archie had a cactus, he'd name it Mr. Prickles. Or Cactus Evergreen. Or—

"Earth to Georgia." Rene snaps her fingers in front of my face.

I shake thoughts of Archie out of my head to focus on my best gal pals. "Sorry. Should have grabbed a coffee on my way. I'm a little sleepy."

"Girl, I have a threenager who has been protesting sleep for weeks. Don't talk to me about being tired."

I chuckle at Michelle as she presses the button for the elevator. She doesn't use my effective method to make it arrive faster, so we're left waiting.

"How is my lil' Sassy Sav? Has she decided what she wants painted on her bedroom wall yet?"

"Sassy is an understatement. One day she wants an elaborate scene with a castle and a thousand bunnies, the next day she's begging for the cast of *Nacho and Friends*, then she decides she wants snakes and butterflies."

"Snakes and butterflies?" Rene and I ask in unison.

"Shawn and I were trying to covertly discuss the birds and the bees. She decided that snakes and butterflies were a better pairing, and really, I can't argue with her."

We all laugh as the elevator dings and opens its doors on the eighteenth floor. We follow the *Paint and Wine* sign to the studio door and enter to find at least thirty other people inside.

"Wow. This place is wild," I say as I take it all in.

"And that's a sign you've gotten boring. If a few dozen people qualify as wild, you need to get out more." Rene leaves me with that declaration and marches ahead to get us signed in at the reception area.

Michelle and I continue our discussion of her daughter's latest antics and a new opportunity she was offered at work.

The three of us met during our time at *The School of the Art Institute of Chicago*—better known as *SAIC*. Michelle pursued a degree in fashion design, and Rene obtained hers in art education. Now they're both working in their respective fields—Michelle as a purchaser for a large department store who works directly with prominent designers, and Rene as an art teacher at a high school in Englewood.

I always want to be everyone's greatest cheerleader, and I'm so happy for them both for pursuing their passion and having it pay off. But I'd be lying if I said it didn't sting a little that I've put so much work into pursuing mine only for my efforts to fall flat time and time again.

Tonight is a pleasant distraction, though. I spend the next two hours indulging in the complimentary wine and painting my version of Claude Monet's *Water Lilies*. I'm familiar with the original because I spent a lot of time examining each brush stroke and color choice during my time at *The Art Institute*. I wouldn't say my version compares to Monet, but I dream of creating work that is hung on a wall somewhere with people flocking to come experience it for themselves, just like they do with his. Especially people like Archie who don't even realize how much a work of art can impact you on a fundamental level.

"This is not fair. Why do we keep bringing this girl to paint nights?" Michelle grumbles as she drops her paintbrush in a cup of olive green water and gestures at my painting.

"You guys keep suggesting it. I just come along for the wine."

"Next time we're going to a football game," Rene adds after setting down her empty wineglass. "It's no fun when I consider myself a decent artist, but next to yours, mine looks like Savannah made it."

"Hey. My child is a prodigy. She can draw the best stick figures you've ever seen."

I listen as my friends exchange playful banter, and I laugh along with them, but my eyes are focused on a couple one row over. The man, who looks to be about my age with umber skin and a neatly styled fade, lifts his hand to brush paint off of the woman's milky cheek with his thumb. She blushes, enhancing her freckles, and looks at him through her lashes with her head tilted downward and a coy smile. The knowing exchange between them—that love—is so obvious, I'd much rather be painting that. No offense to Monet, but his work has already been mastered. No one can out-Monet Monet. I want my work to be my own and capture these moments that I feel are deserving of being frozen in time.

But it's hard to make a living on capturing that in an age of cell phone cameras and filters.

"Hey, what's with the face?" Michelle asks, pouring the last of our shared bottle of wine into my glass. "You look like you could use that."

I smile at my observant friend. "I don't know. Just feeling defeated, I guess. Like I'm never going to catch a break, and I'm wasting my time by trying. Maybe I'm not as good as I thought."

This is the first time I've said those words out loud, because I didn't want to admit it to myself. Let alone anyone else.

"Oh, girl. Look at this." Rene points at my lackluster re-creation. "This is remarkable. It may be a tough industry to break into, but it has nothing to do with your talent. It's more a matter of connecting with the right people and having your work seen."

"Why didn't you say you were feeling this way? I'm sure between me and Rene, we can round up some names of people you can contact." Michelle passes me my wineglass, encouraging me to drink.

Now I feel guilty for being a downer on our girls' night. I chug the last of my merlot before responding. "No, no. It's fine. I'm just being a *winer*." I wink and hold up my glass, hoping they understand my terrible play on words.

They've been around me long enough, they get it, judging by their eye rolling.

"Seriously, you've got too much talent to waste. I wish you would have told us sooner that you were feeling this way. We can help," Michelle adds, tilting her head to inspect my artwork.

"You would make a killing if you had your own gallery showing. Guarantee. Give me a week and I'm going to find some names for you to contact," Rene says, fiddling with the final touches of her painting.

I smile at her, appreciating her confidence in me. Confidence I no longer have in myself. "I'll figure it out. Thanks for the little pep talk." I push my stool back and stand. "Now, enough whining and more wining. Time to make some *pour* decisions."

The rest of the evening, I sneak peeks at the young couple, committing their exchanges to memory so I can draw on them for inspiration in my own work. There's no greater muse than two people in love.

It's just too bad for me that love and passion aren't enough to pay the bills.

Archie

5

UNDER COVERS

It took every ounce of professionalism not to tail Georgia when she left last night. I wanted to follow her and see where she was going, but I knew if she caught me, I'd have no way of talking myself out of it. She would be well and truly convinced I was following her. So I stayed back, ate my dinner from the grocery store deli, and analyzed every bit of evidence I've obtained so far. Which, admittedly, isn't a lot.

Imagine my surprise when she returned home after 10p.m., carrying a replica of Monet's *Water Lilies*. I know that one well because it's one of the most expensive pieces displayed at *The Art Institute of Chicago*. It still doesn't qualify as hard evidence, but it inches me toward being able to request more invasive surveillance equipment.

If I only have two months to solve this case, I need to make the most of it. So at 9a.m., after I've hit the gym for a sweaty hour of circuit training, I return to my temporary home to shower—in what I'd class as the world's smallest bathroom—then venture to Georgia's apartment.

Three taps at the door, and I listen closely for movement inside. Nothing. After thirty seconds, I knock again.

"Coming." Some rustling sounds from the other side of the door and something slams, followed by "Ow!" Whatever she's doing in there, it sounds rushed and panicked.

Perhaps hiding evidence. Though she should have made more of an effort of that last night when she marched in with her painting forgery.

Georgia opens the door another half a minute later and peeks her head around without opening it more than a few inches. Her hair is messy, piled on top of her head in a frazzled ponytail. "Hi. Oh, it's you. Sorry, I just woke up."

"Late night?" I try to glimpse inside her apartment, but the small gap isn't enough for me to see anything.

"Kind of. I did this paint and wine night with my friends, then got home and wanted to capture something else, so I was up until 3:30."

I'm impressed with how smoothly she delivered that statement. My deception-detection training is no help because I don't sense the slightest bit of a lie. But I do notice a smudge on her right cheek and instinctively reach up to wipe it away with my thumb.

Our skin makes contact with a jolt of electricity that shoots up my arm. Georgia freezes under my touch, so I pull my hand away, afraid I'm overstepping. I've never felt inclined to even tell someone they had broccoli in their teeth. What possessed me to touch her?

"Sorry. You had black something..." I gesture at her cheek like she needs clarification.

"Th–thank you."

I shake my hand out to rid it of the weird tingling sensation and refocus on why I'm here. I told my boss I was going to approach Georgia this morning, so something better materialize before I have to report back in. "Coffee. I was stopping by to see if you wanted to grab a coffee. Or whatever you want that comes to around fourteen dollars."

She smiles, and I get the sense her guard is dropping. She pulls the door open a little wider. "Clearly I'm not dressed to go in public. Can you give me fifteen minutes? I promise I'm fast."

I drop my eyes to examine her outfit. She's wearing a short black T-shirt with a cartoon Tyrannosaurus rex and the word "roar" over its head and matching shorts with dinosaurs in domed space ships.

I can't help but laugh. "How do they reach the steering wheel?"

Georgia scoffs, looking down at her shorts. She pulls the fabric out to inspect it. "Pretty sure if they're driving space ships, they've worked out the whole self-drive function."

I take a second to peek behind her now that the door is open wider. Her Monet replica is leaning against something on her dresser. Her floor plan looks similar to mine, which doesn't allow for much delineation of space. Nor a lot of privacy.

"Did you paint that?" I ask, pointing behind her.

She moves to close the door part way, blocking my view of the inside again. "I did. Paint night. They often choose an impressionist to mimic." She turns her head to look behind her, then spins back to address me again. "Fifteen minutes?"

"Yeah, sure. I'll go back to my place. Just knock when you're ready."

She nods, then disappears behind her closed door. I walk to my unit and return inside. No sense in updating Lancaster after that brief interaction, but I make a note to look into this supposed paint night. I don't understand why a trained artist would attend an amateur painting event. That's like an MLB player showing up to Little League. I can't imagine it's much of a challenge.

According to a website for a studio not far from here, they had a Monet paint night yesterday. The timeframe coincides with Georgia's exit and reappearance. I suppose that means she's off the hook for this one. That just means I have to try harder.

Georgia knocks a moment later. She was faster than expected, because she only took eleven minutes. She's dressed in dark denim and a *SAIC* hoodie, looking deceptively innocent.

"Ready?" she asks from behind a tentative smile, drawing attention to her pillowy pink lips.

"Ready." I pat my jean pockets to make sure I have my phone, wallet, and keys, then step into the hallway. "Do you know a good coffee place nearby?"

"I don't go out for coffee a lot, but *Pete's* is pretty good," she replies, ambling toward the elevator.

"Lead the way." I press the call button, but it takes a full minute for the elevator to arrive. I notice Georgia smirk, but I don't ask why.

We step inside and descend to the lobby without saying a word. I'm so intent on watching her non-verbal cues, I'm finding it difficult to maintain small talk. If I'm not careful, this could be our final interaction, so I need to be smart about my approach. This needs to go well enough she invites me to see more of her life.

"Tell me more about yourself. You're an artist from a small town with a black belt in jiu-jitsu, and you like painting while drinking wine. What else is there to know?"

She makes that weird snort-laugh sound she made yesterday. "Wow, you take impressive notes. Good thing I didn't tell you my social security number."

I try not to let my face express that I already have that and every tax return she's ever filed. "Now that's two things you've learned about me. I listen and I have a good memory."

Pete's appears on our left, only two hundred feet from our building. I reach out to pull the door open for Georgia and one other woman who enters behind her.

"Do you know what you're getting?" I ask, sliding in line beside Georgia as she stares up at the rustic menu board.

"Just a large black coffee."

"Black coffee?"

She turns her gaze from the pastry display to look at me. "I thought you listened and had a good memory."

"I do. That's just... not what I expected."

Her eyebrows raise a fraction of an inch, as does the left side of her lips. "What did you expect?"

Suddenly, I feel put on the spot. Like my intention of gaining insight into her has backfired. But I play along. "Maybe a matcha latte with a fancy leaf image on top. Black coffee seems so plain. So un-artistic."

She chuckles—without the snort this time—and steps forward as the person in front of us clears away. "Large black coffee, please. He's paying." She winks at me, which is also a surprise.

"Make that two," I say to the cashier, whose name tag reads *Tasha*. "And an oatmeal with berries, please." I turn my focus back on Georgia and ask, "Do you want anything to eat?"

She glances at the pastry display again, and her eyes settle on a cinnamon bun. "No, I'm good, thanks," she replies, but doesn't sound convincing.

"And a cinnamon bun," I request from Tasha, then wink at Georgia. I don't recall ever winking at a woman before. It's never been a move in my repertoire, but I'll do whatever it takes to play along here. If baked goods and silly facial gestures help me solve this case, I'll chalk it off as part of the job.

A few moments later, we're seated at a table for two along the back wall of the cafe. A law-enforcement habit: positioning yourself in a place that allows for a full visual. The chairs are worn and uncomfortable, but otherwise, the ambiance of the place is nice. It seems like a suitable spot for a surface-level conversation that can lay the foundation for a friendly relationship and lead to getting the answers I'm looking for.

"So I've also learned you're no good at guessing coffee orders. Tell me something else about you, since you know more about me. We need to level the playing field."

I'm not sure if she's interested in me or if she's being deceptive, but I don't want to make her suspicious. Time to bust out the undercover identity Lancaster arranged for me. "I'm a fire-safety inspector at the OFI. Grew up in Ottawa. Second of four kids. Severely allergic to shellfish and cats." Three out of four of those things are true.

Her eyes widen. "I'm allergic to cats too. When I was younger, I begged for a kitten. My parents finally caved. Within an hour, I was covered in hives and struggling to breathe, but I was clinging to that poor tabby, refusing to accept she was the issue. We had to take her back and never got another pet."

The way she speaks with such conviction and passion, even with a hint of sadness in her eyes, it appears she's being honest.

"Very similar to how I found out. My little sister brought home a box of abandoned kittens. Needless to say, it came down to saving me or them."

"I hope your sister chose the kittens."

I laugh a genuine laugh, which is an unusual feeling. Most of the time, with a suspect, every action and reaction are calculated, but Georgia keeps surprising me. "She did, but they had to stay in the garage. Though she put up some good arguments to move my bed out there instead."

"Phew." Georgia smiles wide, creating faint creases around her eyes. "As long as the kittens were okay. Sounds like a real cat-astrophe."

I laugh again, nearly spitting out my sip of coffee. I watch as she rips apart her cinnamon bun, eating one small piece at a time. She tells me about her fervent love for any and all sporting events—something I had gathered from her social media posts.

We discuss my "job" and my dual roles inspecting buildings to ensure they're up to code and speaking in public schools about fire safety. They're all predetermined tidbits of information to share in hopes she'll see my capacity with the OFI as an opportunity to cut me in on future heists.

The strange thing is, I struggle to maintain the lie. There's something so backwards about lying to someone in an effort to make them tell the truth. Or even worse, trying to catch them in a lie. But if people were inherently honest, I'd be out of a job.

A job that is important to me and I will succeed at, no matter the cost.

Georgia

6

MUGGED

For some reason, when Archie speaks about his job, his demeanor shifts. It's almost as if he transforms from a person to a persona. One has feelings and funny memories. The other is regimented and rehearsed. The animation he had in his face talking about his sister and the kittens is replaced by structured sentences void of emotion. Back to the unreadable Archie from three days ago.

I do my best to circle back around to anything other than work, but he keeps asking about mine and sharing more details about his. Details about his I don't want, and ones about mine I don't want to share.

"So, what do you create as an artist? Obviously you paint."

I stuff the last piece of cinnamon roll into my mouth so I can delay answering. Then I take a sip of coffee to hold off another few seconds. "I *can* paint, and it seems to be what I'm asked to do most, but it's not my preference."

"What's your preference?"

"Graphite drawing. There's something satisfying about the sound on the paper that I find melodic and love getting lost in the rhythm of creating."

He studies me for a moment, stirring the remains of his oatmeal, creating a swirl of color from the mixed berries. "So why don't you do that?"

I fiddle with my ceramic mug, trying to choke out the real answer. "There's no money in it. Unless I want to build a career sketching tourists down at *Navy Pier*, it's hard to survive on that alone." That's embarrassing to admit. I might as well just add that I'm obviously not as good as I thought, and my years-long education at a prestigious art school was a massive waste of money. I take another sip of coffee to shut myself up before I blurt that too.

"Adulthood has a way of destroying dreams, doesn't it?" He gives me a weak, one-sided smile before pushing the last of his oatmeal to the side. It looks like it's hardened to the consistency of drying cement. "What kinds of things do you paint, then?"

Another question I don't want to answer. "A little bit of everything." I shrug off any more details on my current work and steer our conversation in a new direction. "What about your work? What made you want to be a fire-safety inspector? I'm going to assume it's because your allergy prevented you from getting any cats out of trees."

Archie leans back in his chair, stretching out both arms to wrap his hands around his mug. "Well, since my kitten-rescuing days were cut short, I became a bit of a pyro. I was obsessed with starting and dowsing small fires. One got a little out of control and my brother had to call the fire department when one side of our garage went up in flames. As part of my punishment, I had to spend twenty hours at the station learning about fire safety." Some joy returns to his face that he'd been missing while we talked about daily work demands.

My body relaxes at seeing his persona disappear. I try to keep the casual conversation going. "Sounds like you and your siblings kept your parents on their toes."

"We did. All of us did our fair share. What about you? Any siblings?"

I smile and nod. "One big brother, Jake. He's a dentist in my hometown. Married. First kid on the way. Living his best life."

"Where is your hometown?" he asks, leaning back in, resting his elbows on the table.

"North Utica. I told you… small town."

He doesn't look surprised by my admission that I grew up one township over from him. "Wow. What are the chances? We were neighbors. Did you go to high school in Ottawa?"

"LaSalle. We were on the west side of town, so it was closer." I look down at my mug and finally see the dark ring encircling the bottom. This little chat with Archie has been nice, but after the physical reaction I had when he touched my face, I think it's smart for me to cut things short. My imagination can get away from me sometimes—something I used to think made me a good artist—but right now, I need to keep it under control. "Thank you for breakfast, Archie. I've got to get back home and get some stuff done, but I'm sure I'll see you around."

Before I stand, he reaches across the table and places his hand over mine. He immediately pulls it back, but the same sensation as the earlier thumb grazing has already shot up my arm.

"Sorry. I was just going to ask for your number. You know… in case I need to find the best taco place or something."

I'm tempted to direct him to one of the many map apps he could access on his phone. But I'm also tempted to give him my number because I'm curious about him. Since we're practically neighbors, it makes sense to have a friend in the building. Meredith from next door has at least six cats in her studio, so I'm not befriending her. Conrad, who lives next to Archie, sets all of my small-town girl alerts off. Practically, it's the smart thing to do—from a fire safety perspective—so I agree. I recite my number and he adds it into his phone, then sends me a text message so I can save his.

With no fanfare or promises to be in touch, I say goodbye and head for the door. I could go home, but I don't want to risk the awkward encounter if Archie's long legs catch up to me in fifty feet, so I make a detour. Before I get to Roosevelt, I decide I'll hop on the subway and go to my favorite craft supply store downtown. I told him I had things to do, but the sad reality is that I've sent out the pathetic number of commissions I had this month and have nothing on the horizon. So while I should not be spending money on craft supplies when I have no income to bank on, I need to do something that inspires me again.

I spend the next hour browsing the aisles of *Brick Art Supply Store*, picking things up and putting them back when I calculate my total. I walk out with some pencils, a sketch pad, and a vision in mind.

Cloud Gate, also known as *"The Bean"* is a landmark surrounded by iconic buildings, and collectively, they provide some inspiring man-made scenery to draw. If I'm lucky, I'll find some tourists who are seeing the sights for the first time. I sit on a bench that provides me with a view of *The Bean*, *The Heritage*, and the *Smurfit-Stone* building. The mirror finish of the monument largely reflects the sky, so as I take a few moments to study the moving cloud formations, a couple walks around the near end and stares at their own reflection. I smile as I watch them marvel at their distorted likeness, making funny faces, and laughing.

Just like I've done at least a hundred times before, I commit their joyful expressions to memory and begin sketching out the complete image. Unlike any time before, I find myself imagining doing the same thing with someone. Not just anyone... Archie. The thought is a blindside. Yes, he crossed my mind last night, but I'd just been caught off guard because a man I only met two days before moved onto my floor. That was understandable. This time, there's no logic to justify him crossing my mind. Nothing except he intrigues me and I want to peel back his gruff exterior to find out who he really is underneath.

That's not a task for today, though.

Back to the task that is. Finding joy in creating again.

The sketchbook I picked up is only eight by ten inches, so I have to budget my space. It fills up quickly as I immerse myself in recreating an image that portrays the marvels of human engineering and the elation created by it.

The couple is long gone by the time I'm done. Chances of running into them again are minimal; that was a onetime happy accident. Though I thought the same about seeing Archie again too.

I pack everything into the plastic bag just in time as rain starts to sprinkle down. I'm tempted to stay and watch it as it bounces off of *The Bean*, but self-preservation moves me to run the near half-mile to the subway station.

My sweater is soaked by the time I arrive at Monroe Station. Thankfully, the train arrives a few seconds later, so I'm not left waiting on the platform. The warm air embraces me as I walk onto the train and find my seat. Again, as I sit in this seat, I recall my first interaction with Archie. I picture his serious face across from me and replay our conversation in my head. It was brief and more of an exchange than a conversation, but he's stuck in my head. The set of his jaw accented by the light stubble. The bulge of his biceps under his crisp suit. The glint in his eyes that says there's more to him than he lets anyone see.

And once something is stuck in my head, the only way to get the emotions out is to put them on paper.

Archie

7

WINDOW OF OPPORTUNITY

Never in my life have I had such a difficult time wording a text. Part of me wants to message Lancaster to ask how to proceed, but my gut instinct says this has to come across as natural. Georgia is a bit of a skittish creature. One wrong word or gesture can send her running off without warning. I have fifty-four days left to crack this case, so I can't afford to scare her away again.

Beyond that, the art thieves hit another target, but we had no idea they did it at the time—we're only learning of this three weeks later. They were in and out without being noticed and left a passable forgery behind. It wasn't until the museum's art restoration specialists went to work on the painting that they realized it was a fake. Upon playback of security footage, in the half-second the crew is on camera before they hacked the computer system, we determined it was the same group who performed the other heists. So now we've realized we only know of twelve stolen works, but we could be missing countless more.

Time is of the essence.

Archie: *Need a good recommendation for dinner. Any suggestions?*

Now we wait.

I walk over to the window to look at my not-so-impressive view and find one thing that captures my interest. Georgia, sitting behind an easel, focused on it with great intensity. I watch her for a few minutes as she moves her pencil across the canvas with a flourish, then places it in her mouth to tweak something with her hand. That's no doubt how she ended up with a smudge on her cheek on Sunday.

She hasn't messaged me since our coffee outing, and I got sick of staring out my peephole, waiting for her to emerge, hoping I could "accidentally" bump into her. That's not progress and I don't have time to waste; I need to take down this crew before they strike again.

The first four incidents, the heist crew attacked the security guards on duty, with one ending up in serious condition. They hacked the security systems and were able to get in and out quickly. The galleries were smaller, high-end locations with less security. The last two, however, have been higher profile targets, and they've been even more efficient each time. Criminals usually progress in their efforts, getting more brazen and confident with each successful heist. Now, with each job, they're leaving behind less and less evidence they were ever there.

They need to be stopped. Between local police and the FBI resources, there's no reason why a four-person crew should be able to evade capture and get away with multiple felonies. If I'm going to work my way up in the bureau and enact change, solving cases like this is necessary to make my name known.

My phone rings, distracting me from the building frustration over this unsolved mystery and the enigma in the rooftop courtyard. I smile at the photo on the screen and answer on speakerphone. "Hey, Nate. What's going on?"

"Good to know my little brother's still alive. Haven't heard from you for over a week."

That comment takes the lightheartedness out of our conversation immediately. I normally make it a point to check in every other day. "Sorry, man. Got distracted on a case."

"Janine and I are in the city for a doctor's appointment and wanted to see if you want to meet. Grab a late lunch or something."

"Doctor's appointment? Everything okay?"

He chuckles and I hear Janine in the background asking which way she should be going.

"Just regular follow-up stuff. No change," he replies. The usual levity he uses to mask his disappointment is obvious in his voice.

"You're perfect the way you are," Janine adds.

"I second that. No change means nothing has gotten worse, so that's something to be happy about."

A notification pops up on my screen with a text message, so I tap it as my brother replies, once again trying to convince me he's looking on the bright side and content with the hand he's been dealt.

Georgia: The Firehouse. *Food is great and you'll love the atmosphere.*

"How late are you guys in the city?" I ask.

"We're in no hurry to leave. Do you have something in mind?"

"I'm not sure. Why don't you guys go to my place? I'll meet you there in a bit. You still have your key, right?"

Nate murmurs with his hand covering the phone, then returns to agree with my plan. We end the call with the understanding I'll be home within the hour.

Now comes part two. When I first texted Georgia, I wasn't sure how I'd convince her to join me for dinner, but this works out perfectly. I hope.

Archie: *Want to meet me there? 6pm?*

Hardly a poetic invitation, but I don't want her to read too much into it. I need her to open up to me. This isn't protocol, but if I play my cards right, it could be the catalyst to get her to let her guard down.

Georgia: *Why?*

Archie: *For a friendly dinner. My treat.*

I walk back over to the window and notice she's no longer outside. Just then, I hear the elevator ding, and before I can get to the door to look out the peephole, there's a knock.

Georgia stands on the other side wearing a gray long-sleeve shirt with black smudges on it. She doesn't have any on her face this time. Her hands are also empty, with no sign of whatever she was working on. "Don't you have other friends you can ask?"

Her question surprises me, but I stutter out a reply, "I've already gone for dinner with my other friends." I blow out a long sigh, really trying to sell my desperation. "My brother and his wife are in town and want to meet up for dinner. I can't handle being the third wheel again." I paste on my most convincing smile, which is easy to do when her indignant scowl is so amusing. "Will you save me? I'll owe you."

"You want me to go on a double date with you and your brother?"

I could say no. I could play this off like that's not what I'm asking—really, it's not—but I don't. "Yes."

She stares at me for a second, then spins to walk toward her door, where I notice a canvas leaning against it. After a few steps, she calls back, "Fine, but I'm ordering the ribeye."

"I'm sorry. You want us to be part of your undercover assignment? You want to bring a criminal to dinner?" Nate stares at me from across my living room. His hair is freshly cut and his face clean shaven. It makes him look younger than me, even though he's two years older.

"She's not part of the Outfit. I just want her to feel comfortable, so I need someone who's familiar enough around me to help her relax. I'm on a tight timeline here; I'm going off-book."

Janine unhelpfully adds, "I say if we can get this guy to go on a date, we take our shot."

"Thanks, J. I can always count on you." I roll my eyes like a petulant teen, which is how she seems to still view me. "Please, Nate. I need to solve this case."

He doesn't reply for a moment, appearing as if he's running a cost-benefit analysis in his head. "What makes you think she's guilty? Or at least what is she supposedly guilty of? I'm not taking my wife to meet a criminal without knowing what we're dealing with."

Janine claps a hand on her chest as her mouth gapes. "I can handle myself, thank you very much."

"That doesn't mean I don't want to protect you when I can." Nate flashes her a tender smile. "I need assurances she won't be in any danger," he requests from me.

"You know I can't tell you details of an active case, but I'd never ask you guys if I thought that was even a remote possibility. Plus, I'll pay for dinner. Whatever you want. Then you guys can stay here tonight so you're not driving back in the dark."

Nate and Janine exchange a knowing look and nod at each other.

"Fine. But if anything happens to Janine, I swear—"

"Nothing will happen. But I do have some ground rules I need to go over with you both."

We spend the next couple of hours rehashing my cover story, making sure they know about my fake job that justifies my unusual work hours, my new accommodations, my vehicle, and everything else they should know to maintain my new identity. Any childhood stories are fair game, but nothing that refers to college years. I don't want either of them bumbling up and talking about my degree in criminal justice when I'm supposed to be a fire-safety investigator.

Once I change into a clean suit, I head back to my apartment building to park there. *The Firehouse* is less than half a mile away, so it's easier to walk instead of dealing with city parking. Janine and Nate go directly to the restaurant to get us a table. Since Georgia agreed to meet me there, I walk the one block west to our location, go inside to make sure Nate and Janine found a suitable spot, then return outside to position myself out of sight to wait for Georgia.

The temperature is unseasonably warm for the first week of October, hovering around seventy degrees. My suit jacket feels stifling for the first time since my senior prom, and I'm not sure why. Once I see a vision in a long-sleeve burgundy satin wrap dress come into view, it makes sense.

Eighteen-year-old me may have thought Amy Brenerhoff was gorgeous, but next to Georgia, who is the embodiment of a femme fatale, I'd rate Amy right around the same as my brother. No offense to either of them, but Georgia is in her own league. With her hair down in loose curls, bouncing with each step, she looks angelic. Her black-framed glasses make her look innocent. The way the silky wine-colored fabric drapes over her feminine curves has me hypnotized. Nothing about her screams criminal.

That's what makes her so dangerous.

But I've never been afraid to flirt with danger.

Georgia

8

STEAK-OUT

Archie is tucked beside a boxwood shrub in a tall planter outside of the restaurant door. He's leaning against the aged brick building, looking at his phone, so I'm not sure if he sees me approaching.

Much like the first time I interrupted his phone scrolling, I clear my throat. "Hi."

He lifts his head and settles his eyes on mine. I feel a flicker of disappointment that he didn't even glance at my outfit. This may be a fake date, but I made a real effort like I would for a real one.

"Hey. You… uh… you look nice," he greets, but it hardly sounds convincing.

"Thanks. You too. Are you waiting for your brother?"

He slides his phone into his pocket. "No, they're already here. I was waiting for you."

"Oh, am I late?" I pull my small purse from my hip, wanting to grab my phone and check the time.

"You're right on time. We were a few minutes early." He juts out his right elbow, signaling me to weave my arm in his.

I hesitate for a second, but decide to commit to the evening. This is the most un-Georgia-like thing I've done in months, and it feels good to be a little carefree. The contact between us creates the same rush of electricity up my arm that I had both other times, and on this occasion, it's through at least three layers of fabric. Maybe it has nothing to do with his proximity and is more to do with nerves.

That's it. I'm just nervous.

Archie leads us to a table where I spot a man who looks like a younger version of him and a woman with beautiful rosy-bronze skin and silky black curls. I suddenly feel inadequate in her presence because she is stunning.

They've nabbed a table right near the large garage doors that open to provide a mix of indoors and out. The slight movement of air that doesn't even qualify as a breeze is still refreshing. The brief gusts at least remind me to breathe, so I'm not smothering myself with my own nerves. I haven't been this anxious since final exams.

"Nate, J, this is Georgia. Georgia, this is my brother, Nate, and his wife, Janine." Archie gestures toward each of them.

Janine half stands to reach across the table and offer a handshake, which, of course, I accept. Then I do the same with Nate, who is seated to my right.

"It's nice to meet you both. I'm sorry for keeping you waiting."

Nate waves off my apology. "We weren't waiting. We just got here a few minutes ago."

Our waiter comes to take our drink order, so Archie asks for a bottle of Spanish red wine and three glasses, and Janine orders a mocktail, since she's driving. Almost immediately after the server leaves, our conversation falls to work. Janine asks what I do for a living, and I pause to contemplate when that became the question people asked out of the gate, as if they need that information to determine someone's worth. Why don't we ask, "Are you happy?" or "What is your goal in life?" Something more profound than just a person's employment status. But maybe that's just me because explaining my current status is complicated. And depressing.

"She's an artist. Though I've only seen one of her paintings," Archie replies after my internal debate renders me speechless for a few seconds too long.

"Ooh, so you paint? I don't have a creative bone in my body. I can't carry a tune in a bucket."

Perfect opportunity to redirect the focus off of me. "I'm sure that's not true. I know a great karaoke place we could try sometime."

Janine guffaws at the same time Nate's eyes open comically wide.

Archie shakes his head adamantly. "No to Janine and karaoke. There's enough suffering in this world."

She doesn't even argue. The girl knows her weaknesses.

"Maybe you could join Georgia for one of the paint nights she goes to instead. At least that would only be an assault on our eyes," Archie suggests.

Nate glares at him from across the table, so I watch the silent exchange between them. I don't feel like he's offended Archie has insulted Janine's artistic abilities. Whatever his issue is, it's over my head.

After a few seconds, it's getting uncomfortable, so I reply, "Oh, sure. My friends and I go to this great place up the road called *Design with Wine*. The wine isn't a requirement, though."

The server returns with our drinks not a moment too soon and, after pouring equal portions into the three thin-stemmed glasses, asks if we're ready to order. Archie nods to me, but I defer to Janine and Nate. They each order a roasted half chicken with sides. I decide on a vegetarian pasta dish because I don't feel right costing Archie a small fortune on a cut of beef I won't be able to eat all of. He lifts a brow at me, silently questioning my choice. I smile in return and close my menu. He orders the wagyu strip loin, which our server scribbles down, and turns to walk away.

"Oh, excuse me?" I call before he gets out of hearing distance. Once I have his attention, I continue while gesturing at Archie, "He's allergic to shellfish. Can you be sure his food doesn't touch anything, please?"

Archie, Nate, and Janine all stare at me like I'm a star exhibit. My cheeks warm under the scrutiny, so I take a sip of wine to hide my embarrassment. Maybe I shouldn't have said anything.

"Thank you." Archie places his hand on mine again when I set down my glass. A combination of the alcohol and the rough texture of his skin sends a zing right up my arm.

"I listen, and I have a good memory." I wink at him, then add, "Plus, if you die, I'll have to pay my own bill." That was supposed to be a joke, but the second it comes out, I regret my choice of words. I don't get a chance to apologize before all three of my tablemates are laughing.

Nate declares he likes me because I'm not afraid to fire back, and Janine predicts I'll be the first person to penetrate Archie's emotional suit of armor. Whatever that means. She obviously doesn't know this is a fake date.

Our food arrives a short time later, so we continue our conversation between bites, and I listen to Nate share stories about all the trouble Archie got into as a child. Archie dished it right back, telling us about Nate's fondness for bottle rockets and BB guns. It sounds like the two of them were going concerns and their two younger sisters didn't help matters. I make far too many punny jokes, but everyone laughs—probably to be polite.

While our plates get cleared away, Nate's expression turns somber, and he shifts from side to side to adjust himself. He looks at me and says, "Most people ask what's wrong with me within the first few minutes of conversation. Thank you for letting me feel normal."

I tilt my head and look into his dark eyes that are not quite as dynamic as his brother's. "You are normal. Why would anyone ask what's wrong with you?"

He's remains silent for several seconds, and I don't understand why. He grabs the edge of the table and pushes himself backwards, displaying his wheelchair.

It makes me angry when I realize he's implying people ask about his disability as if it's a topic of conversation worthy of him not being shown respect. "How does anyone have the audacity to ask you what's 'wrong' with you? Do you ask them what's wrong with them?"

Nate chuckles. Janine places a hand on his forearm once he settles back at the table. The look he gives her at that moment nearly brings me to tears. The sheer adoration and respect he has for her is evident in his eyes. It says more than a million words ever could.

He returns his focus to me once again. "People are curious about someone who is different. It took me a couple of years to come to terms with that."

"That doesn't give people the right to be rude. Asking what's wrong with you? Pshh." I shake my head, still infuriated people see differences as a source of entertainment for themselves and not as part of the beauty in the world. "Flowers wouldn't bring us the same joy if each one was the same. Forests wouldn't hold the same appeal if each tree was uniform and shed their leaves at the same time. People wouldn't spend time and money touring the Savanna if all the animals were identical. It baffles me why anyone would think human differences are less beautiful. That's all I'm going to say about that." I glance at Archie, who has been silent for several minutes, and he's staring at me with an indiscernible expression. Unsurprising.

"Well, thank you for saying that," Nate replies, drawing my attention back to him. "I hope we'll get to see you again soon, Georgia. It was nice to see my little brother smile."

Archie and Nate have another wordless exchange with narrowing eyes and animated brows. I look across to Janine for clarification, but she just offers me a kind smile. I take that as a form of reassurance that there's some family drama I don't need to be privy to. The tension is palpable.

I attempt to break it before things gets uncomfortable. "This was really nice. It was a pleasure to meet you both. Janine, if you're ever up for a paint night and you're in the area, Archie has my number."

She thanks me, and once all family members have exchanged hugs, the lovebirds leave, citing that they want to get back to their accommodations for the night. Most of the evening felt comfortable and relaxed, despite my preference to watch people from a distance rather than interact with them. Now, with just Archie and me at the table, the vibe is drastically different. He shifts to a new intensity. His eyes are more focused. His posture is more rigid. He signals our server to bring our bill, and waits for it without speaking.

I slide my chair out and stand. "I'm going to head out too. Thank you for—"

"Wait. I'll walk you home. It's dark out."

Seriously? I just sat beside him in awkward silence for several minutes and *now* he wants to act like a gentleman? Worse than that, he wants to prolong our time alone together? "It's fine. I walk home at night all the time. Jiu-jitsu, remember?"

He reaches up and clutches my hand in his, stopping me from walking away. Partly because he's holding my hand, and I can't leave without it. Partly because his touch leaves me incapacitated. Mostly because I like how it feels and don't want him to let go.

But he does. He drops his hand to his side and shakes it out like it fell asleep. "Just give me thirty seconds. We're going the same way, anyway." He slips his wallet out of his pocket, then locks his piercing brown eyes on me. "Please?"

I nod and drop back into my seat. My guard is slipping around him already. And I don't think any black belt in martial arts can protect me.

Archie

ON DUTY

Why do my stupid hands keep touching her? One wrong move and I'm going to end this case with a mistrial because of unprofessional conduct. But it's like I've lost all control around her. She's enchanting and hypnotic, and if I'm not careful, she's going to put me in a trance.

On our walk home, I struggle to keep my hand from reaching for hers. But ten feet out the restaurant doors, she shivers and professional boundaries are no longer my concern. I shrug my jacket off and wrap it around her shoulders.

"Thank you," she says so quietly, I barely hear. "And thanks again for dinner."

"You're welcome. I was surprised you didn't go for the ribeye."

"You know what they say." She looks at me for a guess, but I stay silent. "A vegetarian meal is a big *missed steak*."

Her puns are so terrible. It's simultaneously the most adorable and unattractive thing about her. Assuming we're not counting her life of crime in the equation. Once that factors in, puns aren't so bad.

I laugh anyway because a bad pun is still funny. And she has a way of nailing the comedic timing.

We walk another stretch in silence until I break it. "Thank you. For back there… with Nate."

She glances up at me while we wait at the crosswalk. "For what?"

I was sure everything she said to him was just her practiced con personality. That she was playing him, trying to win him over because that's what con artists do. Collect favor with people and keep them in their arsenal for a time when they can use them to achieve their nefarious goals. They usually see nice people as easy targets, and both Nate and Janine fit that criterion. But can she really be that good of an actor? To look so clueless about what I'm referring to?

"Thank you for not drawing attention to his disability. Most people see it as the elephant in the room, and they're all zoologists who need answers."

The light changes, allowing us to proceed across the street. Our building is less than a quarter mile, so I need to capitalize on the evening between here and home.

"Seven years ago, Nate was in a workplace accident. He was working construction on a strip mall when the roof collapsed, leaving him with damage to his spinal cord. Three other guys died. Him and Janine had just gotten married, so it was tough going for a bit."

Georgia keeps her eyes on the ground in front of her as she strolls along the sidewalk, hugging my jacket around herself. "I'm so sorry. That had to have been difficult for everyone."

Suddenly, I feel like a scumbag for sharing my brother's story and using his pain to draw me closer to a target. I've never felt like a worse brother than I do at this moment.

Georgia surprises me by reaching over to interlace her fingers with mine. "He's doing all right, though. Him and Janine seem happy, and that's the important thing, right? I'd say he's winning at life."

I don't let go of her hand. As we walk into our building lobby and I look down at her, I feel like I'm walking a date home. A real date.

That jolts me back to reality. I drop her hand when we reach the elevator, under the guise of needing it to press the button — like I don't have a second one that is perfectly capable of the mundane task. She notices my abrupt disconnect, but I ignore the hurt on her face. I need to get my head refocused so I can end this night on a good note.

We arrive on the fifth floor and I walk her to her door. We stand silently for about ten seconds, which are nine more than what's comfortable. She slides my jacket off of her shoulders and hands it back to me.

"Thank you for coming with me tonight. I owe you again. You're a good friend." I clap her on the arm like a frat brother and instantly wish I could clap myself in the face instead. This is not leaving the right impression, but I don't want to give her the wrong one, either.

This situation is what my mother refers to as a conundrum.

Georgia gives me a sweet smile that looks a lot like a *nice knowing you, buddy* gesture. "Thanks for dinner. I'll... see you around, Archie." Then she unlocks her door and tucks herself inside without so much as a backwards glance.

I may have left out certain details in my report to Lancaster. Like the bit about my brother and his wife working to solidify my undercover identity, but also exposing a large portion of my true one. Georgia now knows more about my childhood than any other woman I've actually dated. My bosses wouldn't be too thrilled about that part, but the ends will justify the means.

I finish in the gym at 6:45 and go back to my apartment to get ready for work. In the midst of choking back the last of my protein shake and trying to find my other shoe, my phone rings.

Based on the time, I assume it's Lancaster, so I don't check the name. "Prewitt."

"I know. We have the same last name," my brother snaps.

"You sound like you're in a foul mood. Are you in the doghouse for something?"

"That woman is not a criminal, Archie. I don't know what you're investigating her for or what you think she's done, but she is *not* a criminal," he repeats. My brother rarely gets passionate about anything other than ornithology or architecture, so to hear his conviction is equal parts surprising and amusing.

"I think I'm better qualified to make that decision. I told you she wasn't a hardened criminal, but that doesn't mean she's innocent."

That's what the evidence points to. Circumstantial, maybe, but she's still the only lead I have at this point. It's only a matter of time before the hard evidence comes to light.

"No, I'm telling you. I looked into her eyes. If she's involved with something, it's not by choice. Maybe someone... I don't know... kidnapped her family. She's being blackmailed."

"Hate to burst your bubble, bro, but white-collar criminals often don't look—"

"I know exactly how they look! Don't patronize me, Archie. You may be the big FBI agent, but you get so caught up in doing your job, you forget how to see people. You're so busy profiling them and compiling evidence that you don't see their souls."

That characterization of who he thinks I am irritates me. I'm not blind to people's personalities or struggles. I'm not bent on convicting an innocent person, but I am determined to convict guilty ones. "Don't let her get in your head because she was nice to y—"

"That's not why. I'm telling you, you're wasting your time. And if I'm being completely honest, if you keep lying to her, you're going to burn a bridge you won't be able to rebuild. From what Janine and I saw, that's one worth preserving."

"Don't be ridiculous, Nate. She's a crimin—"

"No, she's not," he interrupts with conviction. Again.

"Listen, I'm getting a little tired of being cut off and having my ability to do my job questioned, so I'm going to let you go. I'll call you on the weekend. Don't forget to lock up my house when you leave." I hang up the phone and finally find my shoe tucked under my dresser.

My mood for the rest of the day is foul. I have to check in at the OFI headquarters just to keep up appearances and get a briefing on suspected arsons in the city. For years I thought the staff in the fire investigations department were just washed-up old firefighters who wanted to live out their golden years pushing papers, but I couldn't have been more wrong. I earn a newfound respect for everyone in the department.

That doesn't change my mood, though.

Nate questioning my judgment like that was out of line. I have always trusted my gut and I have a strong feeling that Georgia is the stimulus to propel my career forward. These two months will not be a waste of my time.

I haven't seen Georgia since we returned from dinner two nights ago. Correction: she hasn't seen me since two nights ago. I've followed her at a distance and am now witnessing her taking an envelope from a middle-aged man outside of *Adler Planetarium*. I've passed off a photo of him to run through facial recognition software, but it will take a while to get a response.

He looks like your average fifty-something man with graying hair and a robust middle. His body type doesn't match any of the security footage from the previous heists. Maybe they're paying him off to access something of value in the planetarium. No scenario is off the table right now.

Just so I don't let the benefit of the other night wear off or allow our awkward departure to linger any longer, I send Georgia a text.

Archie: *Are you busy tomorrow night?*

The man returns inside. She looks happy with the exchange as she strolls down the Skyline Walk, carrying her large tote bag. She sets everything on the concrete wall, facing out toward the city's towering high-rises along the water, and holds up her phone—presumably to check my message.

She tucks it back in her small shoulder bag, then proceeds to pull art supplies from her tote and set up a portable easel. The knowledge she saw my message and ignored it stings more than it should.

This is just business. It's not personal. So why does it feel like it is?

SKETCHY

It's not my style to ignore messages. The manners my parents instilled in me always win out; not replying is rude. But when Archie walked me home two nights ago, his "good friend" comment made me feel… cheap. Stupid, I know. He didn't make any promises and admitted it was just to save him from the awkward third-wheel scenario. Somewhere on the walk home, listening to him open up about his brother, I guess I got my wires crossed and, like an idiot, held his hand. So when he made it a point to body check me back into the friend zone, I felt foolish.

Now I'm too embarrassed to face him again—even through a text message. I'll have to, eventually. We live on the same floor. Unless I turn into a recluse, chances are we're going to run into each other. For now, I'm going to focus on my task at hand and forget about Archie.

Since this piece is a commission and not just a painting for fun, it's going to take me a lot more hours to finish and perfect. The narrow walkways here don't give me space to set up my easel and stand without being constantly crashed into, and there's no way I'm sitting on this concrete wall for ten hours in one go. So I take out my phone again to snap some photos of the landscape I've been asked to re-create. At least that way, I can work on some bits and pieces at home.

I don't take a single photo before Archie's message taunts me. Am I free tomorrow night? Do I want to be?

Georgia: *That depends.*

He replies immediately. **Archie:** *On?*

I wish I knew. Me getting over my habit of closing myself off and immersing myself in creating? The healing of my injured pride?

Archie: *I have tickets to an IHL preseason game. Nate won them, but they can't upgrade to accessible seating. Want to go?*

My heart hurts for Nate. That's a really unfair reality I'm sure a lot of people with disabilities have to deal with.

Georgia: *I don't want to take his tickets. Can I try calling to see if they can find seats that will work?*

Archie: *He says it's fine. He's not a hockey fan anyway.*

Georgia: *Don't you have friends you can ask?*

Archie: *They're all on shift tomorrow. Too late to swap.*

I love going to hockey games. Out of all sporting events, they're my favorite. My family and I used to come into the city once a year to take in a game and I would look forward to it for months. So, despite my embarrassment over our last encounter, I agree.

With plans for him to stop by my place tomorrow evening, I get back to work. I've got a masterpiece to create.

▰▰ DO NOT CROSS ▰▰

● JUST KIDDING ● KEEP GOING, YOU REBEL ●

Social media is the bane of my existence. From day one, every bit of marketing material for creatives has told me it's a necessary evil for sharing my work. I've amassed a small following, but not enough to gain any traction. Rene is my number one fan who likes and comments on everything I post, telling me how amazing I am. Michelle constantly shares my work, but none of it seems to get me anywhere. My mom also "liked" my page out of obligation, but never says much. A three-person fan club isn't exactly a ringing endorsement. Especially when one is a reluctant follower who doesn't support my choices in real life.

When a notification pops up for a message from Caroline Brown while I'm trying to get ready for the hockey game, I'm not sure what to make of it. She's recently followed my page, but beyond that, we've had no interaction. Being an amateur sleuth, I click on her profile and immediately recognize her as the woman I gave the drawing to last week.

Caroline: *Georgia, I hope you don't mind me messaging you, but I showed your beautiful drawing to some friends of ours, and they'd like to commission you to do one for them.*

I reread the message at least twelve times to make sure this is real. Commission me for a drawing? Is this really happening? I better make sure they don't expect me to draw an entire family portrait for twenty dollars. People tend to underestimate the time it takes to create custom art.

Georgia: *I'd be happy to speak with them. Are they in the Chicago area?*

Caroline: *No, unfortunately not. They're friends of ours from Buffalo.*

Ugh. That means they're probably going to want me to draw them from a picture, which isn't ideal. It's not organic, and unless they're really well done photos, it's hard to capture the emotion I strive to re-create.

But, as the saying goes, beggars can't be choosers. If they're offering to pay for my work, I'd draw the back end of a horse if they asked.

Georgia: *I'd be happy to chat with them and figure out what they're looking for. They can send me an email or give me a call at the info in my bio.*

Caroline: *They'll be so excited. I'm going to tell all of my friends about you. You're so talented. Thank you again for your beautiful drawing.*

She adds a photo of the drawing, now framed and hanging on a wall, surrounded by wedding and family pictures. Knowing they appreciate it enough to give it pride of placement in their home makes me smile.

Georgia: *It was my pleasure, truly.*

I can hardly believe my luck. What are the chances that the one family I chose to draw ends up sharing my art and results in more work? Slim.

A knock at the door disrupts my silent mini celebration.

"One second!" I scan my apartment to make sure nothing is left out that shouldn't be before going to open the door.

Archie is dressed in a jersey, dark jeans, and classic tan Timberlands. He looks good dressed down, but my favorite addition is his plain black baseball cap. "Hi." He utters the single syllable, dragging it out as he scans my outfit from bottom to top.

My fitted white jersey is a contrast to his bright red one. It's only fitted because I've had it since high school—fourteen-year-old me did not possess the same curves. My skinny jeans are a light wash and I've got on my favorite white sneakers that go with everything. It's casual, but the way he's looking at me, I don't know if I chose right.

"Hey," I choke out on account of my dry throat.

"You look…"

I hold my breath, waiting for him to continue, surprised by my ridiculous need for his validation.

"… like you need a foam finger."

Then I deflate like a balloon. "Thanks?" I'm not sure what that even means. Is this too much? Not enough? Why can't I read him? But if a foam finger helps me keep a barrier between our skin, I'll gladly wear one.

I grab my jacket to drape over my arm, march out the door and lock it behind me while Archie presses the button for the elevator.

"Do you want to take transit or drive?"

I look up at him as the elevator doors open. "I don't drive. Starving artist, remember?"

He looks like he wants to laugh but thinks better of it. "I mean my car. It's up to you. I don't want you to think I'm set on kidnapping you."

That's news to me he even has a car. "I haven't taken it completely off the table. The bus makes more sense though. Finding parking will be a nightmare."

We exit into the lobby and cross the polished marble floor to the front doors.

"I can buy a pair of foam fingers with the money I'll save on parking. Maybe even one drink, but we'll have to flip for it." He smirks as he holds the door open for me to exit.

"You don't need to buy me anything, Archie. Do you buy your other friends dinner and drinks and... foam fingers?" I throw his use of the term 'friend' back at him in such a childish way, it only makes me more embarrassed about our encounter three nights ago. I slide my jacket on, even though I'm not cold, just so I can put my hands in the pockets.

We arrive at Roosevelt Station, and the dynamic between us feels much the same as it did when we first interacted here. We've spent time together since then, but he's still very much a stranger. He attempts to make small talk, asking me if I've been to different locations in the city and if I've been to certain art galleries. Every single one he mentions, I've been to at least twice. To be fair, I've been to every art gallery or museum between here and Utica a few times. Some, I couldn't even count the number of visits I've made.

"What's your favorite work of art of all time?" he asks next.

I don't hesitate. "*The Captive Slave* by John Philip Simpson. It's a life-changing experience."

"Is it in Chicago?"

That's a weird follow-up question. Maybe he wants to see it for himself.

"It is. At *The Art Institute*."

He nods as the subway arrives, so we hop on the orange line car and find two seats side by side.

"What makes it your favorite?"

That painting stirs up so much emotion in me, my voice cracks as I explain. "Because what he captured, the emotion in that man's face, you cannot look at that painting and *not* feel every bit of despair he felt. It causes such a visceral reaction that moves people to tears. It's so much more than just a man sitting in an orange jumpsuit. It captures the plight of generations of slaves. The hopelessness and anguish each of them must have felt." I realize somewhere during my monologue, I closed my eyes to picture the painting. My recollection of it is so vivid, it's as if it's right in front of me. "You can feel the chains on his wrists and the tiredness in his soul. It's heartbreaking and life changing and beautiful in the saddest of ways, all at the same time."

"Wow. Sounds like it must be valuable."

"Value of art is subjective. Some people care about the dollar amount, but every piece is so much more than that." I hate it when people boil down a piece of art's worth to its cost or the highest bid it fetches at auction. That's not what makes a work of art impactful. "So much of human emotion is left unsaid. We war with feelings that we never express and fight battles we never win. But it's all there for other people to see if they look hard enough. Art captures that. Whether it's realism portraying it or abstract expression leaving it to the viewer's imagination, it's there."

He pauses for a moment, as if he's contemplating his words. "Would you ever re-create that painting?"

I turn to face Archie, who is focused on me. His signature indifferent expression paired with unreadable body language — slouched back, legs wide, one arm resting on his thigh and the other draped along the back of empty seats beside him. Of everything I've just said, that seems like a weird question to ask.

Before I answer, the train squeals to a stop at Washington/Wells Station, so the shuffling crowds remind us this is where we need to get off. We both exit onto the platform, but the mass of people separates us and, in the blink of an eye, Archie is nowhere to be seen. Great. Not that I'm inept and can't find my way around, but I'll be annoyed if we don't get to see the game. I walk over to a clearing at the edge of the station toward the bus stop we should be waiting at. While I'm distracted trying to pull my phone from my purse, someone wraps my free hand in a comforting grasp. I don't even need to look. I do anyway, just to make sure my brain isn't playing tricks on me.

"I thought you got away from me."

"Archie," I reply with a chuckle, "that sounds like something a kidnapper would say."

"Pretty sure they'd say, 'You're never getting away from me,' with some kind of creepy laugh." He looks down the street as we round the corner, and pulls me into an easy jog. "I see the bus. Come on."

And for some reason, the decision to follow him anywhere feels as natural as graphite on paper.

Archie

11

LIE ABILITY

Nate didn't win these tickets. I paid several hundred dollars for preseason tickets because I remember her saying she loves going to sporting events and thought it would be a way to spend some time with her again. To get some insight into whatever she's got brewing with the guy she met yesterday and why she comes and goes at unusual hours. So far, I don't have answers to either.

We disembark the bus at the stop across from *The Connect Center*, only a few feet from gate three, where we need to enter. Lineups are forming, so instinctively, I grab hold of Georgia's hand so I don't lose her again. I'm telling myself that's the only reason. Entirely professional.

I'm kicking myself for not scanning our surroundings before I asked her if she'd recreate her favorite painting. That was a rookie mistake to ask when there were so many potential disruptions. Now, if I ask again, it's going to seem suspicious.

"Which section are we in?" she asks from her spot tucked behind me, still grasping my hand.

"101. Row six."

"Woah. Right behind the Chicago bench?"

Beats me. I just bought the tickets. Our proximity to the ice didn't play into my decision. "Perks of winning tickets, I guess."

"I still feel bad Nate couldn't come. This hardly seems fair. We get the—hey!"

Suddenly I'm jolted forward from Georgia pushing into my back. I catch myself and spin around to see what happened, only to find two buffoons pushing and shoving each other behind us. I spin Georgia so she's behind me again and shout at the two imbeciles to sort their petty grievance elsewhere before I sort it for them.

"Are you okay?" I ask Georgia once it's safe to turn my back on these two dude-bros, who are apparently at odds over which team is better. Like the entire point of the evening is not to let the teams decide that on the ice.

"Yeah. Par for the course. Happens every time." She shrugs off the encounter, but it has me on high alert.

The doors finally open and people start funneling inside. I hand Georgia her ticket, but usher her in front of me to keep any other rowdy fans from plowing her over. We get inside, where we're directed through metal detectors. Thankfully, I left my sidearm in my apartment so I won't have to justify carrying by showing my badge—which is also in my apartment. That would defeat the purpose of an undercover assignment.

Minutes later, we're getting settled in our seats. The same idiots from the collision outside are three rows behind us. Together. That makes the encounter even more confusing because they came to the game as friends cheering for opposing teams and couldn't even get through the ticket lineup without things getting heated. We're in for an interesting evening.

"Do you want something to eat?" I ask Georgia as she pulls off her jacket.

She scans our surroundings, studying the crowd filling in the rows of seats. "Maybe later. I like to watch the warmups."

Sure enough, sixty seconds later, the players from both teams make their way out onto the ice. Under the bright lights, they skate circles around their halves of the surface, taking easy shots on their goalies and congregating at the boards before darting off at top speeds. It looks like organized chaos to me, but Georgia is fully immersed in the experience. She talks about a few new teammates this year and asks me my opinion on veteran players. Her passion is much the same level as it was when she was discussing art. I enjoy watching most sporting events, but I don't get invested in their roster or placings in each division.

After the warmups are complete, the players file back into their dressing room as pre-game festivities start. I take that opportunity to fetch us some food. The lineups for everything are insane, so the only reasonable choice is a couple of hot dogs. She said she wasn't picky.

I return to our seats, walking past the two frenemies, who each have a full cup of beer and are gesticulating with their hands, sloshing it around like it's not seven bucks a serving.

I slide into my seat beside Georgia, handing her our gourmet meal. "Those guys don't have a pair of brain cells between them."

She stares at the food, looking unsure. Hesitant.

"Is that okay? I can get you something else."

Her mouth turns up into a slow smile. "It's fine. I'm just resisting the urge to torture you with a terrible pun. My friends tell me I'm intolerable."

I try not to react to that. I want to laugh, because her puns are awful, but intolerable is a stretch. "Go on. Let me hear it."

She hesitates before taking a bite of her hot dog. It takes her an unreasonable amount of time to chew the morsel of food she consumed. Then she clears her throat. "I never *sausage* a beautiful hot dog."

An uninhibited laugh bubbles out of me, and it's one of those situations that once you start, you can't stop. "That... was the worst joke I've ever heard." I swipe at my face and look at Georgia, realizing she's laughing just as hard.

"I know. They're only funny because they're so bad. Puns *are* the lowest form of humor." She shrugs off my insult. There's something so endearing about her laid-back personality. She's funny and sweet. The complete opposite of me. I have to stop myself from leaning in to kiss her.

She's a criminal. This is work, not personal. This isn't a date.

Saved by the lights. The arena falls into darkness and spotlights dance around the ice as the announcer calls the officials and the starting lineups for both teams. The deafening roar of the crowd for the home team is overshadowed by the boos for the visiting team, minus a handful of cheers, including the one man behind us.

Neither team scores in the first period. During the first intermission, a promotional team shoots T-shirts into the crowd from a cannon. I catch one, which I promptly pass to Georgia. She unrolls it and bursts out laughing as she turns it to show me.

The cartoon hot dog holds a sign with *Relish the Moment* written on it.

"I didn't think anyone could come up with a worse hot dog joke, but yep, they've gone and done it."

Georgia clutches the shirt to her chest, wearing a huge smile. "Let's be *frank*, here. I'm the real *wiener*." She looks genuinely proud of herself.

"Just when I thought we'd reached the limit for the worst."

The crowd erupts in loud cheers, drawing our attention to the jumbotron. They're panning the arena with the Kiss Cam, searching for unsuspecting couples. A camera zeroes in on a man and woman who promptly start flailing their arms and the woman makes a throat cutting gesture. The man appears to mouth *that's my sister* as he makes an X with his forearms. The crowd has a good laugh at their expense, but the camera moves on. They focus on two more couples who comply. One couple really goes for it, taking their moment in the spotlight for an epic PDA. The second couple shares a chaste kiss, and both have matching pink cheeks I don't suspect are from the cold air.

I'm distracted watching the giant screen when my own surprised face appears. I stare at it for a moment, watching Georgia turn to face me. She looks just as stunning five times her normal size and on a grainy screen. I take a deep breath and turn to look at her.

"We can pretend we're siblings," she blurts.

This is a problem. She's given me an out. I could pass and maintain my professional boundaries. But in the split second I have to decide, I tell myself this is the next necessary step to get her to trust me. Yes, that's why I'm leaning in and placing one hand on her cheek. That's exactly why a tangible electric pulse is humming through my veins when I make contact with her skin. It's certainly why my lips collide with hers and the erupting cheers fade away instantaneously as I taste her for the first time. Thankfully, she doesn't taste like hot dog. Somehow, she tastes like Juicy Fruit gum and banana cream pie. I'm so confused by that, but I can't be bothered to stop to ask. Georgia makes a faint moan as I caress her soft lips with mine. That sound is going to replay in my head for the foreseeable future.

The surrounding cheers come back into focus as Georgia inches her face away. I keep my eyes closed for a few seconds, allowing the sensation of her lips to linger. Until reality kicks back in and I realize I just kissed a suspect in front of twenty thousand spectators.

"I don't think we can convince anyone you're my brother now." Her lips are an even more vibrant pink, turned up in a smirk.

"You're probably right." Though, I doubt anyone would guess the actual nature of our relationship, and I can only hope to keep it that way.

The rest of the game passes in a flurry of excitement. Power plays, two fights, and as the clock ticks away, Chicago is up by two. Georgia reaches over to grab my hand again and it's the first contact we've had since our kiss almost ninety minutes ago. The final seconds count down and the buzzer sounds. Other spectators erupt in cheers and applause as the players form a huddle on the ice, congratulating each other right in front of the bench.

Again, Georgia shouts, "Hey!" just as I feel a splash of liquid on the right side of my face. I look at her to discover her hair is soaked, and all I can smell is beer.

"Are you okay?"

"Ugh. I'm fine. I smell like a brewery, but I've heard beer is good for your hair."

Security comes running down the stairs to tend to the idiot who threw his beer. I'm assuming it's the guy in the losing team's jersey.

I chuckle as I look back to make sure security has removed the beer thrower. "Way to look on the bright side."

"What can I say?" She glances at me from the corner of her eyes and a mischievous smile spreads, creating a faint dimple. "I'm just glad it wasn't *hard* liquor."

No, I won't say it. I will not stoop to this level. I can't resist. "It would hurt a lot less getting hit by a *soft* drink."

Georgia's smile grows exponentially wider. "Archie Prewitt, welcome to the dark side."

I don't think she realizes, but that's exactly what I'm waiting for her to do. "Come on. I'm *hoptimistic* I can get you home in one piece."

Georgia

12

CON ETIQUETTE

A foam finger would have been a smart choice. Hand holding does not seem like a friendly gesture, but maybe that's just me. I've never held Michelle or Rene's hands, yet I've spent ten percent of my evening with my hand in Archie's. It's starting to feel like a natural action.

We're strolling down the street toward home, smelling like beer, still riding the high from the game. And that kiss.

We may not have labeled this a date, but it's the best one I've ever been on. Minus getting shoved and having a full solo cup of beer saturate my head. Even with the hiccups and uncertainty, it has still been a great night.

Archie drops my hand and opens the front door to our building and allows me to walk in front of him. The temperature change has nothing to do with the warming of my cheeks. I'm wondering if he's going to try to kiss me at my door. Should I kiss him? At least give him permission? I swear, if he tells me I'm a good friend, I'm going to call on all of my fake jiu-jitsu expertise and punch him right in the throat.

Who am I kidding? I'd just smile, nod, and usher myself inside so I could watch a Hallmark movie and curse my failed attempt at a love life.

The elevator opens on the fifth floor, so I exit first and walk toward my door. My heart rate speeds up hearing Archie behind me. I get to the door and slide my key in, then suddenly feel a rush of panic at the thought of Archie asking to come in. I don't know what to expect now. This is why I normally don't let dates walk me home, but that's hard to avoid when someone lives three doors down.

My panic causes me to repeat the events of three nights ago. "Thank you for tonight, Archie. I'll see you around." Before he can reply, I slip inside my door and close it behind me.

I sink down against the wall, disappointed in myself for not giving him an opportunity to say good night. Instead of being a mature adult, it's easier to squash potential disappointment or upset by calling it quits before it starts.

It takes me half a bottle of shampoo to get the beer smell out of my hair. Most of my time while scrubbing is spent thinking about Archie's instinct to shield me from those two idiots at the game. He didn't hesitate to stand in front of me and that confirmed the protector vibe he gives off is accurate. I just wish he gave off some other readable vibes.

I throw my jersey, jacket, and jeans in the wash to clean those, then crawl into bed and flick on a movie. It might be easier to navigate this back and forth with Archie if I could throw myself in the washer and come out with a clean slate. Instead, I'll settle into this decades' old sports film and plead with my brain to sleep.

"Do you care to explain to me why you're on SportsCenter with a hunky hunk of hunkiness, covered in beer?"

There's a lot to process in Rene's conversation starter. I blink at the phone, unsure if I want to answer her question or hang up. But she's the type of person who is determined enough for answers, if I don't reply, she's bound to show up at my door. And 7a.m. is too early for that nonsense.

"My new neighbor. His brother won tickets, but he couldn't go because he uses a wheelchair and they didn't have accessible seats—which, I won't even get into how wrong that is—so I went as a replacement." That makes it sound platonic. Friendly. Nothing worth discussing further.

"This new neighbor... does he have a name?"

"Does it really matter? What do you mean I was on SportsCenter?" I grab my remote and flick on the TV, tuning to ESPN. Sure enough, the replay of last night's sportscast is on and there I am, minding my business, cheering for the home team as a full Solo cup of beer comes flying at the back of my head. What a claim to fame. "Ugh."

"So you and Hunky McHunkerson went on a date—"

"It wasn't a date. And don't call him that." I climb out of my bed and wander into the kitchen for a glass of water.

"You leave me no choice. Hunky McHunker—"

"Archie. His name is Archie."

"Ew. That's not a hunky name. What is Archie short for? Archibald? Hunky McHunk—"

"Rene! It's too early for this. Were you calling for a reason?"

"*Le sigh*. Yes, actually. Yours truly, the best friend ever, has some amazing news for you. After our paint night, I put out some feelers and *Smith Goldstein & Co.* wants to present you with an offer to host an exhibit."

Stunned doesn't quite encapsulate the surge of shock that rushes through me. *"Smith Goldstein & Co.* is a top gallery in the city. How...? Why...? I don't understand. They haven't even seen my portfolio."

"You underestimate me, my dear Georgia. One of my co-workers is married to the curator—which I didn't even know until I got held up in the staff room during my lunch break and heard him talking about his wife. So I connected with her and made an informal pitch. Untraditional, yes, but your work speaks for itself. She looked at your stuff online and said if you're interested, she'd love to set something up."

Wow. How is this real life? This is the kind of opportunity I've been dying for since I graduated. I haven't been part of an exhibit since my graduating class hosted ours. To have my own... that's a dream come true. But the self-doubt that has been gripping me for months takes a stranglehold on the small bit of confidence I had left.

I breathe out a sigh, too overwhelmed by all of this information first thing in the morning. "Thank you for trying. Um... But can we plan an evening in? I could use input from you and Michelle. I'm in uncharted waters here. With Archie... and now with this potential offer."

Rene pauses for a few seconds, creating an uncharacteristic silence. "Girl, you need to give yourself more credit. But since I am your best friend ever, I'm at your service. Michelle will call you as soon as she sees you on TV, so you sort out a plan with her. I'm flexible; just let me know what you decide."

A smile overwhelms my face hearing the care and concern in Rene's voice. "Thanks. I could use my trusty sounding boards."

"We've got your back. I've got to run, but I'll talk to you later. Make sure you wash your hair." The phone clicks, and my best friend is gone.

It rings again two seconds later. Not even enough time passes for me to set it down, so I immediately slide the green circle to answer. "His name is Archie. He lives in my building. Yes, I washed my hair."

"Um. I'm sorry. Is this Georgia Dewan? The artist?" an unfamiliar woman asks.

I yank the phone from my ear to look at the number on the screen. An unrecognizable 716 number, and obviously *not* Michelle. "I'm so sorry. Yes, this is Georgia. I thought you were my friend calling to ask why I was on TV."

"Well, I was calling because I got your information from my friend Caroline, but now you have me curious about what this Archie did to your hair that landed you on TV."

I am so mortified. In an age of call display, there's no excuse for not checking the phone before answering. Especially knowing customers could be calling this number—not that I have that happen often. I explain to the stranger, who I learn is named Isabella, about the hockey game and the disgruntled fan, which makes her laugh, and it sounds like all is forgotten. She even hints at turning on SportsCenter to see the clip for herself. Once that is out of the way and we've built some rapport, she explains why she's calling.

"So I'm hoping you can create a lovely family picture like you did for Caroline. You know how young boys are. They never want to sit still or smile nicely for the camera. At least not both at once."

She giggles at that and I picture her two sons, Paolo and Carlo, who are nine and seven, pulling silly faces for family photos.

"I don't have kids of my own, but I grew up with a brother, so I can imagine."

"Boys will be boys. I was hoping, if I send you some videos and photos, you can work your magic and make something for me."

That suggestion makes me so excited. Creative control and not having to recreate a posed family photo make this job far more appealing. This could be the kind of confidence booster I need to push myself to pursue the gallery opportunity. "Absolutely. It would be my pleasure. What size do you have in mind?"

"Well, I don't know what size you normally work with. Caroline's was quite small, and I was hoping to gift this to my in-laws for in their family room. If you could make it thirty-six by forty-eight inches, that would be ideal."

That's a big drawing. Most of my graphite work has been in the eight-by-ten or nine-by-twelve range. But I've also never had a commissioned drawing. Everything custom I've sold for a payday has been a painting. My graphite work, since graduating, has been exclusively for my own enjoyment, with a few being sold online. "I've never done a family portrait that size, but I'm more than willing to."

Isabella claps her hands in the background. "This is so exciting. You don't have to worry about a frame. I'll handle that once we get the hard copy. I do have one other request, though, if you don't mind."

This is usually where people ask if I can do it for free because they don't have the means to pay me and it's "just art". I suppress the sigh wanting to escape. "Sure."

"My husband is quite well known. Mostly in our area, but through a lot of the US. Would you mind signing a confidentiality agreement that you won't share our photos or videos with anyone else? We'd also need you to keep the project to yourself as well. I know it's a strange request, but it's one our lawyers have insisted we make."

Not at all what I was expecting. I've been sworn to secrecy on other projects before, but those all consisted of gifts or nude portraits. None required legal documentation. As long as she doesn't ask me to do it for free, I'll sign whatever she wants. "That's not a problem. I wouldn't share videos or photos, anyway."

"Thank you, Georgia. I appreciate your understanding. I guess the last thing to discuss is payment."

I hate this part. As much as I want my art to be my career and get upset when people ask me to do it for free, I still hate converting creative work into dollars and cents. Somehow, assigning it a monetary value makes it feel cheaper.

Before I can chime in, Isabella continues, "I'll pay you fifteen hundred dollars now, and the rest upon completion, if that works."

The rest? Who does this lady think I am? My name may be Georgia, but I'm not Georgia O'Keefe. Not to mention, this is a new challenge for me, creating something from a combination of videos and photos and at this scale. "That's plenty, Isabella. Fifteen hundred covers my costs."

"Nonsense. This is something I've wanted done for years, and I'm happy to pay for your skills. Is forty-five hundred fair?"

I feel faint. So much so, I have to drop onto my sofa and pinch my leg to see if this is some fantasy dream I'm having. Ouch. No, this is definitely real life. "That's very generous of you. But a dollar per square inch is a fair price. Forty-five hundred is way over that rate."

"Consider it an extra fee for your secrecy. I'm paying for anonymity that I wouldn't find from a local artist."

I'm not even sure what to say. "Thank you. You can count on me to keep it under wraps. Would you like me to send you updates so you can give me feedback, or do you want it to be a surprise?"

"Oh, I trust your judgment. I'm sure whatever you create will be wonderful. I'll send over the paperwork and deposit by the end of today. Once you send back the signed documents, I'll get you the photos and videos. Does that sound good?"

Sounds like a dream come true, honestly. "That's perfect. I'm looking forward to getting started. I'll get my supplies together so I can start right away. Thank you so much."

"Thank you, Georgia. I'm excited to see the end result too."

With that, we send each other off with plans to follow up and get the ball rolling. I take a few seconds to wrap my head around what this means, then I pop up off of my couch and dance around my living room.

I haven't had this much opportunity within my reach since… ever. Maybe persistence will finally pay off.

Archie

13

OUT-LAW

They struck again. The crew hit a small museum that was hosting a famous painting for the next eighteen months, only to have it stolen out from under their noses the day it was put out on display. After all the precautions they took to increase their security and protect the priceless art, they still didn't stand a chance. Now both the museum and the security company are furious because it's somehow the FBI's fault—*my* fault. As if I'm supposed to provide private security for more than a hundred art galleries and museums in the city simultaneously.

Maybe that's why Georgia rushed off the other night. She was on her way out to meet with her co-conspirators. Though, it doesn't make sense to have her as part of the heist process. If she's the artist, it would be more logical for her to just create the work and meet up to exchange with a middleman. If that's the case, she stands a chance at avoiding jail time—which I shouldn't care about either way.

As for my search for potential middle men, I got a report back from the facial recognition software about the man she met with three days ago.

Bernard Shaw. Longtime employee at *Adler Planetarium*. Recently put in his papers for an early retirement and, according to one co-worker, ol' Bernard claims he's about to come into enough money to fund the next phase of his life. A hunch doesn't hold up in court, but my gut is telling me it has something to do with Georgia.

This new revelation leaves me with a pit in my stomach. Each new piece of information seems to point toward Georgia being part of this crew in some capacity. Why else would she be meeting with Bernard outside of the planetarium? How else does someone just come into enough money to sustain them for decades? I doubt he won the Illinois Powerball, and it doesn't appear he has any family members who are well off. Call me cynical, but criminal activity is the next logical conclusion for easy money.

Still, all of my evidence regarding Georgia's involvement is circumstantial. I just finished a meeting with my higher-ups, and so far, they're not impressed with my progress. Lancaster is still pressing me to find hard evidence, but Georgia is secretive. I need to kick things up a notch, and I haven't heard from her since the hockey game.

It's nearing the end of my official workday, so now's a good time to reach out.

Archie: *Which one do you like better? Hey, hops stuff… or… hello, brewtiful? I can't decide.*

I park myself at my desk and rummage through some unorganized paperwork while I wait for a reply. It amazes me how, in this digital age, so many documents and reports are printed and hand delivered. Not only would they be more secure sent digitally, but we'd significantly cut costs *and* save a few hundred trees per year. Add that to my list of future policy changes.

Once I stuff the last rogue document in the appropriate file folder and lock my desk cabinet, my phone pings.

Georgia: *And you said my puns were bad.*

They are. Truly awful. So bad they're funny.

Archie: *That's not an answer. I've been feeling brew and not very hoppy. It's almost unbeerable.*

I can't believe I went through years of university to get my bachelor's degree in criminal justice, a year of work placement as a 9-1-1 operator, and rigorous training to become an FBI agent, just to take down a criminal enterprise with bad puns.

Georgia: *Please make it stop! I see the error of my ways!*

Her reply makes me laugh, but I have a feeling it won't deter her for long.

Georgia: *How can I cure what ales you?*

That was even less time than I thought it would take… by a significant margin.

Archie: *What are you up to tonight?*

It's not until I hit send that I realize I am asking her that as a friend… acquaintance. I'm not asking as an FBI agent intending to arrest her. My instinct is to back-pedal so I can re-evaluate and plan a better method to approach her, but I don't get a chance.

Georgia: *With my friends in the sky lounge on the 16th floor.*

You can join us if you're bored.

Friends. Perhaps criminal friends. This could present an opening to infiltrate her circle. It could also be a really bad idea to go alone, not knowing what I'll walk into. I lean back and look toward Lancaster's office to find her door is open. I jog through the pathway between the crowded desks abuzz with activity and come to a stop at her door.

She's in the midst of writing something, so without looking up, she asks, "What do you need now, Prewitt?" Decades as a special agent has made her alarmingly good at noticing things in her peripheral vision.

"I made contact with Georgia and she invited me to join her and her friends in our building. I just wanted your input."

She lifts her pen to her lips, not speaking for thirty seconds. "Take Sanders with you, but have him wait in your apartment and wear a wire. That way, you'll at least have some backup if things go south."

"Yes, ma'am. I'll check in tomorrow morning."

She nods and lowers her pen back to the paperwork she was focused on when I interrupted. I take that as my cue to leave.

Forty-five minutes later, Sanders, a middle-aged agent with a receding hairline and enough muscle to dent a bus, is on the sofa in my apartment. I change out of my CFD "work" clothes, and I'm wired for sound. He gives a thumbs up he can hear me, so I make my way to the elevator and press the button for the sixteenth floor. The corridor looks identical to the fifth floor, other than the sign that says *Sky Lounge* with a single arrow pointing to the left, rather than apartment numbers.

I enter the unfamiliar room slowly until I take in the scene in front of me. There's a young dark-haired girl—maybe three years old—running around with her arms out, pretending she's an airplane. The head of blonde hair seated on the sofa spins when I enter, followed by the other three adults on either side of her.

Georgia's soft lips turn into a warm smile as she stands and walks toward me. "Hey. You decided to come." Her smile falters, and she subtly shakes her head. "Duh, you're standing in front of me. Apparently, I've given up puns in exchange for stating the obvious."

"I think we both know you're not giving them up."

She chuckles, returning the missing smile. "I promise I'm trying. It's a tough habit to break." She turns her head over her shoulder to look at the three adults and one preschooler watching us. "Let me introduce you."

I release a long breath, hoping it portrays that I'm a bit nervous to meet her friends and not that I'm excited I could be meeting the people I've been searching for.

"Everyone, this is Archie. Archie, this is Rene, Michelle, Shawn"—she points to the little raven-haired girl buzzing around the room—"and Savannah."

We all exchange handshakes, except Rene, who clutches my hand and doesn't let go. "I saw you on SportsCenter, but the camera didn't do you justice."

"Um… thank you?"

"Rene, don't make the guy uncomfortable yet. He hasn't even sat down," Michelle chastises.

Yet? Like that's something that's reserved for after I'm seated? What have I walked into?

"Please excuse her. She's a teacher and is forced to keep her weirdness hidden all day, so when she's set loose, it all comes flooding out." Michelle gestures toward the only other male in the room. "You'll be safe sitting beside Shawn. Unless… you'd rather sit beside someone else." She glances at Georgia, who has yet to reclaim her seat.

"You guys are exhausting." Georgia groans and drops into the seat she vacated when I arrived. "Do you want some champagne? Clearly, these two have had enough. Though, if I'm being honest, they're just as embarrassing when they're sober."

"Oh, honey. If you think that much champagne even gave me a buzz, you don't know me at all." Rene laughs, placing her drink on the table.

The coffee table set in front of the charcoal-colored sectional sofa has an array of plastic cups and a bottle of Taittinger Brut Reserve, three-quarters empty. I decline a drink so I can keep a clear head, then sit on the couch at the bottom of the L-shape beside Shawn. I estimate he's about my height, has reddish-brown hair and a full beard, fair skin, and hazel eyes. I commit his description to memory, hoping I can get some more information—ideally his last name or social security number.

"I got fizzy juice," Savannah adds as she climbs onto the couch beside me. The little girl is petite, like her mother, and has a mix of her parents' features. She raises her sippy cup to show me.

"Wow. You're a big girl now." I scan the room and notice a bottle of sparkling white grape juice on the console under the wall-mounted TV.

Savannah clutches her cup to her chest like a prized possession, smiles and nods. It's been a long time since I was around a child her age, but I remember my sisters being the same way. Nate and I always wanted to go off and be kids, getting into whatever trouble we could find. Elle and Penny just wanted to be grownups. Now that they are, they've both realized it's not all it's cracked up to be. Savannah leans against me, so I lift my eyes to look at her parents and see if they have any issues with their small child snuggling up to a virtual stranger, but neither seems bothered.

Before our conversation goes beyond surface level, Georgia's phone rings and she hops up to answer it in the far corner of the room. She doesn't get more than a concerned greeting out before she steps onto the outdoor lounging deck surrounding the north and east sides of the building.

"Must be big news," Michelle declares.

Rene shrugs one shoulder and sips the last of her champagne. "Maybe it's a call about that big job she got. She's pretty excited about the payday."

That piques my interest. "Big job?"

Rene offers me a mischievous smile. "Yeah, she—"

"I'm officially an auntie!" Georgia sing-songs as she returns inside.

Rene and Michelle both jump up from their spot, squealing and running over to their beaming friend.

"Boy? Girl? Tell us everything." Michelle is bouncing with excitement.

"Girl. They named her Leah. Both baby and mom are doing well, but that's all I know. I need to try to get home in the next few days to meet her."

My instincts are confused around Georgia—like a compass being swayed by a magnet—but just because her friends gushed over a new baby and have a child in tow does not mean they're innocent.

The three women buzz between each other as Savannah sips her juice, tucked in beside me. I listen intently to the conversation while trying to appear indifferent. When I hear Georgia mention she's unsure how she'll get home, I know it's my shot to spend some more time with her and get insight into this *big job* Rene mentioned.

"I'm going home this weekend. Why don't you come with me?"

Georgia

14

IN-LAW

The bus from Chicago to North Utica is so much longer than driving. It detours through Rockford, and it's expensive, but with Isabella's deposit, I *can* afford it. There's not any real reason I can't take the bus. Except... I don't want to. As weird as our interactions have been, the prospect of spending time with Archie is... intriguing? Exciting? Alluring? All of the above.

"You're really going home?" I ask, though I'm certain he wouldn't be offering to drive me if he wasn't. No one is crazy enough to take a three-hour round trip with these gas prices if they don't have to.

"Yeah, Nate asked me to come help him with a few things, so I was going to leave Friday after work and spend the weekend."

My friends are staring at our interaction like we're the latest blockbuster, designed for their entertainment. I give them the *be cool* look in hopes of avoiding any more awkwardness.

Savannah is snuggled in beside Archie, and I convince myself that her stamp of approval is enough to agree.

"That would be great, if you don't mind. I know it's a little out of your way, but I'm sure someone could pick me up from Ottawa if you don't want to do the detour."

Archie stands and walks toward me, with Savannah close behind. "I normally stay at the *Grand Wolf Resort* when I visit anyway, because I like running the trails along the river. It's no trouble."

"Well, that's settled then," Rene adds as she wraps an arm around my shoulder. "Word of caution: don't let Georgia choose the music or you'll be listening to singer-songwriters the entire way."

Archie chuckles, which causes a warm, blooming sensation in my chest. "Taylor Swift has some catchy songs."

I smirk at Rene, knowing she's going to have something to say about it.

"No one said anything about Taylor Swift. I'm talking K.D. Lang and Joni Mitchell. She's an old soul."

Archie's raised eyebrows and wrinkled forehead are comical for the split second they last. I have no shame in my music choices, but it's a challenge to keep myself from laughing as I watch his otherwise stoic expression shift from confusion to curiosity. I could explain to him that my mom went through a singer-songwriter phase and that's all I listened to from grade four until the end of high school. I could explain that she is musically gifted and used to strum along and sing those artist's songs as if she were recording their studio albums. But I don't want to justify my preference. For some reason, it matters to me whether he'll question me about my likes and dislikes or just accept them.

"They don't make music like they used to." Archie smiles at me, prompting Rene to wrap her opposite hand around my left arm and squeeze. "But the driver chooses the playlist. That's road trip 101 rules." His smile grows wider, and Rene's grip gets tighter.

Michelle clears her throat, drawing our attention. I turn to see her linked arms with Shawn, who has Savannah's giant bag of entertainment on his shoulder. "We've got to head out to get little miss ready for bed. Send us lots of baby pictures so I can catch baby fever and beg Shawn for another."

"Then Savannah will bring you back down to Earth and remind you why you decided you only wanted one," Rene quips.

"Most likely, yes." Michelle leans forward, kissing us each on the cheek and offering a hug.

Shawn follows suit.

Savannah is holding the bottom hem of Archie's flannel button-up, as if it's some kind of security blanket. "I'm not weady fo' bed. Awchie, do you wike snakes and buttafwies?"

Michelle starts hacking like she's choking on air, and Shawn does a combination cough-laugh.

"Snakes and butterflies? Yeah, sure." Archie glances down at Savannah; his eyes lit with the same curiosity he had a moment ago.

She nods. "Mommy wikes birds and bees, but I wike snakes and buttafwies."

Rene, Archie, and I turn our attention to the young parents and giggle over how uncomfortable they look.

"You can always count on kids to turn an encounter awkward." Michelle claps her hands and addresses Savannah, "Let's go, stinker. You've got preschool tomorrow. Say good night to everyone."

Savannah blows a kiss at each of us before reaching up to grab her mom's hand without further debate. At least, until they reach the door. "Mommy, I don't stink. I had a baf dis mowning."

The three of us remaining laugh at the exchange again, watching as the young family disappears into the hallway.

Rene hollers at them to wait as she scrambles to grab her purse from the sofa. "I might as well head out too." She retrieves her cherry red bag and returns to faux-kiss my cheek. "Nice to meet you, Archie. I'm sure I'll be seeing you around." With a wink, she's out the door, leaving Archie and me alone.

"I guess congratulations are in order. I missed that earlier." His dark eyes bore into me, making me confused if he's being genuine or if he's angry about something.

"Uh... thank you?" I maintain eye contact for a few seconds, but his expression doesn't change. "Have I done something wrong?"

Finally, the glower Archie is sporting disappears. "What? No... sorry. Just a tough day at work."

My experiences talking about his work haven't been great, but his job as a fire inspector is important. Maybe he needs a listening ear.

"Do you want to talk about it?"

He glances over at the mess on the coffee table and walks over to start cleaning up the leftover cups. "Nah. Boring bureaucratic stuff getting in the way of front-line work. Nothing I can do about it." He grabs the stacked cups in one hand and the quarter-full champagne bottle in the other. "Do you want to finish this?"

I hate to waste. "You know what they say... no *champagne*, no gain."

Archie groans and shakes his head, but he's smiling wide. "Road trip rule 102: no terrible puns."

"Deal." I smirk at him when he raises an eyebrow—likely on account of my easy concession. "I won't tell any terrible ones. You'll get my best material."

He acts like he hates my lame jokes, but his chuckle betrays him.

We spend a few minutes cleaning up the lounge. Archie asks me about my own projects, but because of Isabella's request to keep things quiet, I evade his questions. Not that I'm afraid he'll rat me out to my client, but I want to respect what she's asked, and I'd rather err on the side of caution by not sharing any details.

Shortly after, I say good night and head back to my apartment to finish the remaining champagne and replay the advice my friends gave me regarding Archie. The consensus was to "go for it," because "what's the worst that can happen?" They should know by now I have a very active imagination and can come up with some pretty gruesome worst-case scenarios.

Then again, they've never steered me wrong. So I'll just have to wait and see which direction this weekend steers us.

DO NOT CROSS

● JUST KIDDING ● KEEP GOING, YOU REBEL ●

Friday evening, Archie leads me down to his parking space. He loads our suitcases in the trunk while I climb into the front seat. The interior is immaculate, but that doesn't surprise me. Archie seems like the type who is very meticulous.

"Ready?" He climbs into the driver's seat and presses the ignition button.

"Yep. I'd say I was born ready, but I couldn't even hold my own head up." I freeze for a split second, hating myself for already breaking road trip rule 102. Rene and Michelle's advice has gotten into my head. "But I'm ready now. See? Full neck control." I bobble my head to prove my point.

"Oh-kay. I'm glad you got that sorted. Based on the one piece of your art I've seen, your hand-eye coordination is a lot better too." He shifts the Jeep in reverse and backs out of his parking space, then eases toward the automatic exit door.

We sit in silence as Archie weaves through the evening traffic until we're outside of the city limits. His music choices leave a lot to be desired, but I'm not going to argue with his classic rock playlist. It's no Carole King; that's for sure.

After the guitar intro to a recognizable hit from the eighties, Archie turns the volume down to ask, "So, how is Leah doing? Are they home from the hospital?"

"Yeah, they went home yesterday. Casey and Jake live with my parents, so my mom was overjoyed when I spoke to her."

"I bet. There's something magical about the first grandchild… from what I've heard. My parents don't have any yet."

It's nice to get a little more insight into his family. He lights up when he speaks about them, as opposed to when he talks about his job.

We maintain an easy conversation while we drive, discussing different sports teams, our SportsCenter mishap, Savannah's antics, and how I met my friends. We even talk about work for a short time. For someone who doesn't seem to enjoy his work, he sure brings it up a lot. And because I can't really discuss mine, I don't have much to say.

Archie pulls into my parents' driveway, stopping in the only open spot.

I notice the new minivan behind my parents' SUV and chuckle. "My brother swore he'd never drive a minivan. One kid and he's been converted."

"They have good safety ratings and they're handy for carrying baby gear. I can see why."

That answer surprises me more than the actual minivan. So much, I don't have a retort. Instead, I ask, "Do you want to come in?"

Archie shifts in his seat, but his facial expression is relaxed. Calm and cool. Reserved. "Sure. I don't want to impose, but I'll come in to congratulate the new parents… and grandparents."

I smile at his acceptance.

He grabs my suitcase from the back, then we walk to the door. I tap lightly before walking inside without waiting for an answer. As soon as we step into the foyer, my nose tickles and I can't hold back the sneeze. My mom walks around the corner from the kitchen wearing a frilly apron and Crocs with gemstone bumblebees on them. Right behind her is a pair of cats. Two long-haired, blue-eyed beige cats with dark faces and tails. I don't know much about cat breeds, but I know I'm allergic to them.

"Oh, Georgie!" My mother pulls me in for a hug while her feline companions stare at me like they're plotting my death. Good news for them, they just have to exist to accomplish that.

"Who are your little friends, Mom?"

She lets go once she's squeezed the remaining air from my lungs, which I'm not sure I'll be able to replenish. "These are Casey's cats. She always wanted a Himalayan, and in a stroke of luck, Jakey found these two, along with three siblings, tied in a pillowcase behind his practice. Can you believe that? How could anyone be so cruel?" It appears my mother has just noticed I didn't come in alone. "Who is your little friend?"

I'd laugh if I wasn't struggling with burning eyes and a closing throat. "This is Archie. He lives in my building, but he was coming to visit his family in Ottawa for the weekend, so he gave me a ride."

My mother seems disappointed by that. "Well, isn't that the sweetest? Thank you, young man."

"My pleasure, ma'am. It was no trouble. Congratulations on your new granddaughter." Archie's voice is scratchy and his eyes are watering.

"Oh, thank you. Can I make you something for dinner? We've already eaten, but I can whip something up for you both."

Some welcome home. They knew I was coming and ate before I arrived. As if the cats weren't bad enough.

"Mom, Archie is allergic to cats *too*." I say *too* in a way like I'm reminding my mother that I have a severe allergy she seems to have forgotten about.

Jake peeks his head out from the end of the hallway to the left of the foyer. "Hey, Georgie. When did you get here?" My typical all-American brother with broad shoulders and animated blond hair looks as tired as I've ever seen him. Even through dental school, he didn't look this ragged.

A series of sneezes prevents me from answering for a full thirty seconds, so I try to rush out a reply before the next wave hits. The longer I'm in this space, the worse it will get. "Just a few minutes ago." I walk the few steps to give my big brother a hug. "Congratulations, Daddy. Where's your baby girl?"

"Her and Casey are sleeping. You just missed them. They dozed off maybe five minutes ago."

My shoulders slump. "Oh. I guess the anticipation will last a little longer, then." I turn to face Archie, who is still standing right at the door, his face puffing up by the second. "Jake, this is Archie." I again explain who he is, then the two of them greet each other. "Can you put my suitcase in my room?" I ask Jake. "I'll hide out in there until the baby wakes up."

Jake lifts his hand to the back of his neck and scrunches his face. "Uh, your room is Leah's nursery now."

"What?"

"Well, you barely ever come home. It didn't make sense to crowd the baby in our room when there was an empty room sitting next door."

That never occurred to me. It makes perfect sense and I'm not upset about it, but home visits will be more of a challenge. "Where am I supposed to sleep?"

"I'll make up the couch for you. It's no trouble at all," my mother replies.

My lungs feel tight and the pressure in my face from my irritated sinuses is enough to make Guantanamo Bay seem like a better alternative. "You want me to sleep on the couch... with your cats?" A quick scan of the living room confirms that the cats have free rein of the furniture. They've both made their way over there and are each curled up in the two armchairs that flank the stone fireplace.

"Oh. Right... I thought maybe you'd grown out of your little allergy by now." Jake shrugs a shoulder like my need for oxygen is a minor oversight.

Archie chimes in for the first time in several minutes. "Why don't you come stay with me at my hotel?"

15

INN MATES

"**I**n your own room. Not *with* me, with me," I rush to clarify. I don't want Georgia getting the wrong idea; I definitely don't want her mom and brother to, either. We may be adults, but that is not an avenue I want to walk down, considering she is my suspect.

Jake looks every bit the tired new dad he is as he steps into the brighter hallway light. "Sorry, Georgie. I thought you knew about the cats and the nursery. You haven't been home for so long, we assumed…"

"It's fine. I just… I was hoping I'd get to meet Leah tonight, but I guess she'll still be here tomorrow."

"Uh… actually, tomorrow we're supposed to go visit Casey's parents in Jonesville. They haven't met Leah yet."

I'll blame the tightness in my throat on the cat dander floating around, but it's partly because I feel bad for Georgia. "I hate to say this, but my allergies are really flaring up, so I'm going to step outside while you guys sort things out. It was nice to meet you both. Congrats again." I don't make a habit of leaving a suspect to discuss things without me being able to hear, but if I don't get out of this house, they'll be dragging my hive-covered, wheezing body out in an ambulance.

I step out the door and immediately feel the soothing relief of the cool autumn air. My lungs greedily inhale deep breaths, but that does little to ease my itchy eyes and nose. I stand on the porch, trying to hear what is being said inside. It sounds like Marina offers to give Georgia money for a hotel stay, but she declines and tells her mom she can afford it on her own. Her mother tells her how proud she is, which irritates me, knowing where that money came from.

Though, if this dismissal from her family is a regular occurrence, I have a little more sympathy as to why she resorted to criminal activities instead of asking for help. It's sobering to realize the picture my background checks painted is very different from reality.

A few minutes later, Georgia struggles through the door with her suitcase—likely on account of her burning red eyes rather than her being incapable. She doesn't say a word to me as she walks back to the Jeep and loads her luggage in the back. We climb in and I back out of the driveway without speaking. I'm unsure if her sniffling and watery eyes are because of the cats or the situation.

"Are you okay?"

She shakes her head. "Casey has never liked me and I don't know why. It feels like… never mind."

"You can tell me. Sometimes it helps to talk things out." I surprise myself by saying that because I care, and not because I want insight.

She breathes a loud wheezing sigh, staring out the window as we travel south. "Casey has a complicated family life. Her and my brother were high-school sweethearts, so my parents have been a huge part of her life. It always felt like she was competing with me to be the best daughter… which is stupid… but now it seems like I've been replaced."

A building to the right catches my eye, so I pull into the parking lot and stop in front. "Don't put too much stock in my opinion, but I'm sure your parents are just trying to make the best of the situation because Casey is living in their home. It's easier to keep her happy because they're around each other every day."

She only acknowledges my take on the situation with, "Yeah, I guess." The glow from the pharmacy sign casts a red light on Georgia's sun-kissed skin. Somehow, even in a red glow, she's beautiful. Unsuspecting. Innocent looking. "What are we here for?"

"Allergy meds. I don't know about you, but I'm about to scratch my eyeballs out."

She laughs and sniffles again, indicating she's suffering just the same. "Good thinking." She opens the car door and adds, "Come on. I'm getting chocolate."

We spend fifteen minutes filling a cart with antihistamines, snacks to suit our tastes—I'm salty, she's sweet—and bottled water. A few people eye us suspiciously as we walk past, laughing and sniffling, both red-eyed with scratchy voices. It's an oddly domestic scenario, and if she wasn't a criminal, I could see myself doing this type of thing regularly.

"Are you okay?" Georgia is looking at me with concern obvious in her irritated eyes.

I could be honest and shake my head like she did earlier. Tell her that I'm not okay because I don't want to arrest her. That I don't want to close this case, but I can't ignore ongoing criminal activity. I took an oath, and that has to mean something. *I will support and defend the Constitution of the United States against all enemies, foreign and domestic…* So instead, I say, "Yeah, I'm good."

She seems to accept that answer with a shrug and tosses a package of strawberry Pop Tarts in the basket. "Breakfast."

The earlier upset Georgia showed disappears a little more with each processed food she adds. As if carbs and trans fats are the cure to family drama. If only that were a real solution, half of the people in the country would carry a lot less emotional baggage.

We step up to the checkout and Georgia starts placing things on the counter. "I'm not accepting any arguments; I'm paying for this. It's the least I can do in exchange for gas money… and to make up for the itchy eyes."

The itchy eyes are irritating, sure. But going into her parents' home granted me this opportunity to stay in proximity to Georgia for most of the weekend. An allergic reaction is a small price to pay.

The problem is, I'm not sure if I'm happy about it so I can get more information on my case or so I can get more time with her.

In an unexpected turn of events, the hotel I booked a room in has no other vacancies. Georgia and I exchange looks between each other and the receptionist, but it seems as though one room with two beds is the best they can do. She doesn't look thrilled.

Georgia avoids eye contact as we ascend to our third-floor room. Whatever the poster stuck to the elevator wall is for, it's captivated her for the sixty-second trip.

"You can shower first if you want. You suffered from cat exposure longer than I did," I say, trying to break the building tension.

"Thanks."

Well, that plan fell flat.

We enter the room, which has two rustic queen beds only a few feet apart. I wanted to keep her close, but this is not what I had in mind. At least if we had separate rooms, I'd be able to slip out of undercover mode for a few hours. Now, I have to maintain this lie until we leave on Sunday. Something good better come from this.

As we agreed, once we arrange our luggage and decide who gets which bed, Georgia goes into the bathroom and turns on the shower. I pop a few antihistamines to combat my burning eyes, but I know that gives me a matter of time before I'm out like a light.

Thankfully, Georgia is fast. She walks out of the bathroom with her hair wrapped in a towel, wearing only her *Relish the Moment* T-shirt that hangs down to her upper thighs.

"Sorry, I wasn't expecting to share accommodations with anyone other than family." She looks embarrassed by her wardrobe choice, but I quite like it. Too much.

"Doesn't bother me at all. I suppose I'll have to sleep with a shirt on too."

Georgia is rummaging around in our shopping bags but stops to turn around and give me a smile. "Don't let me change your plans, Archie. By all means." She grabs a piece of chocolate from the bag and pops it in her mouth.

Suddenly, I have a major craving for chocolate.

Shower. Now. Before I do something I regret.

I take my time in the shower. Partly to wash away the cat dander, and partly to stay on the other side of a door from Georgia. My objectivity gets more compromised the more I get to know her, but if I back off now, everything will be for nothing. Months of bureau resources, wasted. Taxpayer dollars, gone. My credibility and chance at a promotion, shot.

So I suck it up and get my head back in the game. When I exit the steamy bathroom, Georgia is splayed out on top of the blankets, fast asleep. Even her little snores seem innocent.

Nothing about her screams criminal, but her name had to have come up for a reason. I owe it to the victims of the crimes to do a thorough investigation.

I tell myself that's why I tuck her in, then watch the rise and fall of her chest until I doze off.

I'm the first one awake, so I climb out of bed to get some coffee on. The sound the coffee maker makes when struggling to expel the last of the water causes Georgia to stir. She wakes with a yawn and a stretch.

"Good morning. I made coffee."

"Oh, I could definitely use some. I always seem to get an allergy med hangover." She swings her feet over the edge of the bed, then pads her way toward me.

"Same," I reply, trying to look anywhere but at her bare legs. "Do you want to grab breakfast?"

Even with her residual puffy eyes and bed head, she's beautiful. The kind of understated beauty that can make a man derail his career if he allows himself to get distracted by it.

She flashes a tight-lipped smile while sweeping some dangling hair behind her ear. "I bought Pop Tarts, remember? I'm good."

"I'm not sure that qualifies as breakfast. You're destined for a sugar crash before noon."

"Well, then I'll have a nap. It's not like I have anything to do today." She takes a sip of black coffee, wincing at the taste of it. "Don't let me keep you from your day," she concludes with a huff.

Little does she know, she is my day. I step forward, fighting the urge to touch her. "Hey. What's wrong?"

She scoffs, but I don't get the impression it's directed at me. "They knew I was coming. They called and *asked* me to come.

They know I don't drive and that getting here isn't easy. They also know I'm severely allergic to cats and don't have a lot of money to burn. Yet they chose to eat dinner as a family without me. My dad chose to go out right before I was set to arrive. Jake and Casey *chose* to make plans to go see her parents today, even though they live twenty minutes away, and she doesn't even like them." Her eyes are welling up with tears, and it bothers me that her family has upset her this much. Based on how everything has transpired, her feelings are justified. "This was a waste of time, a waste of money. Worst of all, I came all the way here and I'm not even sure I'll get to *see* my niece. And given how often they come to the city, you can bet I won't see her until I come home again."

When a tear trickles down her cheek, that's my cue to step in. Rationality is out the window as I wrap my arms around her and let her sniffle against my chest. The way she fits against me is like a missing puzzle piece sliding into place. Like a complete picture that finally makes sense. It's terrifying. I'm more familiar with her than she is with me, after weeks of searching through every aspect of her life. But I want to share something with her that is wholly me. Not Special Agent Prewitt.

"Grab some comfortable shoes. I want to show you something."

She swipes at her face and nods. "Okay."

And the way she's come to trust me both thrills and sickens me.

Where is he taking me? I may have grown up in this area, but my time south of the river has been limited. This part of the county has a lot of hiking trails, nature reserves, waterfalls, and canyons. If I preferred to draw landscapes, it would have been an ideal location to find inspiration, but my focus is more on the look of awe on people's faces when *they* see the natural wonders around.

But as Archie holds my hand, leading me down River Trail, I'm taking in the beauty surrounding us. The rock formations that have been created in distinct layers after thousands of years of compression. The impact of erosion and extreme weather that have upset trees that have stood for decades. The water trickling down rock faces, changing the landscape with its persistence. It's all beautiful in its own way; though I'm not sure any of it is what's having a calming effect on me.

"We're almost there."

I look ahead and see gray sky peeking in between towering trees. We pass a sign that reads Lover's Leap Overlook with an arrow pointing in the direction we're walking. A lump forms in my throat. I know it's just a silly name, but given the tingle blazing through my veins from having Archie's skin against mine, there's a chance it could be prophetic. Because no one else has ever given me butterflies with a hug before.

We reach the wooden platform that has been crafted into the aged rock, and Archie draws my attention to a small island that sits in the center of the river. I know it well as *Plum Island Eagle Sanctuary*. Something that I've known was here and seen from the north side of the river plenty of times. But this perspective is magical.

Archie turns around to speak, but his words trail off as he places his finger over his lips, then points behind me. "Look."

I spin slowly, placing myself in front of Archie, facing an imposing elm tree leaning out over the cliff-side. He steps closer until his chest brushes against my back and leans down until I feel his breath on my ear. His proximity sets every nerve ending in my body alight.

"Do you see him?"

My eyes trail up the tree until they land on a bald eagle perched about forty feet from the ground. "How do you know it's a 'him'?"

Archie huffs a chuckle, again blowing his breath across my neck and ear. "Females have deep-set beaks, and they're usually bigger, so I'm just guessing."

"Oh." I wasn't really expecting him to have a logical answer for his assumption. "How do you know it's not just young?"

"They have different coloring until they're about five years old, so he's fully grown."

"Oh," I repeat.

We stand there watching him for several moments without moving. The eagle makes subtle movements of his head, but he's statuesque and stunning. It's a privilege to watch the majestic raptor in his element. I'm content to stare at him clutching the tree branch, but without notice, he takes off with his impressive wingspan and soars out over the choppy river. In a display of utter elegance, the eagle flaps its wings and picks up speed before diving toward the water, and with a last-minute adjustment, breaks the surface with his feet. He flies off toward the island with a helpless fish in his grasp. He disappears into the lush trees covered in varying colors of foliage.

Goosebumps erupt along my arms—unrelated to the cool breeze sweeping by.

"Wow," Archie states from behind me.

I'm speechless… and in tears. An after-effect of waking up emotional and witnessing that awe-inspiring display.

For the second time today, Archie asks, "Hey, what's wrong?"

"Tha—that was incredible. It was… beautiful."

He uses a gentle hand on each of my shoulders to turn me back to face him. Then he moves one hand to either of my cheeks, wiping my ridiculous tears with his thumbs. "It was. So are you."

All the emotions I'm feeling get stifled by the overwhelming desire to kiss Archie again. If my years of studying human expression are worth anything, I'd say he feels the same way. It's been six days since we had our first kiss, but it has crossed my mind at least twenty times a day, and with each replay, it steals my breath all over again.

But I chicken out, despite Rene and Michelle's advice playing on a loop in my mind. "What time are you supposed to be at Nate's?"

Archie's gaze moves from my lips to my eyes and his mask is back. The one he puts on that makes his feelings unreadable. "Whenever I get there. He's not in a hurry."

Instead of remaining face to face, I turn back around and walk to the railing to watch Plum Island. I'm hopeful that from this vantage point, I'll be able to see a few more eagles. There's a sliver of blue sky to the east, bringing promise of some much needed sunshine. It's reflective of this weekend. Though there have been brighter moments, it has still been gloomy.

I spot an eagle perched in a tree below the overlook's deck. He's watching out over the water, unfazed by our presence a mere fifty feet away. I direct Archie's attention to the dignified bird, so he inches forward to join me at the edge of the balcony.

"Did you know eagles mate for life?" he asks unexpectedly.

I give him a sideways glance, not wanting to take my eye off of the eagle for more than a second. "No, I didn't." Nor did I expect this nature walk to turn into an ornithology lesson.

"Most bird species are. I watched a documentary that showed the distress birds feel when their mate passes away, and the excitement they show when they're reunited after a time apart. I think that's why they call this Lover's Leap."

"Oh," I say again, as if my brain is only capable of forming one syllable. That makes more sense than referring to the humans who visit—making it seem like the site of a tragic Shakespearean play.

My phone rings in my pocket, so I pull it out to see who is calling just as the eagle takes flight and soars past us, headed toward the other side of the river. I flash the screen at Archie to show him it's my mom and I'm not answering to be rude. He returns a reassuring smile as I tap the green icon.

Our conversation lasts four minutes. It's just enough time for the emotions I've been distracted from to reappear. I stuff my phone back in my pocket, releasing an involuntary grumble.

"My dad had to go to Rockdale for a work emergency and won't be back until late tomorrow. Jake and Casey are staying late at her parents', so my mom is going out with some of her work friends. So glad I came home." I roll my eyes, refusing to let another tear fall.

Archie stands upright, lifts his arms from the railing, and closes the gap between us. His handsome features are the essence of compassion, with his eyebrows pulled straight and together, and his jaw relaxed. "If it makes any difference, I'm glad you're here," he utters in a voice that is smooth like a smokey whiskey. It gives me the same kind of buzz.

I want to put more stock in his words. I want them to mean something. But Archie is so hard to read. So what if he's wiped my tears, made me laugh, and come to my rescue when he didn't need to? So what if his touch incapacitates me with the surge of electricity that courses through me deep down to my bone marrow? So what if he brought me here to lift my spirits, allowing me to witness one of the most incredible scenes I've ever seen?

Instead of acknowledging his comment, I ask, "Should we go back?"

Archie scans the landscape—I'm assuming he's looking for eagles—then uses his thumb and forefinger to rub at the stubble on his angular chin. "If you're ready to go, sure."

We walk along the decking that makes up the trail at the edge of the cliff, completely silent until we reach the paved pathway.

Archie is the first to speak. "We can stay until late tomorrow so you can see your dad and niece before we head back."

I shake my head. "No, I can't. Thanks for the offer, but I have work I need to get back to. Deadlines. Really, I shouldn't have taken the weekend off to come here, but I thought... Well, you know."

He raises one dark eyebrow over his scowl. "What kind of art job has such a strict deadline?"

I could explain what I'm working on. I could tell him that being freelance at anything doesn't mean you get free rein of your own schedule all the time. That a commission the size I'm doing will take me a lot of hours to complete. But I don't.

Instead, I change the subject. "Are you going to see your sisters and parents while you're here?"

Archie is walking a half step behind me, so he takes a few longer strides to draw even. "Yeah, I'll see them tomorrow morning. My mom insists on hosting brunch when I'm in town."

I choke down the disappointment I feel knowing my family can't even *not* make plans when I come visit. Like they put effort into avoiding me, when Archie's family encourages time together. "That's nice."

"Do you want to come?"

That question surprises me. Do I want to? Sure. Who can say no to brunch? But whether I should is a different question. "No, thank you. I appreciate it, but I should keep myself available to see Leah tomorrow if I get a chance."

And once again, Archie's mood transforms faster than an eagle catches its prey.

Archie

17

JAIL BAIT

My brother still isn't speaking to me. I've talked to Janine more often than I've talked to Nate ever since our heated conversation about Georgia. He didn't ask me to come like I claimed he did, but I'd feel bad being so close to home and not stopping in to smooth things over.

That's why I'm parked in front of his house, wondering what I can say to fix things. We had a few wrestling matches as kids, but we've never had a major disagreement. We're as close as two brothers can be, but in this instance, I need to trust my professional experience over my brother's gut.

I turn off the ignition and step out of my Jeep, now that I know how I'll start this conversation. I knock at the door three times, and Janine answers a moment later. She smiles when she sees me, but it's not full of the warmth it usually is.

"Hi, J. Is he here?"

She holds a hand out to welcome me inside and stops me for a hug. "Tread carefully. He's been in pain the past few days and he's already not happy with you."

Nerves cause my stomach to turn sour—not because I'm nervous to speak to Nate, but because I'm always anxious when Janine reports new pains or health issues. Nate doesn't tell me much regarding his symptoms or treatment.

I walk into the living room to find my brother leaning back in a recliner, watching a documentary on flamingos. He's always been interested in birds, which is how I know about eagles. When he spots me, he reaches for the remote and turns the volume up. Suddenly the living room is filled with the booming voice of an Englishman narrating the dangers of marabou storks and salt flats for baby flamingos.

I reach over to swipe the remote from Nate and press the power button. "Don't be an idiot. Aren't you happy to see me?" I flash him a toothy grin, trying to ease the grimace on his face.

It doesn't work. He retorts, "No."

"That cuts me deep. Come on; I came all this way to see you."

"Have you stopped investigating Georgia?"

I exhale and drop onto the left side of the sofa, closest to Nate's chair. "No. I have to follow the evidence." Granted, I still don't have any real evidence, so I have to follow logic and potential leads. Georgia is still my best shot at finding answers.

"Then we have nothing to talk about."

Janine peeks her head around the archway from their kitchen. "Can I get you something to drink?"

Before I can answer, Nate responds for me, "He's not staying."

It stings to be dismissed by your brother and best friend. More than I realized. "Nate—"

"I'd never tell you how to do your job. Never. I trust your training, and I know you've put in a lot of work to be good at what you do. But this one time, I need you to listen to me. That woman is not a criminal. She's a good person."

"Criminals can still seem like good people. A lot of them even do good things. Do you really think there aren't community centers and hospitals funded by the mafia? You think every person donating money to certain causes came across a hundred percent of it legally?" I try to keep myself calm as I justify my choice to my brother, but I get a little passionate in my delivery. I take a few seconds to compose myself before continuing. "I'd never show up at your job and tell you how to draw blueprints. I'm going to solve this case with or without your support. And really, if Georgia isn't guilty, then she has nothing to worry about."

"You're the idiot here, Arch. I'm not worried about her doing jail time. I'm worried about you screwing things up and losing your chance with her. She'll never forgive you when she finds out who you are."

Sometimes my brother is too perceptive; you'd think he's the FBI agent.

I stare back at the black TV screen instead of facing Nate's penetrating glare. "What am I screwing up, Nate? She's a suspect in a crime. I don't need a chance at anything except catching the people responsible."

"You might have gotten the looks in the family and I got the brains, but you cannot be *that* stupid. A blind man can see you have a thing for her. And apparently you *have* to be stupid not to see that she does too—for reasons I'll never understand."

"You're wro—"

"Oh, shut it, would you? Can't you just accept that I'm right? If you don't want to see that, don't come crying back to me when it all blows up in your face." Nate's gray eyes bore into me with renewed intensity.

For the first time since I accidentally gave him a black eye when we were play-fighting as kids, I shrink back. "She *has* to be guilty."

"It's you who's wrong here, little bro."

DO NOT CROSS

● JUST KIDDING ● KEEP GOING, YOU REBEL ●

We returned from Utica two days ago, and I haven't seen or heard from Georgia since. She was able to meet her niece Sunday morning, but when I picked her up after brunch with my family, she was silent and detached, spending nearly the entire drive staring out the window. Even Joni Mitchell didn't get a rise out of her. I'm not sure what happened, but I don't think it was the introduction Georgia had hoped for. At least she had some allergy medication to take *before* she went inside.

So we got home mid-afternoon on Sunday and I walked her to her door. She thanked me quietly, pulled her suitcase inside, and disappeared into her apartment.

Luckily, I got approval to place a motion-sensored security camera in the hallway outside of her door so I can monitor when she leaves or has visitors. It was difficult to assess case files and investigative reports while trying to track Georgia's whereabouts without technological help. But so far, her door hasn't even opened. Unless she's scaled the exterior walls of the building, it's safe to assume she's inside working on whatever her *big job* is. I've been occupying my time by investigating other tips that have come in and coordinating with the police department to comb through any new information they've obtained. These criminals are getting more efficient and skilled with each job, which makes catching them more difficult.

In a last ditch effort, I submit security footage from the weeks leading up to the last two thefts that was captured by surrounding businesses. I'm hopeful the audio-video forensics lab can pinpoint any suspicious vehicles or people around the buildings. I made the same effort with the first few targets, but they didn't come up with anything useful. At this point, though, it's worth a shot. There have been times when a stray cigarette butt solved a case.

I can only hope that something pops up and gives me a new direction to investigate.

Instead, a notification pops up on my phone, indicating the motion sensor has been triggered. Every other instance has been a different fifth-floor resident, but this time, it's Georgia. Not only is it her, but she's carrying a plastic-wrapped canvas and a tote bag.

She eases herself and the artwork into the elevator, never turning it sideways so I can see it. But she'd be the world's dumbest criminal if she walked out of her apartment in the middle of the day with a forgery. This crew would not have evaded capture this long if any of them were parading their activities around in broad daylight.

The elevator doors close and Georgia disappears, leaving me curious what she's up to. I gather my belongings, exit the building, and climb into my Jeep to head to my temporary home. Before I pull out of my parking space, I send Georgia a text.

Archie: *Any plans for dinner tonight?*

She doesn't reply by the time I reach our building. Weird.

I go up to my apartment to shower and change, then wait on the couch, watching TV for twenty minutes. Still no answer. This would be a lot easier if I had a tracker on her phone, but I haven't provided enough cause to have that luxury. So I sit and wait. And stress. And watch the local news station, reading the headline ticker as it repeats the same stories multiple times. *And* check my phone every thirty seconds.

The faint sound of the elevator ding permeates my door at the same time the motion sensor alarm goes off. Georgia is back—no canvas, but still carrying her tote bag. Obviously, she delivered the art somewhere. Now the first potential lead I could have had in a while is just a wasted opportunity.

A rookie mistake, and I am no rookie.

Georgia

18

RESISTING A REST

This drawing for Isabella is going to be the death of me. With the amount she's paying me, I want it to be the literal picture of perfection. Since I delivered my last commission two days ago, I have spent more than twelve hours combing through family photos and watching the videos she sent, trying to piece together their family while capturing their expressions from candid moments. Isabella said their favorite place to visit is the Canadian side of Niagara Falls, so I've tried to position them all in front of the impressive waterfall. As much as I love graphite drawings, though, I'm questioning whether the pigments of tinted pencils are really doing the falls justice. And because I'm sworn to secrecy and don't want to betray that, plus Isabella wants the image to be a surprise, I can't ask for a second opinion.

I need to trust my instincts.

By 1a.m., I have an indent in my arm from the mahl stick I have angled over my work to prevent smudges. There is still a lot to do, but I'm pleased with my progress. For an image this size and the work I've had to put into creating a mosaic of happy family moments, it's turning out to be a long process. I knew it would be, but it's a different standard than drawings I create just because I want to. This can't get tucked into a drawer or crinkled up and thrown out if I'm not happy with it. It *has* to be perfect.

I decide to call it a night because my eyes are struggling to focus, so I take a quick shower, then climb into bed and turn on SportsCenter to lull me to sleep.

DO NOT CROSS

● JUST KIDDING ● KEEP GOING, YOU REBEL ●

I'm jolted awake at 7:40 by a knock at my door. Something that rarely happens, but since Archie moved in three weeks ago, the frequency has increased. This guy needs to learn to send a text. I'm assuming it's him without even looking through the peephole. Since I didn't put any of my supplies away last night, my art is still out in the open and in direct view from the door. I crack it open just enough to see Archie's energized face in the hallway.

"Hey. Did I wake you?"

"I'm an artist, Archie. My sleep hours are all over the place."

"Sorry." He has the decency to look down and appear a little remorseful. "What are you working on?"

For a split second, I consider betraying Isabella's confidence and showing my progress to Archie to get his opinion. But two things stop me: he's not an art expert, and I barely know him. It's one thing to take a chance if it were my own private moments, but these are not mine to share. "Just a commission. Nothing too exciting."

He tries to peek his head around the door, but proves unsuccessful. "Let me see."

"Archie, I can't. I promised my client to keep it confidential. When you're a starving artist and someone wants to pay you decent money for your work, you don't ask questions."

He tilts his head to my left, his brows raised, creating forehead creases on his otherwise smooth skin. "Come on. I won't tell anyone. It's just... all this time, I've never really seen your work."

Instead of conceding, I come up with a new plan. "I have a better idea. Do you have an hour to spare? I want to show you something."

He lifts his left arm to look at his watch. "Yeah, I guess. Unless I get a call from work."

Right. I forget that most people have regular jobs with regular hours. "Okay. Give me ten minutes. We can grab coffee on the way."

I close the door, then rush to get ready. I hop around the living room, pulling on a pair of black leggings, slip on a royal blue tunic sweater, then repeat the hopping for my socks and shoes. My teeth are gleaming after I exert an unnatural amount of force while brushing. Since my hair is a disaster, I grab a navy beret to hide the worst of it, slide on my wool coat, and exit my apartment.

As opposed to last time, when he was waiting in his apartment, this time Archie is in the hallway.

"Sorry. I tried to be fast."

"You were," he confirms. "You good?"

I'm irrationally excited about this impromptu outing. He took me into the forest and I followed him, so I appreciate his reciprocity.

We opt to take the subway because parking is a headache, and it allows us to grab a coffee at *Pete's* on our walk to Roosevelt Station. Our conversation bounces from random sports news to more personal questions about tattoos and scars. For someone whose life revolves around art, I haven't permanently inked any on my body, but I have plenty of scars.

Then, like he so often does, he dives into a topic I'd rather avoid. "How was your visit with your niece?"

Apparently, my silence on the drive home didn't make it clear how it went. "She's cute… Tiny. Dark hair and eyes, like her mom."

Silence.

"I got to hold her for about twelve seconds before Casey claimed Leah needed a diaper change and a nap. She disappeared into the bedroom and never came back out."

Archie flashes me a sympathetic tight smile, but says nothing.

"I understand babies need diaper changes and naps and feedings. I understand that they shouldn't be tossed around between new people and treated like a commodity. But I'd have been happy just to sit beside her bassinet or look at her while someone else held her. It didn't feel like she disappeared because of what Leah needed." My entire rant pours out with increasing pitch and volume as we climb the stairs to the station.

The train arrives right as we reach the top step, which almost never happens to me. We rush to get on before the doors close and take our usual seats, across the train car from each other—this time because they're the only seats available. The trip is quick, but crowded. I underestimated the amount of pedestrian traffic in the downtown core on a Friday morning.

We emerge a few minutes later at Adams/Wabash Station and struggle to navigate the crowd to exit. Thankfully, this time we stick together.

"Are you taking me to the orchestra?"

I glance at Archie to see him smirking. "At 8a.m. on a weekday? No. Just trust me."

He walks in stride with me toward our destination. We stroll through the north and south lion sculptures marking the entrance to *The Art Institute*, where I see a familiar face. I grab Archie's hand and pull him toward Pierre.

"Ah, Miss Georgia. Long time, no see," the brawny French-Canadian greets.

I give him a brief hug, feeling guilty I haven't stopped by for quite a while. "I'm sorry. You know how it is. Life tends to derail us from doing the things we want."

"Only if we let it, Miss Georgia. Only if we let it."

Archie stiffens beside me, which I feel through my hand before I notice. Again, his demeanor is shrouded in mystery.

I take the opportunity to introduce the two men. "Archie, this is Pierre. Pierre, Archie."

They shake hands and exchange pleasantries. I'm surprised by the unspoken camaraderie they seem to have. Like they're both brave men of service in different areas and take their jobs seriously.

After a brief conversation, during which we exchange updates on the goings on in our lives, I ask Pierre, "Can we get inside for a bit? Archie has to be at work in forty minutes, so we won't be long. Promise."

Pierre crosses his arm and sets his face in a serious scowl before it morphs into a massive smile. "*Oui, oui*, Miss Georgia. You know the rules, yeah?"

I return his smile, assure him we won't touch anything, and confirm we're only going to one specific area, then we'll let him know when we're done. He knows how much I value every piece of art in this building. I spent many hours here while I was studying, drifting from room to room, letting the artwork speak to me. Pierre and I connected over my favorite painting and became familiar acquaintances.

Archie follows me inside, and I navigate my way through the vast corridors until we're standing in front of one painting that never fails to speak to my heart.

"This." I stare at the image of the man in an orange jumpsuit, looking up at the Heavens as if he's begging for mercy.

"This... your favorite work of art?" Archie stands beside me, studying the painting.

"It gives me chills every time. The subject, Ira Aldridge, was actually an actor who posed for the painting. He wasn't born into slavery, but he was a major part of the abolitionist movement. It's a testament to his acting skills, how convincing he is, and how well Simpson captured it."

We stand in silence for about five minutes. Archie takes the time to read the information posted near the painting and really scrutinizes the work. I resist the urge to talk and allow him to immerse himself in the experience.

When he speaks again, his words stall, and he has to clear his throat. "It's hard to believe that this painting was hidden from public view for 180 years. I get why it's your favorite. The emotion in his eyes... it's heartbreaking."

I step up beside him, stopping four feet away from the gallery wall. "You wanted to see my work. I can't show you what I'm working on, but this is what I want to create. Works of art that express the emotion someone is feeling with no other context beyond what you see. To portray feelings so real, people looking at it can feel them too."

He turns from the gold-framed masterpiece to look at me while I speak. He looks like he's hanging on to my every word. "You will. Just seeing how passionate you get talking about it, I know you will. You can capture that depth of emotion and make other people feel it too. You're amazing, Georgia."

I've had so many doubts about my artistic ability lately, and despite Archie only seeing my one drunken paint night Monet, his words flood me with confidence. And it turns out, it's not my friends' assurances or Isabella's faith in my abilities that give me the boost I need. It's Archie's eyes that portray a raw honesty and tell me he believes his own words.

So I look at *The Captive Slave* and the other works surrounding us, imagining my own art hanging in place of each one. The overwhelming emotions give me goosebumps. I'm going to take this opportunity at *Smith Goldstein & Co.*

Archie

19

CELL SERVICE

She knows a security guard and is friendly enough with him to be let into the museum at a time they're not open to the public? Not just let in, but given free rein of the place with no supervision. Pierre didn't even seem to think twice about letting me inside, just because he trusted her. In the brief conversation we had, Georgia asked him about his wife and young daughter, so I don't think the two of them ever had a romantic history.

But that's what con artists do. They build trust among unsuspecting people who can benefit them, then those people end up taking the fall.

There is so much about what just transpired that is suspicious, and now I have to do a full work-up on Pierre. *The Art Institute* hasn't been a victim of a robbery yet, but that doesn't mean it's impossible. A determined band of criminals can bypass even the most sophisticated security systems. If they have guards allowing them to walk in the front door, that makes things a lot easier.

Our entire journey back to our apartment building, I'm running through different scenarios and potential avenues I can pursue in my investigation. Where else has Pierre worked? How long have they known each other? He's obviously not from Chicago, so does he have a criminal history wherever he's from? I'm champing at the bit to get started on my work for the day.

Georgia and I part ways in the lobby after she informs me she has a lot of work to get done, only driving my curiosity regarding her *big job*. It doesn't make sense to keep her work so secretive unless it's a forgery of a famous work of art.

I descend to the parking garage in the opposite elevator as she ascends to the fifth floor. She may not want to share her personal work, but her willingness to share her passion for art with me may just be her downfall.

On my way to the FBI headquarters, I stop at OFI to get an update on fires in the city and progress related to their cases. From what I've learned so far, arson cases may be harder to solve than mine, with even less likelihood of finding solid proof. I walk out with surface-level knowledge of the most recent investigations—just enough to satisfy any curious questions, though Georgia never seems interested in talking about my "job".

I occupy the first five hours at headquarters investigating Pierre, searching through his green card application and contacting local police from Montreal to inquire about his criminal record. Everything I turn up points to him being an upstanding citizen on both sides of the border. He moved to Chicago when he was twenty because his now wife earned an athletic scholarship for pole vaulting at a local university. He's been employed by *The Art Institute* for nine years. Usually, when someone seems too good to be true, they are. He'll require a deeper dive.

Shawn and Michelle, on the other hand, don't come up as squeaky clean. Shawn is a computer programmer by trade, specializing in high-end security system programming. Go figure. He also has a criminal record for shoplifting when he was seventeen. It's not a smoking gun, but it does point to a criminal past, even though he hasn't been arrested for the past decade. Michelle doesn't have a criminal history, but her capacity in her job grants her access to international trade routes. Retail establishments have used the guise of their businesses to hide criminal activities for decades. Between that and her educational background, she has the means to ship priceless works of art out of the country.

Nothing concrete. Nothing that will please my superiors. Nonetheless, progress is progress. Part of being a good investigator is being really good at accepting failure. A complex case requires a lot of failing before succeeding.

Lancaster has been on my back the entire day, questioning each new request I run through different departments. I waste a lot of time justifying each inquiry. In her defense, she's trying to maintain a strict budget, but micromanaging has never been her style, so it's a little suffocating.

Thankfully, now I have a reason to get out of the office, and I'm on my way to meet with my criminal informant, Bobby. He was busted six months ago in an identity theft scam where he was collecting social security numbers for children and using them to open up credit cards. Since most parents don't check their child's credit report, he got away with it for several years. Thanks to one diligent parent, we were made aware of the situation and arrested Bobby for identity fraud, which could have landed him fifteen years behind bars. Like most criminals, he was willing to sell out his more successful competition to avoid doing time.

One look at him, and anyone would understand why he'd want to avoid prison. He's no more than 120 pounds and has a high-pitched voice indicating he skipped puberty altogether.

I pull up to the curb near the alleyway Bobby and I agreed to meet in. The few hundred yard's distance allows me to scan my surroundings as I approach and make sure I'm not being set up. The coast is clear, so I turn right into the alley and call Bobby's name. He steps out from behind a large restaurant dumpster.

"Archie, I'd say it's good to see you, but I'm trying to behave myself... don't wanna lie."

"Feeling's mutual, Bobby. What have you got for me?"

"Right to business. Do you have an off switch somewhere? No small talk. How 'bout the weather? What have you been up to? Nothin'?" The scrawny, shaggy blond steps toward me with both hands in the pockets of his oversized coat.

"Woah, Bobby. Hands where I can see them. We've been over this."

Like a CI on thin ice, he complies, holding his hands up so I can see they're empty. "It's chilly. Just keeping warm."

"Right. Let's try again. What have you got for me?"

He releases a heavy sigh, indicative of a man who is pretending to be annoyed about selling out his competitors. "My sources say they're going to hit a private residence with a few prize pieces."

I study Bobby's face to gauge whether he's telling the truth. So far, the information he's given me hasn't resulted in any hard evidence. But the look on his face tells me he's being honest. There's a chance his information isn't accurate, sure, but the direct eye contact and steady posture tells me he believes what he's saying.

"An art collector? You're sure?"

"Pinky swear, Archie. You know I can't give up my source, but I have it on good authority they're making their move soon."

"I've never made a pinky swear in my life, but I appreciate the sentiment. Any idea what or who they're going after?"

Bobby looks at the ground, kicking a small rock so it pings off of the dumpster. "Sorry, man. I tried to find out but couldn't get it out of anyone and didn't want 'em thinkin' I was a rat. The only thing I know is that their artist has been workin' on two forgeries."

I want to hit back with a snarky retort about him *being* a rat because the fact Bobby got off scot-free irritates me beyond measure, but I need the slimy crook to be my eyes and ears right now. Beyond that, mention of their artist creating forgeries brings my mind back to Georgia and her secret project. "Keep yourself safe, Bobby. Call me if you hear anything else."

None of what Bobby shared is particularly helpful. I can ask around at different galleries to get the names of private art collectors, but it's unlikely Lancaster will sign off on surveilling all of them for several days. All I would accomplish is risking exposure if any of the crew works at a gallery, meaning there's more risk than reward. They must know by now that someone is onto them. You can't just walk out of several art facilities with their possessions and injured security guards without attracting the attention of law enforcement. That doesn't mean I want to give them confirmation I'm looking for them. The last thing I want is for them to pick up their operation and move to another city before I catch them. That means someone else has to start over from scratch and waste more resources before we lock them up.

I slip into the driver's seat and clench the steering wheel. I take a few deep breaths so I can refocus my attention and come up with a plan of action.

Before I can do that, my phone rings from a private number, which usually means it's someone from the bureau. I slide my thumb across the screen to answer and hear muffled talking in the background. "Hello?"

"Special Agent Prewitt?" a deep voice asks.

"Who wants to know?" I reply, unwilling to give confirmation until I know who is on the other end of this conversation.

"This is Special Agent Kensington from the Buffalo field office."

Weird. I don't have any interest in anything going on in Buffalo. "What can I do for you, Kensington?"

"Well, I think we can be mutually beneficial. You've flagged a local artist in relation to an active art forgery case. Miss… Georgia Dewan?"

My chest tightens when he mentions her name. "Yes. Why?"

"We've been running wiretaps on a money laundering operation here, and she's recently been in contact with our number one suspect."

That one sentence steals the air from my lungs. There are only so many coincidences before it's not an accident anymore. If she's involved with money laundering, she could be higher up in the Chicago crew's hierarchy than I realized.

"What details can you give me?"

"Not a lot. You know how the bosses are with the red tape. She had a fifteen minute phone call with our suspect's wife back on the tenth, but we weren't authorized to tap the wife's line, so we only know the conversation happened. Any details of what they discussed are speculation, at best. We were wondering if you've gotten wind of anything on your end."

I blow out another deep breath and use my free hand to pinch my temples, trying to alleviate the tension in my head. "I'm working on getting an in, but you know these organizations don't just welcome anyone with open arms."

"That I do. I'd appreciate it if you kept us in the loop. Between you, me, and a lamppost, this operation is running fake cash over the Canadian border, and with the rise in digital payments, not many people check cash anymore. Nothing will stop them until we do."

"Copy that, Kensington. If I hear of anything related to Buffalo or your case, I'll pass it along."

"Thanks, Prewitt. I'll do the same from my end. Stay safe and watch your back."

Kensington ends the call as I sink back into my seat. I've never wanted to bust a case wide open so much and so little at the same time. Regardless of her level of involvement, I need to do my job and let things unfold. She's just another case. Another criminal who needs to be stopped, and that's the career I chose.

Georgia

20

CLEAN GETAWAY

This drawing is finished. I stand back and admire my work, analyzing the composition of lighting and layers. I've spent more than fifty hours on it since returning from Utica to get it ready to ship to Isabella. I still need to apply a fixative to seal it, but there's no way I'm spraying that in my apartment, so I'll have to do it outside on the next sunny day and hope no one else sees it.

I send Isabella a quick message to ask if she wants me to send her a photo of the completed drawing before I seal it, in case she wants to suggest any changes, but she replies moments later saying she still wants it to be a surprise.

For all the self-doubt and discouragement I've felt over the past few months, this moment, staring at a happy family in front of Niagara Falls, brings me so much contentment. This is what I'm meant to be doing, and I just need to find other people like Isabella who appreciate it.

Hopefully, with this exhibit at *Smith Goldstein & Co.*, I'll be able to find more clients who value my work. Now, the only hurdle is creating a body of work that is both a variety of subjects, but a consistent, recognizable style.

I tuck my easel and stool along the half-wall that separates my bed from the living room. This seems like a time to celebrate. I've finished hundreds of paintings and drawings before, but this one feels special. Like the dawn of a new era of Georgia Dewan, transitioning from a girl who was creating anything that provided a payday to a woman who creates with heart and purpose. It's a momentous occasion.

The weird thing is, when I think about celebrating, it's Archie who comes to mind. He was the one whose final vote of confidence really ushered me into this new stage. I've been a hermit for the past week since we went to *The Art Institute*, but we've been texting every day. He's been torturing me with his terrible artist puns, making me question everything about my personality. I've been pretending like they don't make me laugh out loud, replying in kind with fireman one-liners.

But instead of giving in to the effects of my confused endorphins, my good sense wins out and I call Rene. She's been my loudest cheerleader since freshman year, and this moment feels like something I should celebrate with her.

She invites me to a football game this Sunday, which I'm always down for. Her dad bought season tickets two decades ago, and he gives Rene a few pairs each year. It's always a highlight to go because the seats are amazing. That gives me a little more than two days to work on my plan for the gallery before I take Sunday evening off.

There's one thing I've learned in my years of creating: if the inspiration well is overflowing, don't plug the source. Cultivate whatever creativity you can in the moment because it can dry up just as fast.

 DO NOT CROSS 

● JUST KIDDING ● KEEP GOING, YOU REBEL ●

"Where is my other jersey?" I ask nobody as I rifle through my closet. It's literally thirty inches wide. How did I lose an orange jersey?

After far too long digging through and getting frustrated, I concede and grab a plain navy hoodie to pair with my dark jeans and sneakers. The game is scheduled later in the evening than I'm used to, but that's another perk of keeping weird hours. I'm adaptable. An 8p.m. kickoff won't stop me from celebrating everything I've accomplished this week.

I grab a tote bag with some art supplies I no longer need that I promised Rene I'd donate to her classroom, then finally rush out the door.

Before I press the button for the elevator, I hear a throat clear. I spin around and find Archie in navy track pants and a pure white T-shirt, leaning against his door frame. What's concerning about *his* sudden appearance is the sudden appearance of butterflies in my stomach. The rapid fluttering that accompanies hearing his voice and seeing his perfect cheekbones and chiseled jaw.

"Hey." I use my free hand to give him a lame wave.

"Hey, stranger. I was beginning to think you actually had been kidnapped and someone was replying from your phone."

"Sooo… you just kept texting instead of knocking on my door to make sure I wasn't being held captive somewhere?" I mean, not that I don't appreciate him giving me space to complete my project, but if he—

My thoughts are stopped by his rumbling laughter.

"I could tell it was you by your terrible jokes."

"Terrible?" I scoff. "Don't blame me for your *terrible* sense of humor."

He holds both hands up as if I'm placing him under arrest. "Where are you headed?" he asks, stepping forward.

"Out with a friend."

There's something about how he asks me that makes me not want to disclose my full plans. The way his eyes narrow and his posture goes stiff. When I met Archie weeks ago, he was impossible to read, but his micro-expressions have become more noticeable during our last few encounters. Maybe it's because we've kissed, so I'm more in tune with him, or maybe he's letting his guard down; I don't know. But in this instance, it makes me want to maintain a little mystery.

"A friend, huh?" The corners of his mouth curl upward.

The faint smile prompts me to share a little more. "Rene." I reach over and press the call button for the elevator. "And I'm running late. I'll text you tomorrow?"

"Sure. Be safe, yeah?"

That's a strange send off.

"I will. Night, Archie."

The elevator doors open, and I step inside. He returns my earlier wave and sentiment as the elevator closes.

Twenty-five minutes later, I meet up with Rene outside of the VIP parking area and hand off my art supplies. She drops them off at her car and we head in through the special entrance for season ticket holders. I love going to sporting events of virtually any kind, but there's something about the VIP treatment that makes the experience even more exciting.

"So, how's Archie?" Rene asks when we get settled in our seats.

"I'm fine. Thanks for asking." I roll my eyes, but don't miss the subtle fluttering again, just from the mention of his name.

"Girl, I know you're fine. You're sitting right beside me, 'bout to watch these *fine* men run around in their tight pants. We're all fine here."

"I'm pretty sure most of the people, myself included, did not come for the tight pants, but okay." I smile at her and laugh when she shrugs off my comment. "To answer your question, I don't know. Aside from a quick trip to *The Art Institute* last week and a two-minute encounter tonight, I haven't seen him since we got back from Utica."

"What? Girl…" She drags out the word in her unique Rene way that says I'm about to get an earful. "You're telling me that Hunky McHunkerson done drove you all the way home, took you on an eagle-watching adventure when your own family couldn't give you the time of day, brought your behind all the way back, and you haven't seen him since?"

I choose to ignore the Hunky McHunkerson moniker because I can tell she's already worked up. "Pretty much. I had that big project I had to get done, so I was working on it every waking minute. We texted."

"Unh-unh. That fine specimen is interested in you."

"I don't know. There's just something… mysterious about him that I can't figure out."

"So spend time with him and *figure it out*. Tall, handsome, mysterious? Sounds like the trifecta to me."

The PA system crackles to life over the Shakira song, announcing the teams as they run onto the field to the sounds of sixty thousand cheering fans.

Once the opening lineup is announced, Rene turns back to me. "Plan a date night with him and spend some time alone, not interrupted by work or family drama. You might be surprised… or you might decide you don't like him and that's that. But don't miss out on the chance just because he's mysterious. Crack that code like DaVinci."

I consider her words for a few seconds before I reply. "DaVinci didn't crack—"

"That's not the point. You know you're not exactly bursting with every detail of your life, either, right?"

This is true. Part of that is because I keep my expectations low with each commission, so I don't feel disappointed when each one is done and it hasn't resulted in my big break. To manage those expectations, I don't share a lot. And part of it is because I feel like a perpetual letdown to my family, so I keep things to myself. Each reminder they get that I'll never be a dentist or engineer only seems to displease them more. Keeping things to myself is safer.

However, my friends have always been encouraging because, as creative types, they understand. Archie may not be an artist, but he's been nothing short of supportive in the few weeks I've known him.

Finally, I nod. "Okay. But I need you to help me make a plan."

Rene starts bouncing in her seat. "You got it, Boo. Let me tell you, this number eighty-eight is giving me some inspiration." She points out to the tight end lined up next to the right tackle.

"He could have the personality of a brick."

She shrugs her shoulder again and flashes me a smirk. "Bricks are useful too."

The whistle blows for the third down to start, so Rene stops talking to focus on the center snapping the ball back to the quarterback. He dances around for a few steps before throwing a perfect arcing spiral twenty yards up the field to Rene's new fixation. He clutches the ball to his chest while jumping to avoid a tackle and takes off like a bullet into the end zone.

The entire stadium erupts in cheers, celebrating the first touchdown of the game.

"I think he was showing off for you."

Rene is fanning herself with her hand, which is comical because it's barely above fifty degrees. "I think I'm in love with a brick."

I'd laugh if she didn't look like she was dead serious.

Two-and-a-half hours later, we're staring at the scoreboard that reads 17-20. There are six minutes left in the game and Chicago has one last chance to score. In a spectacular play that results from an epic fail on the defense's part, Mr. Brick re-creates the same play from earlier, but from a longer distance. He weaves through the opposing team's linebackers, past the safety, and into the end zone. The entire stadium explodes with excitement as eighty-eight celebrates with his teammates. Despite the other team's best efforts, they can't capitalize in the remaining seconds, and the entire Chicago team bursts onto the field to celebrate as the timer winds down.

Nothing compares to the energy at a sporting event when the home team wins. It's electric, with a joyous hum buzzing between players and spectators. It's addictive.

"He did it!" Rene squeals, like she has a personal investment in this man's success.

"He did. That was amazing."

We stand, soaking in the cheers of the crowd until the last player runs off the field, waving to the fans.

Rene turns to me and grips my left arm. "You never know how the game will turn out when you start watching, but you stay anyway because there's a chance your team will win. Just give him a shot. You win some; you lose some. But you'll never score on a shot you don't take."

"That was a lot of sports metaphors in one sentence."

She releases my forearm, only to slap my bicep. "Seemed more appropriate than saying every masterpiece starts with a single brush stroke. You never know how it will turn out."

Her metaphors are even more impressive than my puns, and that's saying something.

"Hopefully we can kick something off and don't fumble."

My best friend wraps her arm over my shoulder and pulls me toward the exit. "Thatta girl."

21

GUILT BY ASSOCIATION

It's hard to prioritize maintaining my cover when Georgia walks out wearing dark clothes, carrying a bag of art supplies, and acts so elusive about her plans. I can't justify following her, though, because if she spotted me, my cover would be blown and I still don't have anything concrete.

But once again, she comes back after midnight, wearing a huge smile, with her art supplies missing. What am I supposed to make of that?

Now I'm lying awake, unable to sleep, running over everything bit of circumstantial evidence that has come up so far. But that's the problem. I've been here for weeks, and still have nothing more concrete than when I started.

Instead of tossing and turning any longer, I pull out my phone to check the security cameras at my house and set another reminder to stop in to water my remaining houseplants. It may seem like a strange hobby, but my boss back during my 9-1-1 operating days had an office full of plants. He insisted that they helped take his focus off of the stress of the job and kept him present, understanding what was out of his control. I adopted the same hobby, and with each tough case, I've brought home another plant to care for. I believe I'm up to thirty-three. This case will definitely result in a few more.

I start running through each of my plants in my head like counting sheep, and eventually drift off to sleep.

DO NOT CROSS

● JUST KIDDING ● KEEP GOING, YOU REBEL ●

Monday mornings are different when you're undercover. Because you don't really have designated days off, the stress of a new week doesn't just appear. Instead, the stress of solving the case without your cover being blown hovers over you in an unrelenting cloud, seven days a week. In addition to that, I have to pretend to have an exhausting regular job, so I'm forced to leave my apartment instead of staying where my actual job requires me.

I pull into OFI headquarters' parking lot, find a spot, then head into the fire inspector's office to check in with the chief. Our conversation is short and to the point, which I appreciate. He's a busy man with no time to waste, either, so asking him to spend even a moment on this sham of a job is a big ask.

On my way out, my phone dings with a text message.

Georgia: *Can you clear your schedule for me tonight?*

I trip on a step leading out of the building, almost dropping my phone. Clear my schedule?

Archie: *What do you have in mind?*

I tuck my phone in my pocket and climb into my Jeep, turning the ignition. Before I can pull out of my spot, she replies.

Georgia: *Do you trust me?*

If I'm being honest, no. I can't tell her that, but she's secretive, suspicious, and likely involved in multiple felonies. But maybe this is her way of inviting me in.

Archie: *Yes.*

Another lie that will linger between us.

Georgia: *Meet me in the sky lounge at 7?*

So much for my plan to check in at my real home tonight. That will have to wait until tomorrow. Considering the last time she invited me up there, it was to meet her friends, I mull over the possibility that they'll be there again. That perhaps, this is the break I've been waiting for. And while that fills me with professional optimism, it also drowns me in personal dread.

DO NOT CROSS

● JUST KIDDING ● KEEP GOING, YOU REBEL ●

Lancaster insisted I bring Sanders for backup again, so he's seated in my apartment, tuned into my wire.

I press the button for the sixteenth floor and rocket upward in the elevator to meet Georgia. I've anticipated this meeting all day, and spent several minutes practicing my reaction face for when she admits she's part of a criminal enterprise and wants my expertise as a fire inspector to help.

But when I open the door to the sky lounge, what I get is nothing like I'm expecting.

There are no friends. No hushed conspiracies being discussed. No one, except Georgia, in a stunning black slip dress. She has her hair curled, and must be wearing contacts, because she doesn't have her glasses. The unimpeded view of her eyes allows me to see her smokey eye shadow and long lashes.

"Hi," she greets with a smile.

"Hi." I do a full scan of the room, making sure I'm not missing anything. "What's all this?" I nod at the counter in the kitchenette area that is covered with dishes.

"I know I've been quiet pretty much since we got back from our trip home, but I wanted to properly thank you."

My stomach sinks. Not because she wants to thank me, but a combination of disappointment this isn't the *in* I was hoping for and because she looks genuine. "Thank me for what?"

"Everything. Taking me home, helping me out with that whole fiasco, the eagles… and for what you said to me at *The Art Institute*. It all really means a lot to me."

I think back to that morning last week and can't recall saying anything noteworthy. "You don't have to thank me… but I'm starving, so I won't say no."

She grabs my hand and tugs me through the doors, onto the terrace. "You might not consider it a thank you once you taste any of it, so don't get your hopes up."

There is a table set in the center with candles, two glasses, and a bottle of wine. This isn't a business proposition; it's a date. And like every other conflicting moment with Georgia, I'm a mixture of disappointment and excitement.

"Sit here. If you can open the wine, I'll grab the food." She looks at me, but quickly averts her eyes. The sky is dark, but the moon is bright and the lights inside illuminate her blushing face.

I place my thumb along her chin and tilt her face so she's looking at me again. "Thank you for this." As sad as it is, I've never felt so appreciated, but how she sees things and my actual intentions for them are very different.

"This is supposed to be my thank you. You can't thank me for thanking you." Her eyelids flutter and she tugs on her bottom lip with her teeth.

It takes incredible restraint not to kiss her. Something I've been wanting to do since the hockey game, but I certainly won't with Sanders listening in on the evening. "I'll get the wine," I say, breaking the building tension.

Georgia walks inside, closing the door behind her. I mutter into the wire that there's no one here and give Sanders permission to sign off. Since he can only hear me and can't reply, he shoots me a text saying he takes his orders from Lancaster, so he'll stick around. Do-gooder. I grab the corkscrew and open the bottle of red wine.

She returns wearing a shawl and kitten print oven mitts, carrying a ceramic dish, which she places on the table, still nibbling on her lip. "Lasagna."

"Kittens?" I gesture to her oven mitts.

"Savannah picked them. She thought it would make me happy since I can't have a cat." She places the oven mitts down beside the dish and begins slicing the perfectly browned pasta.

"Probably because she couldn't find ones with snakes and butterflies," I reply.

Georgia chuckles but the moon is behind her, so I can't see her expression well.

"That child will move mountains when she's older. She's so stubborn and determined, Michelle says she has to remind herself daily that those qualities will serve Sav well someday."

"Determination is a good thing."

She slaps a hardy helping of pasta onto my plate, scoops some Caesar salad into a second dish and slides them toward me. "It is, in some cases, but not when it comes to overruling bedtime."

I laugh, trying to fill our wineglasses, while she dishes up her food. Then she finally takes a seat across from me. Now I can see her entire face, with the left side lit by moonlight and the right by the faint interior lights.

Over our meal, we maintain casual conversation. With my recent check-in with the chief, I have fresh details to share about my "job". Georgia gives very vague details on her *big project*, just saying that she hopes it opens up new opportunities. As much as I press for specifics, she doesn't give anything away. I try to work everyone in her life I've met to this point into conversation, asking about Michelle, Shawn, and Pierre specifically. It's a difficult dance to probe for answers without coming across as suspicious.

If Georgia is hiding any information, she's a very good actress. She seems to enjoy talking about her friends.

Everything from their time in university to their more recent outings—which she claims flip-flop between paint nights and sporting events. No mention of forging famous works of art or break and enter.

For the duration of our meal, I drop subtle hints that I'm morally ambiguous and that I'd like to find a way to make extra cash to help my family out, but she doesn't bite. Instead, she looks sympathetic.

It's concerning. Not only because I've got my real-life brother wrapped up in this ever-growing lie, but I've stooped to guilt-tripping to build a case. I normally wouldn't be concerned with what weighs on a criminal's conscience, but it bothers me using this method with Georgia. She seemed to care about Nate, and exploiting that feels cheap. But I've got a case to solve by any means necessary.

Together, we clear the table, taking the dishes into the lounge kitchenette, and placing them in the sink. Georgia runs some hot water over them but abandons them to drag me back outside. The temperature is unseasonably warm, yet still chilly.

"The city is beautiful, isn't it? I never thought it would warm on me because it's a far cry from Utica, but it feels like home now. Like every time I'm back in the city limits, it wraps its arms around me and pulls me in, so I never want to leave again."

I wish I had the same affection for Chicago. Being in my line of work, I see the dredges of society. Criminal underworld, shady businessmen, deceitful people who walk around with a smile that hides their true intentions. It takes a toll, and my escapes from the city often give me a moment to breathe. I can't tell her that, though.

"It is." I stare out beyond the railing, taking in the lights between us and Lake Michigan. During the day, this position is a nice view of the water, but right now it's full of light pollution, making it impossible to see more than a few stars. That's one thing I miss about Ottawa.

Georgia shivers beside me, which awakens my inner gentleman. I attempt to shrug off my jacket, pausing halfway, realizing I have a hidden wire in the breast pocket. I have two options. Leave it and hope she doesn't notice, or yank it out and stuff it in my pants' pocket. I opt for the latter, stealthily grabbing it and hiding it away.

I slip the jacket over Georgia's shoulders, and she nuzzles into it with a quiet "Thank you." The sight of her wearing my clothes again is surprisingly intimate. Attractive on a whole other level than her in this dress. It's as if a primitive urge ripples through me, creating waves from my bones to my skin.

That reaction is squashed by the buzzing in my pocket. And another buzz. Several in quick succession tell me Sanders isn't pleased the wire is dead. I have a sudden flash of him bursting in here, gun drawn, with Lancaster on the line, blowing this entire case to smithereens. That can't happen.

I start with a faint cough, working up to an aggressive, hunched over, gasping for breath type. "Wa—water."

Georgia spins in a hurry and darts inside with my jacket trailing behind her like a superhero cape. Or super villain. I'm not sure yet. I take the split second to pull out my phone.

Sanders: *Wire is dead.*

Check in.

Prewitt report.

Don't make me come up there.

Great. He sounds like my mother.

Prewitt: *All good. Stay put.*

Georgia comes running back out a second after I slip my phone into my pocket and resume my coughing fit.

I take a healthy sip, add in a little throat clearing for effect, then set the cup on the railing. "Thank you. Not sure what happened."

"Maybe it was the kittens," she jokes, adding an irresistible smile.

And I don't want to resist anymore.

Georgia

22

CON DESCENDING

He's kissing me. Our lips haven't touched since the brief moment at the hockey game over three weeks ago, under the scrutiny of thousands of spectators. This is entirely different. This time, his hands are caressing my waist underneath his jacket. His tongue swipes the seam of my lips, and I'm powerless to resist letting him in. He doesn't hesitate, leaving me struggling to stay upright. The buzz zipping through me is no longer on account of the three glasses of wine I drank to calm my nerves. Not only are his lips responsible for my buzz, but they've also shifted my body temperature from cool to inferno. I'm at risk of incinerating his blazer.

I'm not sure how much time passes before we break apart. The cool air fills the space between us, making me miss his body heat immediately.

For a moment, I want to bask in the contentment that follows, but when I open my eyes to look at Archie, all I feel is a flood of anxiety. One that mimics the feeling when the bus driver slams on their brakes and you aren't sure if you'll stop in time. That fear-fueled moment not knowing if you're about to crash. His face is a mask of conflicting emotions. He blinks several times in succession, tugs the collar of his shirt, and avoids looking at me.

Guilt? Regret? Which one is unclear, but I know whatever he's feeling isn't good.

This was a mistake.

Instead of waiting for him to shoot me down, I act first. "I'm going to call it a night."

He breathes out a long sigh, still looking over the edge of the terrace. "Georgia…"

"It's fine. You don't need to explain yourself. I didn't knock your socks off or whatever. Message received." I'm not one to jump to conclusions, but this situation calls for a little self-preservation. I don't wait to hear his reply before I'm headed for the door.

Archie calls after me, but I don't stop until I'm inside and toss his jacket on the back of the sectional. Then I spot the sink full of dishes I either have to wash here or carry them back downstairs. Staying here will only open the door for more awkwardness, though.

As I stack the dishes so they'll be easier to carry, shoving what I can in a tote bag, Archie walks inside. He looks like he's gone six rounds in a battle with his better judgment and lost.

He still avoids eye contact. Apparently, his shoes are extra interesting, because he can't tear his focus from them. I kind of want to kill Rene right now. She's the one who talked me into this, and I'm the fool who listened. Granted, she's not familiar with my kissing skills, so she couldn't have known I'd fumble the entire evening on that part.

"Georgia?" Archie finally turns to face me.

My cheeks burn hot under his gaze. A combination of being stupidly attracted to him and utterly embarrassed that he looks like he wants to vomit.

"Yes?" I ask on a sigh.

"Can I help with the dishes?"

Seriously? Is this guy serious right now? The *dishes*?

"It's fine. I'm used to doing things alone. Perks of the job." I mean every ounce of snark that escapes. It's probably immature, but I don't care.

"Georgia…" he says for the third time, each one being a unique expression of the same two syllables. Each one expressing a note of despair. "It's not whatever you're thinking." He steps closer, rounding the counter covered in dishes.

My body tenses as he approaches. It almost feels like a warning. A subconscious alert telling me to guard my heart from his hot and cold behavior. But that same heart wants to hear him out.

"Then what is it, Archie? Why did you look like you were about to puke for five solid minutes? Hmm?" I shove the cooking utensils into the tote bag, and now I'm ready to take my leave. Yet, here I stand, waiting for an answer.

"I…" He pauses for a few seconds, and in that time, regains his composure, putting his mask back on. "I got burned by my last relationship. She wasn't completely honest with me, and I get the impression you're hiding something from me too."

That's rich, coming from the guy I can't get a read on to save my life.

"Sounds like you have trust issues, Archie. I'm not the one who burned you and you can't put that on me. So, if you'll excuse me." Without waiting for him to reply, I walk out the door and struggle down eleven flights of stairs so I can be sure to avoid ending up in the elevator with him.

Once I'm safe inside my condo, I change into pajamas, wash the dishes, and decide I'm angry my slight alcohol buzz was ruined. I open the freezer and pull out a bottle of vodka I was gifted from a distillery I made a painting for. I pour myself a drink, then pick up the phone to call my best friend, who may not be in possession of that title much longer.

"This can't be good if you're calling me this early," she answers.

"I hate you right now."

"What happened? Lay it on me."

I proceed to tell Rene every detail of our dinner; including what I wore, a detailed description of our kiss, and Archie's confession afterward.

"Do you want me to tell you what you want to hear or the truth?"

I should have known she'd have some wisdom to share that I might not like. Though, after this failed evening, her 'wisdom' is questionable. "Give it to me straight."

"That's my girl. You're right that his issues aren't on you. However"—she draws out the word, which makes her sound a bit like a Disney villain—"you aren't exactly an open book, so you can't blame him for hesitating if he's been hurt in the past."

"I don't blame him for anything. If he has issues with not trusting people, that's not my fault. Some things I *can't* share, or others I don't want to until the time is right. I shouldn't have to compromise any of that to ease his insecurities. I barely know the guy."

Rene fiddles with something in the background, then I hear SportsCenter come on her TV. "I get that. I'm just saying maybe be a little more patient with him. Don't cut and run because he doesn't accept everything at face value. You know everyone has a different learning style, and sometimes we have to adjust our teaching method."

Of course, she'd turn my dating life into a teaching scenario. Like I want to have to teach a guy how to date me. At least it wasn't a sports metaphor.

"I'm just not sure it's worth my time. The whole hot and cold thing is exhausting. He sends more mixed signals than a drunken quarterback." Well, now I've gone and done it. "You know what I mean."

"Only you can make that decision. I think you should give Hunky McHunkerson another shot. But since you brought up football, let me talk to you about number eighty-eight real quick."

Rene's fairytale—or delusional—love story is a nice distraction. I drink far too much vodka as I listen to her gush over her latest crush and hear about every aspect of his life she found online. She's flirting with stalker territory. Unlike her, I can't bring myself to tell her to rein it in. I allow her to live in her fantasy world for a bit while I sink into a drunken one.

We finish our call a short time later, and I lie on the sofa until I doze off.

I awake to a pounding headache, a crick in my neck, and knocking at my door.

Only one person would be insane enough to disturb me at 7:30a.m. I debate answering or not, quickly allowing curiosity to win out.

Sure enough, I tug the door open a few inches to find Archie on the other side, wearing his CFD coat, holding a pair of takeout coffees.

"Hi." He holds out one cup to me, which I reluctantly take.

I blink a few times, trying to clear the fogginess from my vision. How does he look so put together? He wasn't drowning his sorrows in ninety proof alcohol last night; that's obvious.

"Hi," I finally respond.

"Do you have a minute?"

"Archie, you woke me up sixty seconds ago. The only thing on my schedule is going back to bed."

He drops his eyes, but I'm not sure if it's because he feels bad or he's checking out my wardrobe choice. My avocado print shorts and T-shirt seem to amuse him.

"Can I come in?"

I turn back to examine the condition of my apartment. All of my art supplies are put away for the first time since I moved in, so it actually doesn't look so bad. "Sure."

He looks surprised by my agreement, but doesn't hesitate walking through the door. We walk past my unmade bed, into the living area, and each take a seat on opposite ends of the couch.

I set my coffee beside the empty glass that contained vodka several hours ago. "Thanks for the coffee."

Archie is busy scanning my space, like he's cataloging every item. He won't find much of interest. "Nice place. Did you make this?" He points to the colored graphite drawing of pedestrian and vehicle traffic on a busy downtown street. Everyone is slightly blurred to depict the hustle and bustle of city life.

"I did. That one is called *Apathy*." It's actually one of the pieces I plan to present to *Smith Goldstein & Co.*, but I don't tell him that. That is a major life event that is still undetermined, so I don't want to share with anyone in the event it doesn't work out. The only thing that would make it more disappointing is to have to share that failure with more people.

"That's amazing. I should get you to make something for my house—my apartment." His eyes bounce around the room again, landing on the only other piece of art I have hanging. "And this one?"

I sigh, looking at the drawing of a homeless mother and her child. "Yes. I call it *Perseverance*."

Archie leans forward, elbows on his knees. "What made you draw such a depressing picture?"

"It's not depressing at all. Yes, the reality of it is heartbreaking, but there's also great beauty in what it represents.

That day is forever imprinted in my mind. One of those moments that made me stop to appreciate everything I have." I take a sip of my coffee, enjoying the warm liquid and hoping it helps dull my headache. "Health, passion, friends, opportunity. I was feeling down on myself that day because I had paid a fortune to attend an artist market as a vendor. I left with ninety-five percent of my inventory, and barely made enough to cover the vendor fee."

Archie sits frozen, focused on me.

"I went to the event with high hopes and dragged everything home feeling like the world's biggest loser. But as I was drowning in my own misery, I walked past this mother and daughter, and they were both smiling. Their clothes were dirty, and the child was running in the alley, eating a slice of plain bread, but she looked happy. I guess it just stuck with me as a reminder to be grateful for what I do have, because you're never truly down and out until you give up on yourself."

"You have a unique eye, Georgia." He takes a sip of his coffee, which he tips quite far back, so I assume it's nearly empty. Then he steadies the cup on his knee as he turns himself a few degrees away from me. "I'm sorry about last night. You were right." His leg starts bouncing, but his face—as per usual—is a case study in stoicism. "Can we try again? Saturday?"

Do I want to go down this road again? Can my brain—and my heart—handle the ups and downs? Well, I don't get to think it through before my perfidious mouth blurts, "Okay."

Archie

23
BREAKING OUT

My instincts are shot when it comes to Georgia. I should have never kissed her. Not back at the hockey game and certainly not on the terrace.

At Quantico, we're taught about lines we blur and ones we don't cross. Kissing a suspect because I *wanted* to is a hard line. It wasn't necessary to preserve my cover or obtain valuable information. It happened because I was selfish and stupid. Then I was at a distinct disadvantage because I could have wound up in a bad position if she kept kissing me like that. One only an irresponsible agent would end up in. So I tried to put some distance between us, which I can't afford with a deadline.

That scenario is especially problematic now, as I take in the crime scene from another art heist where two forgeries have been left behind. Another perfectly executed break and enter into a private residence. Initial assessments indicate the owner has no idea when the paintings were switched, and only discovered anything amiss when he had an appraiser come in this morning to assess his collection.

It takes hours to interview the property owner, Tom Conti; the lone security staff, Mr. Choi; and the appraiser, Guillaume. After the crime techs process the scene and I grill them for any kind of lead, I've got no helpful information, and a lot of 'I don't know' answers. Few fingerprints, which likely all belong to the owner, no footprints around the exterior of the house aside from the security guard's, and no busted door locks or windows. It's concerning how efficient these people are, and they're getting better.

Sanders: *Got something.*

The do-gooder is proving himself useful, sifting through hours of security footage. It's hard to watch running backwards, but without a definitive timeframe, our investigation will go stagnant quickly, so I'm grateful to have another set of eyes.

Prewitt: *Be right there.*

I walk out of the elaborate mansion that costs more than I'll make in a lifetime, to meet Sanders in the AV van. He's seated in front of three computer screens, each frozen in the past.

"Looks like the heist happened on Sunday."

Every time I start to think Georgia isn't involved in this, another situation comes to my attention that changes my mind back. I'm getting whiplash from the back and forth. "What time on Sunday?"

"Sometime between eight and midnight. The cameras went dark just after eight and didn't come back online until 11:54."

Our condo building is about thirty minutes from here on the red line. That puts Georgia's timing in line with the theft.

"What are you thinking?" Sanders asks.

I shake my head to clear thoughts of Georgia. "Nothing. Just trying to think what other businesses are around that may have cameras."

"I already have a tech running through some footage from two doors down."

This could be the break I've been waiting for. The answer to the question that has plagued me for months: Who is responsible for these crimes? Yet, I don't feel the slightest bit enthused anymore.

How did I allow myself to get so distracted? How did I allow one woman's lips to make me betray the oath I've taken and the promise I made myself to avenge Nate?

"Okay, let me know what they find. Maybe we can get a partial plate or vehicle model to run down."

Sanders nods and returns to his examination of the video footage alongside another AV tech and instructs the young woman to rewind to Saturday evening.

I make my way back to speak with the security guard again. He somehow skipped over the fact that the camera cut out for four hours on Sunday evening. If he's any good at his job, he should have realized that.

"Mr. Choi, can I have another minute of your time?" I ask, leaning my head into the security room.

He jolts in his chair, immediately looking at the floor and fiddling with his necktie again—something he did several times when we spoke before. "Uh, sure. I doubt I have anything else useful."

I remain standing, leaning against the desk that holds the computer monitors, crossing my arms. "Sometimes we don't realize we know something helpful in the moment."

"Yeah, okay. I'll help however I can." He still avoids eye contact, but straightens his posture in his rolling chair.

"Have you been having any issues with your security cameras lately? Any scheduled outages for maintenance or problems you're aware of?" I attempt to phrase the question in a non-accusatory tone, but judging by Mr. Choi's wince, I fail.

"Not that I know of, no. I'm not in here every day, though."

"Why are you the only security staff? Has it always been just you?"

Mr. Choi starts twisting in his chair, turning it in one direction, then the next. "No, we had four staff, but boss man let the rest of them go, one by one. I thought he was going to can me too and get a dog."

Really, a dog would have been a wiser choice.

"Why did he let everyone go? Do you know?"

The robust Korean man freezes in his chair and looks at me for the first time since I re-entered the room. "Budget cuts, I guess. Boss owns a furniture company. Times have been tough."

That's ironic, considering the paintings stolen are allegedly worth a cool million. His gated home in the heart of Lincoln Park is four levels, over eight thousand square feet, and has a wine cellar in the basement with a wine collection that rivals my lifetime salary. But that does fit with the narrative of the appraiser coming in to assess the paintings for sale.

It's hard for me to press Mr. Choi when I'm not getting the impression he is involved in anything. He genuinely seems like a man who is concerned he's going to lose his job. For the sake of being thorough, I'll run his financials, but I doubt it will turn anything up.

"Thank you, Mr. Choi. I'll be in touch." I exit the main floor security room and walk through the elaborate kitchen into the backyard to comb the property one last time. At least if we could find a point of entry, we'd have something concrete beyond a timeframe. Not a single window or curtain is out of place. I tug my jacket closed and stare at the stone facade, willing it to speak to me. Instead, my phone buzzes.

Sanders: *Came up empty on video footage. I'm checking with other neighbors now.*

Six weeks ago, that message would have frustrated me or encouraged me to dig deeper. Today, it fills me with relief.

DO NOT CROSS

● JUST KIDDING ● KEEP GOING, YOU REBEL ●

Sanders and I wrap up our business at Tom Conti's house and head back to headquarters. Lancaster has been down our throats for the last three hours insisting she wants progress. Sanders wasn't even supposed to be on this case for more than a few occasions when I needed backup, but the big bosses are calling for someone's head. Lancaster sent him with me today as a courtesy, and he was helpful.

"Thanks for everything today, Sanders. I appreciate it," I confess as I pull into the parking lot.

"Any time." He stays silent for a few seconds, but I can feel him staring at me. "You wanna tell me what happened with your wire the other night?"

No. "Exactly what I wrote in the report. I took my jacket off, so I stuffed the mic in my pocket. There were no threats present." I pull into my designated spot and put the SUV in park. "Is there something you want to ask me?"

"It's a little odd to be standing out on a balcony the last day of October and taking your jacket off... without a reason to."

I turn to face my co-worker, who has been at this job longer than I have. His powers of perception are finely tuned to root out deception.

"Fine. I took it off because Georgia was cold and I was trying to maintain my cover. She'll be more likely to open up to me if I'm nice to her."

He arches a bushy blond eyebrow. "Is that what it is?"

I narrow my eyes at him in return, because I do not like being on the other end of an interrogation. Especially not when this is my case. "Yes. I know which lines to blur."

With one hand on the door handle, Sanders replies, "Just make sure you know when they have to be brought back into focus." With those closing remarks, he steps out and walks to the elevator.

I wait a few minutes until he disappears before I follow. The ride up in a confined space is the last thing I want right now. He couldn't have heard me kiss her. There's no way the wire was still working, or he wouldn't have been texting me when it went dead. So why does he seem so suspicious?

He's better at his job than I gave him credit for. I need to get my head back in the game and focus on the end result of this case. Not on Georgia's lips. Or how well she fits in my arms. Or how she smells like grapefruit and mint. I can't get distracted by the moments she seems like a sweet girl-next-door type and need to follow the evidence. More of which piled up today. There is only so much circumstantial evidence we can reveal before it starts to look like hard proof.

I finally make my way up to my desk, wanting to look through Mr. Choi's financials, add a few follow-up questions to ask him, and research this art vendor market Georgia mentioned yesterday morning. I task Sanders with running down the former security staff and the scenarios surrounding their termination. More directions for this investigation to go in hopes we can find answers.

The people responsible will be brought to justice—no matter who they are.

Georgia

24

STAINLESS STEEL

Today I have two nerve-wracking events happening.

First is a meeting with the curator at *Smith Goldstein & Co.* to discuss details of my potential exhibit. I have a portfolio of smaller graphite drawings and photos of a few larger ones I have finished. Whether it will be enough to cement myself an opportunity to share my work is one question weighing on my mind.

The second, and perhaps more anxiety-inducing happening for the day, is meeting Archie for drinks. I haven't seen him since Wednesday morning, but in all fairness, I haven't left my house. Ensuring I have a well-rounded collection of art pieces has been a lot of work, but I'm pleased with my portfolio.

I enter the prestigious *Smith Goldstein & Co.* building and take in the opulence of the space. The gleaming maple floors, immaculate gallery lighting, ornate wooden ceiling, warm white walls, and leather benches placed in front of a few select pieces make this the real deal. The kind of place I've dreamed of having my work showcased.

From my quick scan of the room, I can see they have a wide selection of mediums. Marble sculptures, abstract oil paintings, photographs, full walls of graffiti prints, and more. I don't see any graphite drawings. So what I'm about to present could be perceived as unique and something they're looking for, or out of their element and I'll be back at Square One.

"Can I help you?" a petite woman with black hair pulled tightly in a pristine bun asks. Her smile is radiant behind her crimson lips, and her dark skin glows under the lighting.

"Yes, please. I'm looking for Mrs. Robbins. I'm Georgia Dewan."

Her smile ratchets up even brighter, making her eyes join in. "Oh, Georgia. So nice to meet you." She reaches her hand out to shake mine. My kind of girl. "I'm Sephora Powell, director of sales."

"Nice to meet you, Sephora." I finally allow myself to return her smile, which helps ease my nerves.

"Have a look around. I'll let Sandra know you're here." She spins on her red-soled heel and confidently walks toward the back of the gallery.

My early perusal of the space didn't take in the immensity of the room. It must stretch back a hundred feet and is about forty feet wide. For a downtown Chicago space, it's massive. The sculptures in various mediums, ranging from clay to metal to marble, are all set on pedestals, protected by plexiglass covers. The wall art is blocked off by velvet ropes so people can't get within arms' reach. This place is *legit*.

A dignified middle-aged woman who reminds me a lot of my mother steps out from behind one of the display walls. "Georgia?"

"Yes." I turn to face her, offering my hand.

She gives it a firm shake, but her demeanor isn't as friendly as Sephora's. Mrs. Robbins is intimidating. "Come into my office. We can speak in there."

I follow Sandra, feeling myself shrink with each step. My self-doubt comes rushing in, weighing heavily on my shoulders and making each step laborious. We walk into an office that consists of two parts. One area has a large table a few feet out from a blank white wall, and at the far end, sits a large stainless steel desk that looks like it could be a feature in the gallery.

"Rene tells me you're very talented, Georgia. She spoke very highly of you."

Well, Rene's judgment is not something I have confidence in right now, so while I appreciate her boosting me up, this may be another situation in which I'm doomed to drop the ball she's hiked my way. She's lucky I love her.

"Friends will do that. She'd say the same thing if I told her I wanted to be an opera singer, and trust me, that wouldn't go well for anyone."

Sandra chuckles as she seats herself on a wheeled stool at the corner of the large table. "Why must artists always be so self-deprecating?"

"It's a requirement for art school. First question on the application, actually."

"Well, Georgia, I hope your art impresses me as much as your sense of humor. Show me what you've got." She gestures to the table. "Whichever you prefer. Lay them out flat or hang them."

I look up at the wall and see adjustable clips, and since most of what I have in my portfolio aren't originals, I don't have to risk ruining them. I walk over to the wall and hang four of my drawings—well, photographs of my drawings. Then I place the remaining six on the table, half of which are originals.

Sandra stays silent as she carefully slides my work toward herself and examines each one. She takes less time on the photographs, and I'm not sure if it's because there is less detail or if she's less impressed. By the time she stands to round the table, I'm chewing a hole through my bottom lip.

"You capture emotion very well."

"Thank you." I stand and wait for the 'but' statement.

"Rene was right. You are very talented."

A sigh rushes out of me fast enough, I practically deflate. "Thank you," I repeat.

"I'll be honest, Georgia; there isn't much of a market for graphite. It's stunning and your ability to capture the realism of certain moments is phenomenal, but selling it is the hard part."

Now I'm deflating for a different reason. I have a feeling I'm about to be told to change my medium and give people what they want, or go back to school for something more practical because I'll never make a career of this.

"But luckily, I've never been one to cater to what people want. I give them what they don't know they need, and this body of work you have, they need it."

My jaw drops, but it's lost all muscle control, so I can't close my mouth. Another stroke of luck, Sandra is looking at my art instead of my goldfish face.

It takes far too many seconds for me to compose myself. "Wow, that's… thank you. That's such a compliment."

"Well, it's not without critique." She spins around and points at my one drawing of a Chicago police officer on a horse smiling down at a little boy holding a balloon. "Everything you've brought, except this one, is depressing. The emotions each one evokes are distinctively sad. I want to give you your time to shine, Georgia, and find you your audience, but I need some range. Don't fill my gallery with stuff that's going to send everyone straight to the nearest pub to drown their sorrows."

Yikes. Am I really that depressing? Archie said the same thing about the drawing in my apartment, but to me, there is beauty and love evident in those moments. Humans often underestimate how strong they are until they're in desolate circumstances. But maybe I need to focus more on the obvious moments.

"I can do that. I can create a range. Do you have a timeframe in mind? And a number you're aiming for?"

"I'd like you to have at least fifteen distinct works. They should all be cohesive and shout Georgia Dewan from the paper, but I want variety. We have an opening in six weeks, if you think you can make that happen."

Six weeks to create five additional works? That's a really tough ask. But this is an opportunity I can't squander.

"Okay. I'll come up with a few new concepts and run them by you?"

"Sounds good to me. Check in with me in two weeks and we'll see how you're getting on, okay? I've got some other stuff to get to, so I'm going to pass you over to Sephora to work up a contract that covers all the messy stuff. Commissions and what not. She'll take care of you." Sandra leaves me with a tight smile, a firm handshake, and a ball of nerves.

My contract discussions with Sephora occupy the next sixty minutes of my life, and by the time we're done, my head is a jumbled mess of numbers. She kept asking me about pricing and commission percentages like it matters to me. Any income is better than zero, right? I'm hardly in a place to argue the difference between twenty-five and thirty percent.

In the end, it's all settled, except for the fact I have a lot of work to do.

On my way out the door, I yank my phone from my jacket pocket and my shaky hands nearly drop it. I step outside, releasing a deep breath, allowing it to dissipate in the cool air like a fog. Once more, and my hands are steady so I can call my best friends.

Michelle picks up on the second ring, and after she gives me the all clear she can talk for a minute, I add Rene to the call.

"I've been dying all morning. Tell me everything," Michelle demands once Rene picks up.

"Me too. Dish, girl. We need to know, like yesterday."

I decide to take a detour to Oak Street Beach instead of going directly to Chicago Station, just so I can have a minute to decompress from the excitement and anxiety brewing inside me. "Well, good news and not so great news. Good news is, I signed a tentative contract."

Both women squeal in the background, then Michelle shouts something to Savannah about not ripping heads off of her dolls. That's mildly concerning.

"Ohh-kay. You should keep an eye on that. You're raising a potential serial killer," Rene responds.

"Oh, stuff it. She's explaining to me why her dolls drew all over the wall, because they're stupid and don't even have brains. Ugh, this child exhausts me."

This conversation has taken its own detour.

Rene and I both stay silent until I attempt to get it back on track.

"Anyway, not so great news is that I have two weeks to present her with a better range of material because she says everything I showed her today is depressing."

"What? That's not like you. I thought your whole thing was that look of love. Finding happiness in people's eyes and trying to capture it." Michelle shouts at Savannah again, but she's covered the phone so I can't make out what she's saying.

"I thought that's what I was sharing. I mean, aside from the one drawing of a couple crying over a tombstone, which I perceived as a great representation of love, I thought most of them showed those emotions in small moments, you know?"

Rene scoffs, then adds, "Art is based on perception, Boo. She might be an expert, but that doesn't mean she sees your vision."

"That might be true, but if she didn't, with her discerning eye, I can't expect the general public to see it. So I'm going to try to come up with some more material and give her that range."

"Well, if anyone can do it, it's you," Michelle says.

"She's right. You've got this, Boo. Just don't let anyone else get in your head. Find your own inspiration and create what you want to create. That will resonate with people a lot more than some forced work to fit a brief, okay?"

I thank both of my friends and say goodbye so they can get back to their day.

Oak Street Beach is nearly abandoned now, short of one guy about my age playing fetch with his fluffy dog. I take a seat on my usual bench and watch them for a moment, trying to force inspiration, then remember Rene's words. Now that this possibility is looking more like a reality, I don't want anything to risk messing it up. I also don't want to go spreading the news like wildfire, only to have Sandra tell me in two weeks that my concepts are rubbish and terminate my contract.

After thirty minutes, my face is frozen from the cold air off of the lake pelting my cheeks. I turn back toward Chicago Station to head home so I can prepare for the next nerve-wracking event of the day.

25

BEHIND BARS

Georgia enters the bar, wearing a pair of tight dark jeans, a wool coat, and a hesitant smile. I have no doubts that I screwed things up earlier this week, but now with this new theft to investigate, I need her to trust me.

I stand to greet her from my spot at the end of the bar, which warms her face a little. Her hesitant smile morphs into a content one, relaxing her tense eyes.

"Hey. Thanks for meeting me." I lean in to give her a hug, resisting the urge to plant a kiss on her cheek.

"Hi. This is some place, huh? They really took the phrase *raise the bar* seriously." She pats the unusually tall bar for emphasis. "Have you already ordered?"

"No, I just saved us seats." I pull out the exceptionally high bar stool for her to climb onto. And she literally does have to climb.

"Seriously, was this bar built for the Chicago Bulls? This can't be regulation." She gets settled in her seat, and she looks like a toddler with her legs swinging beneath her.

"Chicago does love its sports teams. I wouldn't be surprised."

The bartender makes his way over once we're settled in and takes our orders. Georgia asks for a gin and tonic, and I request a beer.

"You know who else is super tall?" she asks once the bartender turns away.

I shake my head. "Who?"

"Volleyball players. Wow! I went to the professional beach volleyball tournament at Oak Street Beach this summer and I felt how Savannah must feel around us adults. My neck hurt from looking up at everyone."

"Really? I don't think I've ever watched volleyball before, so I never noticed."

Her jaw drops. "Never? Oh, man. You're missing out. Volleyball is a totally underrated sport. Great action. Incredible athleticism. So much fun."

I stare at her for a moment, trying to differentiate the Georgia who presents herself to me and the potential—likely—criminal I'm supposed to bring down. In the beginning, I was so convinced it had to be her because I was desperate for a lead, but now, even despite all the evidence, I just don't see how this woman could be a part of this. It's messing with my head and I'm afraid Nate is right.

"I'll have to check it out sometime to see for myself."

"Definitely. Next summer, if the pro tour comes back again, we'll have to go one day." She smiles at me in a different way from moments earlier. This one is full of excitement and truth. Her eyes sparkle under the hanging overhead lights, casting a shadow on her face that somehow still looks angelic.

"It's a date." I swallow deep after I blurt those words. It scares me when I realize I meant them. That I can see myself taking Georgia out in eight months' time, for reasons not connected to any investigation.

The bartender arrives with our drinks before we go any further down that train of thought.

I take my first sip, trying to settle my conflicting emotions. "So, what were you up to all day? Anything exciting?" That question also spurs a lot of regret, because I can't exactly tell her that I spent the better part of the day at my real house, arguing with my nudist neighbor about his refusal to close his curtains.

His exact response was, "If you don't like, don't look." No, Bruce. I don't like it at all, but it's a little hard *not* to look when you keep all of your lights on and walk around after dark in the buff. That imagery requires a good chug of my beer.

All the while I'm trying to scrub Bruce's naked form from my mind, Georgia is silent. I glance away from my beer to look at her, and she's also taking a healthy mouthful of her drink.

She sets down the tall glass with a sigh and clears her throat. "Nothing exciting, no. Just trying to find some inspiration for new projects. Trying to build my portfolio and stuff, you know?"

Well, at least she's opened the door to discuss art. None of our conversations thus far have made my next question a natural thing to ask.

"I don't really know how the artist life works. How do you find clients or make sales?"

Georgia muddles the slice of lime in her drink, watching it intently. "I'm still figuring that part out, to be honest. If I knew the secret, I might be able to afford an apartment with a bedroom."

That's a curious answer. If she was bringing in money from criminal activities, I don't imagine she'd stay in an apartment just for affordability's sake. Another hint that she's not guilty. Still, I need definitive proof either way.

"The *big job* you had when we went home, how did that come about?" I take a casual sip of my beer, trying not to look too eager for an answer.

She mimics my gesture, creating a long pause. "Where do you see yourself in ten years?"

I'm not sure how to come back from that. She's obviously trying to redirect the conversation, and I need to know why she won't discuss this *big job*. What's the reason behind it being so secretive? But if I repeat myself, she'll realize I'm being intentional in my line of questioning. Not only that, but where I see myself in ten years is being well on my way to a position as deputy director so I can make policy changes that actually lead to criminals being punished.

Since she wants to operate the same way, I supply a vague answer: "Wherever my job takes me."

"So that's it? Your job is your goal? You'd move away from Chicago if they sent you somewhere new?" She pushes her empty glass forward, gesturing to the bartender for a refill.

Again, I don't know how to answer that because I work for a federal agency that *could* send me anywhere, but she thinks I work for a regional one. "I don't think the CFD would send me anywhere outside of Chicago, but whatever role they needed me in, I'd do it. It gives me purpose, and I feel like I'm making a difference."

She studies me as she absentmindedly swipes the condensation on the outside of her empty glass with her thumb. "Your intentions are noble, young Archibald, but you need more to your life than work. Trust me."

My desired line of questioning is no longer my strongest *desire*. I inch forward off of my stool, but they're so obnoxiously large, I'm no longer on the seat by the time my feet touch anything. "What else should I have in my life, Peaches?"

She swallows hard. I trace the movement of her throat as she does. My eyes keep lowering until I see the rise and fall of her chest; lower still and see her legs separate to allow me to come closer. I shouldn't. I told myself I'd keep my composure and not put a conviction at risk, but I'm a mere mortal and Georgia is looking at me like I'm her source of life. When she peers down at me and licks her lip, I don't want her to do that herself.

Just as I'm about to tug her forward and take over that job for myself, the bartender slams her drink on the counter, drawing her attention. I glare at the smug guy with half a mind to arrest him for obstruction of life-saving acts. But I should probably thank him.

Georgia looks back at me, but the moment has passed. She clears her throat and takes a sip of her new drink. If her body temperature rose as much as mine did, no doubt she needs it to cool off. "Why Peaches?"

I hop onto my stool and slide as far back as possible. "Georgia peach. Peaches."

"How original." She rolls her eyes, but her wide smile tells me she's not the least bit annoyed.

Truth is, it just came out. I didn't put any thought into it, but she looked tempting, like a perfect, ripe peach and I'm disappointed I didn't get to take a bite. "Noted. Georgia doesn't like Archie's choice of nickname." I turn forward and tilt my head back to take a gulp of my beer.

"No, Georgia thinks it's… She likes it just fine," she replies, playing along with my third-person narrative.

I'm suddenly so tired of this ginormous bar and extra tall stools. It's like someone picked this place up out of the middle of Texas and dropped it in Illinois. It's all presenting problems tonight that I should be grateful for because it forces me to keep my distance, but I'm resenting each oversized item.

"I want to take you somewhere."

The left side of her mouth lifts into a half-smile and she snort-laughs. "I thought this was you taking me somewhere."

"No. Yes. It is, but I want to take you somewhere else." I chug the last of my beer, which prompts Georgia to follow suit. I jump down from my stool and help her from hers, toss some cash on the bar to cover the tab and a tip the bartender is lucky to be getting, and we're on our way.

Like previous experiences have gone, she trusts me. She doesn't ask any questions or offer any resistance. She's willing to go for the ride, wherever that may be. If she trusts me this way, wouldn't she trust me enough to offer some insight into her criminal activities? Wouldn't something have clicked by now that was more than circumstantial if she really was part of this?

Maybe I was wrong all along and Georgia isn't the link to the heist crew.

But it's hard to ignore the puzzle pieces that have been collected, and all seem to create a picture with her face on it. It's also hard to ignore how her hand fits in mine as I drive through the downtown core. It's even harder to ignore the way my heart races in my chest when she looks at me as she does when I pull into a parking spot at *Navy Pier*.

"Are we playing tourist?" she asks, her face lit up with a smile so wide, it reaches her eyes.

"You'll see." I hop out of the Jeep and walk around to her door, where she's already waiting. "Are you warm enough?"

"I'll be fine as long as we're not going swimming."

I chuckle at her deadpan expression. "No swimming. I promise."

"Okay. Lead the way. I trust you."

Those three words feel like a gut punch. I could let it fuel my guilty conscience and ruin the evening, or I can trudge forward, carrying the weight of the hatred I feel for myself for deceiving her. I choose the latter. "Come on."

We walk along the pier until we arrive at the ticket booth for the *Centennial Wheel*. Georgia stays silent as I purchase a gondola for us that is scheduled to lift off in fifteen minutes.

"I can't believe you're taking me on a giant Ferris wheel. You fell into a tourist trap." Her words lack any harshness. She's smiling, and I hope that means she's excited.

"Sometimes we have to live a little."

We waste ten minutes browsing the other attractions. It's cold and nearing the end of the day, so it's not busy. I've wanted to check out the *Centennial Wheel* since it opened, but never had a good enough reason to splurge on it. Tonight is the perfect opportunity.

We navigate the sparse crowd to get back to where we climb into our private gondola. The doors slide closed and our smooth ride into the dark sky begins. It's a slow ascent while other passengers load, so it takes several minutes to reach halfway up. We're already a hundred feet in the air, which is plenty high enough to see the lit up skyline.

"I love this city. The sights, the sounds, the people. There's so much beauty in it."

An artist's eye is more discerning when it comes to finding beauty in everyday things, but that's not the only reason I see things differently. The only beauty I see is a blue-eyed blonde sitting close enough I can wrap my arm around her. So I do. I drape my right arm over her shoulders and pull her close. I should stop there, but I can't. She's too tempting. I kiss the soft skin in front of her ear, just under the arm of her glasses.

She turns toward me, and I finally get the uninterrupted moments I've been craving since the bar. And it's worth the wait. I kiss her while we rotate through the sky, and the view I was excited to see has no appeal. Georgia's lips against mine make me forget about everything. Supervisors, policies, goals, fears. They all disappear until the only fear remaining is if she'll ever forgive me when she finds out who I really am.

Georgia

26

END OF A SENTENCE

I have four of my five new pieces conceptualized for the gallery exhibit, but I'm struggling to come up with one more. If I don't have something to present Sandra with next week, she'll probably rescind my offer and tell me to get my act together. I need some inspiration.

Georgia: Are you busy?

I don't even know what I'm doing right now. Thankfully, a reply comes back within seconds, not giving me an opportunity to regret my decision.

Archie: No. Just back from the gym.

Georgia: Can I come over?

What kind of inspiration do I think I'm going to find inside his tiny apartment? Doesn't matter. Too late to turn back now, unless he says no.

Archie: Sure. When?

Georgia: Now?

Before I lose my nerve and come up with an embarrassing excuse why I need to stay home.

Archie: *Give me ten? Need a shower.*
Georgia: *Okay.*

I will not sit here and think about sweaty Archie straight home from the gym. I will not imagine sweaty Archie getting in the shower. I will not imagine freshly showered Archie standing in a towel, with his muscles flexing and relaxing with each movement while he combs his hair. I *will not* imagine myself touching those muscles.

Yes, yes, I will imagine each of those things. For ten solid minutes until my heart is racing as I walk the few feet to his door.

He answers seconds after I knock. Fully clothed, much to my disappointment. Or perhaps my relief, so I can still form words.

"Hi." I flash a pathetic little wave.

He smirks and imitates my gesture, but it somehow looks cute when he does it. "Hi. Come in."

I walk into his condo, which I had seen from the door before, but it's even smaller in reality. A fire inspector must not make a lot of money if this is what he's settled for. Either that or the rental market is even more of a challenge than I realized. I've been in my place for five years, so it has been a long time since I had to hunt for an apartment.

"Do you want me to order food or something?"

I stop at the window to look at the same view I have from mine. "It's up to you. I'm not really hungry."

Archie walks up behind me. I smell his body wash before I feel him. I'm at war with myself, wanting him to come closer and wanting him to keep his distance. It's alarming how much I've been craving his presence since the *Centennial Wheel* a week ago.

He makes me decide which one will win the battle when he asks, "What *do* you want, Peaches?" He's close enough, his presence is consuming me. The conflicting feelings make way for one dominant one.

"I–I want you to kiss me."

He steps even closer until his body is against my back. With one gentle movement, he sweeps my hair off of my shoulder to expose my neck. His hot mouth connects with the flush skin below my ear. He teases me, sucking and nipping along that area. "Here?"

"Yes," I gasp.

He continues his trail, closer to my ear, then starts along my jaw. "Here?"

"Mm-hmm." I'm struggling to maintain any level of coherence.

Then, without warning, he stops.

I'm just about to protest until he spins me to face him. His eyes are dark with desire, which are a contrast to his pink lips framed by his rugged facial hair.

"Where else do you want me to kiss you, Peaches?"

At this point, I'd settle for anywhere, just to have his lips against me. He could kiss my big toe and I'd be happy. But I don't bother answering him with words. Instead, I tug on his fitted CFD T-shirt and pull him toward me until our mouths collide.

The second our lips make contact, Archie sighs, which, paired with the rough bristle of his facial hair and taste of mouthwash strong enough to sting my tongue, I'm lost in a sensory overload. He explores my mouth with an expertise I'm convinced only he possesses. Gentle nips. Sweet caresses. Passionate groans.

Time and space come to a screeching halt when he pulls back. His shirt is wrinkled in two circles from me clutching the fabric for dear life.

"You're killing me, Peaches," he whispers as he steps closer again. "You have no idea how bad I want to kiss you here." His mouth plunges back down to my collarbone, forcing me to throw my head back.

"Archie," I whimper.

He doesn't stop. I lose all concept of the world that exists beyond where Archie's lips are connected to my skin until I'm straddling him on the sofa. His lips separate from my neck and I take stock of where I am—physically and emotionally. In Archie's apartment; more specifically, on his lap. Falling hard and fast for a guy who is still such a mystery. I move to jump off his lap because that realization scares me, but he places one hand on each side of my hips, holding me steady.

"I like you right here."

Oh, trust me. I'm not complaining about my seat, either, but it's going to melt all of my self-control, and until I get a consistent read on this guy and learn more about what makes him tick, that's not going to happen.

I give him a quick kiss and shimmy off of him, dropping onto the other cushion on the loveseat. "What inspires you?" That seems like a safe direction for our conversation to go that will cool the temperature significantly.

He leans in toward me. "Your lips."

I laugh and push him away with one hand on his firm chest. "No, seriously."

"Seriously."

"Archie." I sigh, but there's no hiding my smile. "How do you keep inspired? What pushes you to be a good person? Or to keep going to the gym? Or get up to go to work every day?"

I instantly regret bringing up his job, because every hint of enthusiasm he had seconds ago disappears like a light has gone out.

"Can I be honest with you?"

"Uh… please." That's kind of a ridiculous question.

He takes a deep breath and focuses his attention on Christofern across the room. "After Nate's accident, the people responsible were investigated, and it turned out they were trying to cut costs. They used cheap materials that weren't to code and paid off the inspectors. That's why the building collapsed." His voice comes out a little louder than a whisper, and he only blinks once. "Anyway, those people, everyone involved, got a slap on the wrist. Three men died and my brother's life was changed forever, but they got away with it. So, ever since, my biggest inspiration has been trying to make a difference, so things like that can't happen again, and people are punished according to their crimes."

I'm confused how his role as a fire inspector even makes a difference in that area. Nate's accident wasn't a fire issue; it was a building issue. A moral issue, obviously, but nothing to do with the fire code by the sounds of it. "I'm sorry, Archie. I can imagine it's really frustrating when justice isn't served, but is vindication for your brother the only thing motivating you? Is that what Nate wants?"

Just like on the terrace ten days ago, his post-kiss face is a stark contrast to the euphoria I felt for the last few minutes. His narrowed eyes tell me he's not happy about my question.

"What Nate wants for my life isn't a factor." His tone is dry and lacking any emotion. Almost robotic in his delivery.

"But if you're hanging onto this revenge plot, dedicating yourself to getting vengeance, are you not just forcing him to keep reliving it instead of moving on with his life like he's trying to do?"

He shifts a little farther away without tearing his glare from me. "You're saying if someone else was at fault for you losing your right hand and you couldn't create art anymore, that you'd just let it go? You'd want everyone else to let it go too?"

Maybe I have no right to say anything because I haven't experienced what Archie's family has, but it bothers me that someone I care about is so focused on atonement, he can't see the harm in it. "I'm not discounting what Nate lost. Nor how the situation must have affected your entire family. Not for one second. What happened was unfair, but in the short time I spent with Nate and Janine, I don't get the impression they're dwelling on it. They're moving forward and living their lives. I just want the same thing for you."

Silence. For far too many seconds. I'm about to slink out of Archie's apartment because I'm convinced I've overstepped, but I'm not sorry for what I said.

He surprises me by reaching his arm over and pulling me against him. "You're right." He exhales a long breath, which makes me relax against his shoulder. "I'm beginning to think you're always right, Peaches. I'm not saying that I can just drop the issue because you make a valid point, but I'm willing to make more room for other sources of inspiration." His devilish smirk makes it clear exactly what he's implying.

"Like…?"

Without another word, he dips his head forward, twists me until I'm back on his lap, and he's sending bolts of pleasure down to my toes by kissing me like that's his actual job. His rough hands sneak up the back of my shirt and graze along my skin. The sensation urges me to bite at his lip. His groan of approval makes his apartment feel like we're in a Caribbean villa, not in Chicago, in the middle of November.

We're jolted back to reality when Archie's phone buzzes in his pocket, rumbling against my thigh.

I lean back and swing myself over to dismount his lap. "You should get that," I say, trying to catch my breath.

He leans forward to give me a quick kiss. "There's no one else I want to talk to right now."

"Archie…"

"Peaches," he growls, diving forward until I'm leaning back and his body is pinning me in place. "It's Saturday, and I don't want to think about work or anything else."

Well, as much as it seems like a good idea to stay here and make-out until my face goes numb, I came for a purpose. "Tell me something about you that no one else knows."

He hovers over me, staring into my eyes, allowing me to really look into his. I've studied them before, but not from this distance. He's also never shown a hint of vulnerability like he is now. "When I found out I was allergic to cats, I hid in my room and cried. Which was hard, because Nate and I shared a room."

That's not what I was expecting, but I suppose it is an answer. "Why?"

"I don't know. The idea of having a pet to care for was exciting. That probably sounds stupid, because I was twelve, but there's just something about taking care of a living thing that depends on you, you know?"

I glance over at his plants, now understanding his obsession with them a little more. It appears young Archibald had the same protective instincts grown Archie has. That little bit of insight into him helps to form a more rounded picture of the man I've struggled to get to know. Just like everyone else, he's more than what appears on the surface, and for the first time in my adult life, he's someone I can see myself taking the time to study each layer. Right down to the base sketch that gets covered up completely, but forms the structure for an entire work of art. I want to see it all. The best part of this new information is the inspiration it floods me with.

"Yeah, I do."

27
CONCRETE EVIDENCE

For someone who has spent the better part of his adult life trying to look after his brother—though he's never asked for it—I sure have come to depend a lot on him lately. Since yesterday, Georgia's words have been replaying in my mind that by clinging to this vengeance mentality, I'm forcing Nate to relive events he wants to move on from. So I've asked him and Janine to come to my house so I can obtain some big brother wisdom.

According to Georgia's brief text exchange this morning, she's locking herself in her apartment and diving into her work, but she didn't tell me anything about it. She just thanked me for providing some new inspiration. As per usual. I've heard that artists are mysterious and secretive about their work, but she takes things to a whole other level, which doesn't help matters when I'm trying to prove she's not involved in these crimes.

I pull into my driveway behind Nate and Janine's van and look to the right. Sure enough, Bruce is parading around buck naked in his living room, behind a window big enough he might as well be on a jumbotron. I don't know if he's doing a Richard Simmons workout or what, but he's so sweaty, I can see the sheen from here.

With my right eye closed and my head turned as far left as possible, I walk to the side entrance along the driveway. I go up the ramp and enter my kitchen to find the lovebirds settled in my dining room.

"Hey. We grabbed lunch," Janine greets, holding up a paper bag and gesturing to the table.

I walk over to give her a hug and Nate a fist bump. He showed up, which is something, but I still get the impression he's mad at me. I'm not sure how he'll take it when I tell him he might be right, but I still can't confirm or deny that with enough evidence to do anything about it.

We sit down and dig into the shawarma and salad, all while carrying on vague conversations. Apparently, our sister Penny has a new boyfriend. At twenty-two, I figured it would happen, but Nate doesn't seem thrilled about the guy. Clearly, he has strong opinions about his siblings' love lives.

Once we're finished, Janine stands to pick up the dishes.

"I'll get that, J."

"I see your brother every day. We came all the way here so you guys could visit and that won't happen if you're in the kitchen. Let me handle it. You guys go chat."

My brother really did win at life when he asked Janine to be his date to the homecoming dance as a junior. They've been inseparable ever since, despite the hard times they've gone through. Their love for each other has stood every test.

"Thanks, J." I stand to give her another hug because I greatly appreciate her.

Nate and I move into the living room, where he situates himself in the front corner near the windows. "What in the name of...?"

I follow his eyes, even though I know what I'm going to see. It only takes a split second for my eyes to land on Bruce's bouncing belly. Thankfully, that's all I catch an eyeful of this time. "I don't know when he turned into a nudist, but I'm starting to think this house was cheap because of him and not the structural issues."

"Why is he so sweaty?" Nate is staring with his nose turned up and his face scrunched.

"How would I know? I'm not going to ask him."

Nate's laughter starts out slowly, but once he gets going, it turns into a fit of giggles. Reminiscent of Nate as a carefree kid. He's slapping his knee, tears streaming down his face, howling. It's impossible not to join in. I drop on the couch, careful to choose an angle that doesn't look into Bruce's windows, and allow myself to really laugh. It feels good. Not just for myself, but hearing my brother too.

Janine walks into the room with a dish towel over her shoulder. "What is going on in here?" she asks with a wide smile.

All Nate can do is lift his hand to point.

Curiosity wins out, and she strides over to the window to see what the fuss is about. "There's nothing th—" She freezes for a second. "Oh. Wow... Well, good for him. You've gotta admire his confidence." Like the mature, sensible person she is, Janine doesn't find the same humor in it Nate and I do.

I guess, when it comes down to it, we'll always be the troublesome Prewitt boys.

Once our laughter dies down and Janine disappears again, Nate turns to me with no hint of amusement left in his voice. "So, are you going to fess up?"

That forces any residual chuckles I had to die in my throat. "To Georgia?"

"No. Well, you should, yeah, but that's not what I was talking about. I mean, why did you ask us here?"

Suddenly, being the recipient of my brother's stare makes me wish he'd turn his attention back to my perspiring neighbor. "I want to make things right again."

"Arch, I'm not sure what to tell you. I'm not mad at you for doing your job, but I am worried that your obsession with it is going to ruin something good."

"Nothing has ever mattered more than doing my job." Until now, I realize after I finish my sentence.

Nate leans forward, resting his forearm across his thighs. "And now?"

It's alarming how perceptive he is. Really, I should get him a job at the bureau. It would be so much easier if I could use his instincts as concrete evidence; if they mattered for anything more than his opinion.

"Georgia is the one who will suffer the consequences when you realize she's not guilty of whatever you think she is. I can't even give you a good reason why I'm so sure of that, but I'd bet my house on it." His confidence in each word leaves no room for doubting his assurance she's innocent.

"You think I want her to be guilty? Do you actually think that I want the woman I'm falling in I—" I stop myself short, surprised by my almost confession.

Nate gawks at me with his infamous big brother *told you so* stare. "Go ahead. Finish your sentence."

I swallow the words back down. "I can't."

"Can't fall in love with her?"

I nod without looking at him. "My heart and my head say two different things. My heart wants to believe you're right. But my head... It's battling between doing my job and doing what I want."

Nate is a romantic, as evidenced by how in love he is with his wife. I can already anticipate his solution to my problem before he says a word.

"Sometimes we have to listen to our heart. Throw logic out the window."

"Hearts make bad choices."

"I disagree." He pauses, waiting until I lift my eyes to look at him before continuing. "When my accident first happened, all logic told me to end my life. My *head* told me things would never be the same and that Janine could move on, find someone to have a better life with. Someone who could climb Machu Picchu or ride in a rodeo. But you know what I learned?"

My insides twist in a knot hearing Nate admit that. "What?" I choke out.

"She didn't want to climb Machu Picchu or ride in a rodeo. She wanted *me*. And I know things aren't perfect. There are things that will always hold us back, but what we have is enough. If I had listened to my head, rather than following my heart, I wouldn't be here."

This is news to me. I know Nate went through bouts of depression for a couple of years after his accident, but that was understandable. In addition to medical intervention, we all rallied together to help him. I didn't realize he was considering taking his life. It goes to show, you can know someone, yet not know them at all.

I feel like the world's worst brother for not knowing any of this sooner. "Why didn't you tell me?"

"That's not really the point. But that's the funny thing about depression. It convinces you that things won't get better, so there's no use weighing anyone else down with the constructed reality it creates. Janine pulled up a blog with an epic bucket list to prove a point, and aside from one or two, there was nothing holding me back from the rest of them. She made me focus on everything we could have and not on what I lost. Because at the end of the day, it was what I still had that really mattered."

My eyes are watering by the time Nate finishes his brief speech. I blink a few times and clear my throat before replying.

"Do you feel like I've held you back? Like my thirst for justice has kept you from really moving on?"

He takes a deep breath, leaning back and focusing his eyes on the fireplace. "Sometimes."

I drop my head against the back of the couch and close my eyes. "Nate—"

"No, don't apologize. You're a good brother, but at the end of the day, the only person it's really holding back is you."

Janine walks into the room, drawing our attention. I flick my gaze back to Nate and watch his eyes light up at the sight of her. His lips turn up in an unmistakable grin.

She doesn't pay any attention to me as she walks across the room to the man who holds her heart. "We'll have to go soon. It gets dark early."

"Yeah, I think we're good here." He turns to look at me. "Right, Arch?"

"Yep," I reply, rubbing my hands on my knees as I stand. "I don't want to hold you guys up. Thanks for coming so last minute."

"There's nothing we wouldn't do for you," Janine replies before pulling me in for a final hug. "Except driving at night. That's where I draw the line."

Fifteen minutes later, I'm standing alone in my driveway after moving my Jeep for Nate and Janine to leave. I have so many conflicting and confusing thoughts swirling in my head, I don't notice my neighbor approach until he's standing four feet away. That's not a good thing for an FBI agent—especially one working undercover, who should always be on alert.

Thankfully, Bruce appears fully clothed. "You've been working a lot lately, huh? I've barely seen you home."

"All part of the job. Sometimes it calls for long hours."

He shakes his head, which makes his third chin wobble with the movement. "I hope that means you'll take some time off soon, Archie boy. Remember, don't give your life—"

"To a job that doesn't give it back," I finish. "I know."

If only it were easy enough to walk away without consequences. Right now, I'm left with an impossible scenario that can't be solved by a few days off. And it's time for me to sort it out.

IN THE LOOP

It's weird how natural it feels being in Archie's space. His view is nearly identical to mine, and his apartment is even smaller—which I didn't think was possible—but being here with him for the fourth time this week feels as much like home as my space ever has. It's probably less to do with the physical location and more to do with the contentment that washes over me being in his presence. I rest my head on his shoulder and cuddle in next to him on the loveseat as we watch the second period of the hockey game, eating potato chips and drinking craft beer.

He drapes his arm over my shoulders and caresses my bicep with his thumb. "Do you want me to pour some beer on your head for old time's sake?"

I snort-laugh and roll my eyes, turning my head to look at him. "Don't you dare. If that's not a case of *deja brew*, I don't know what is. I'd never forgive you."

Instead of the laugh at my stupid joke I'm expecting, Archie's face morphs into a mask of anxiety. He refocuses his attention on the TV without responding, but his hand is fidgeting with the hem of his waffle-knit Henley, and he's chewing on his bottom lip.

With Archie, I take two steps forward and one step back, which still may be progress, but his shifts in demeanor are exhausting. Every time I've tried to ask him about it, he tells me it's work related and not to worry. But what does a joke about pouring beer on my head have to do with work? It's not a fire hazard. How does he go from light-hearted and fun one second to nervous and dismissive the next?

He did the same thing the other day when we were in the sky lounge with my friends. He just shut down and left me trying to analyze what went wrong.

Quite frankly, I've had enough of being dismissed by people who I thought cared about me.

We sit in silence until the second intermission, and that marks the end of my tolerance for his standoffishness.

"Are we going to talk about whatever's bothering you, or should we just sit here in silence?"

He shifts out from under me to stand and walks over to Vincent van Grow on the kitchen counter to touch the soil. I know for a fact he coddles his plants and has a regular watering schedule for them. He's avoiding me.

After my trip home last month, maybe I'm a little more sensitive, but I'm not going to dedicate time to people who don't value me enough to dedicate effort back.

I release the throw pillow I am clutching over my chest like a shield and toss it on the couch as I stand, then walk toward the door. "I'll leave you to take care of your plants."

Archie doesn't chase me, but he calls my name before I reach the door.

I spin around to glare at him—hopefully making it clear I'm not impressed.

"Listen… I… uh." He scrubs the back of his neck with his hand, pausing his words and actions simultaneously as if someone pressed his stop button.

"I'm listening."

He turns his focus to his zebra plant by placing both hands on the edge of the counter and leaning forward. He sighs, then continues speaking. "I like you, Georgia. Really like you… and I'm afraid you won't—"

My phone dings, which stops Archie mid-sentence.

"Won't what?" I prompt.

He shakes his head without looking up. "You should get that."

Him dismissing me again compounds my anger. I'm not shocked by him admitting to liking me. We've spent enough time together, I had already assumed as much because I really like him too. At least, when he's not being infuriating and impossible to read. So, to make myself appear indifferent to his admission, I pull my phone from my sweater pocket and read the notification. I gasp as I read the words *Priceless art stolen from Smith Goldstein & Co.*

"What is it?" Archie now moves closer; the earlier traces of uncertainty are gone.

"The gallery I—" I stop myself before spilling my secret because I'm still not ready to share my potential career- and life-altering opportunity in case it doesn't work out and I'm left feeling like an immense failure. "An art gallery in Streeterville was robbed."

Archie scrambles to pull his own phone from his pocket, reads something quickly, then returns his focus to me. I know he's had a vague interest in art, but he hasn't shown enough to justify the flurry of questions he tosses my way. When, where, how, what… everything but the why. I take a seat on the couch part way through his interrogation because he insists on asking the same questions multiple times until he's satisfied with my answers. A combination of his surprising enthusiasm and position on the counter-height stool at his kitchen island makes our conversation a bit intimidating.

It takes a lot of dancing around the truth to avoid telling him I set up Google alerts on that gallery because I'm supposed to be having a show there in four weeks. A lot of half-truths and withholding to avoid sharing how this theft affects me personally.

I try to detour the conversation away from my firsthand relationship and back to the big picture. "It makes sense thieves would target Chicago. We have the most expensive art collection of any city in the world."

"Really?"

I nod. "Really. Even Paris and New York play second fiddle to Chicago when it comes to the dollar value of art here. It is a remarkable place to be an artist. Albeit, saturated and competitive."

He leans forward to rest his elbow on his knee and his chin on his hand, much like *The Thinker* by Rodin—except Archie is fully clothed. "If you were going to steal any piece of art in the city, which one would you take?"

That question, again, surprises me. "For one, I'd never steal art because I wouldn't betray other artists that way. Not only that, but I believe in art's power and influence, which can't be replaced by any dollar amount, so stealing it would be pointless."

Archie studies me intently, but doesn't interrupt. It appears he's run out of questions.

"But if I were going to target something, I wouldn't go after the most expensive pieces. Logically, that's a waste of time because they would be heavily guarded, largely studied and documented, and nearly impossible to sell. I wouldn't even go after anything at *The Art Institute* or other large museums because their mission is protecting their pieces of art, not selling them."

"Not even if you had an inside man?"

I raise a brow at him, curious why he's so interested all of a sudden. "Are you planning to steal a Monet, Archie?"

He lifts his head from his fist and sits upright. "No, I'm just wondering. I thought art heists only happened in movies." He lets out an awkward laugh, adding to my confusion.

"Art is a valuable commodity. There have been thousands of successful thefts throughout history and a lot of lives lost in the process. It's really sad, because artists just want their work shared and enjoyed, not turned into a reason for violence or murder." One of my art history courses had a section on thefts and forgeries. I've also spent enough time touring the city's extensive list of art galleries and museums and been around enough artists to know that's a universal constant.

He studies me for a few seconds, as if he's assessing my comments. His phone rings before he can respond, so I'm again left wondering what he's thinking.

"Hello?" He listens for several seconds, then replies to whoever is on the phone, "I'm just here with Georgia, but I'm sure she'll understand." He continues with a few *mm-hmm*s and *uh-huh*s before he hangs up the call. "I'm sorry, Peaches. My sister is in a bit of a situation and asked me to come help her."

"Oh." I try not to let my inner pessimist convince me he's making an excuse to get rid of me. "Penny or Elle?"

"Uh, Penny. Some drama with a new guy she's seeing." He stands from his stool like he's not giving me a choice in the matter. "I'll text you when I get back if it's not too late."

If he thinks I'm going to sit around and wait for him, he's mistaken. No matter how much I like him. "Don't worry about it, Archie. I've got work to get done, anyway. I should be spending my time on that." Then, like I attempted to earlier, I walk out the front door of his apartment.

This time, he doesn't call after me.

"I don't understand. Why don't you just tell him about the exhibit?" Rene asks while adding some viridian green to her work in progress.

Tonight we're painting an abstract pine forest, which isn't really my preference, but I don't come for the art. I came for a distraction after Archie's dismissal two nights ago and the fact I haven't heard from him since. Not to mention, I was supposed to present my final pieces to Sandra yesterday, but that has been delayed because of their robbery.

"I've told you. The gallery hasn't made it official, and with this theft, I don't know if they ever will. I can't handle letting everyone down. It will be bad enough you guys know if it falls through. Which, FYI, you need to be on standby for with a few bottles of merlot."

"Oh, stop," Michelle chides. "Whatsername already said it was basically a done deal. They just haven't done the press release. Big whoop. You're making excuses not to tell him, which begs the question: why?"

Am I? Is my refusal to confide in him more than what I've been telling myself? I mean, I haven't told my parents either, and with them, it's definitely because I'm afraid of disappointing them. Rather, continuing my streak of being a perpetual letdown. That was my justification with Archie too, but maybe it's more than that.

"I don't know. He's…"

Both of my friends abandon looking at their canvases and stare at me.

Rene wafts her hand. "He's *what*?"

"Nothing has changed from before, even though everything has. I know that doesn't make sense, but he has this mysterious side to him that's hard to navigate. So, when he asks me to do something, I have this confidence that I can trust him. But with keeping secrets, I guess I'm holding on a little tight."

Michelle surprises me by replying, "If you can't trust him in everything, you can't trust him at all, babe. That's just the cold, hard truth."

I drop my paintbrush on the paper towel in front of my table-top easel. Suddenly, my artistic inspiration is gone. "I don't know what it is. He's great and I enjoy spending time with him, but I have this nagging feeling that keeps holding me back. Maybe that's all it is with him too. How do you decide who spills their guts first?"

"You shouldn't have to decide. You just spill because you trust the person and don't want to hold back. Especially in your case, when what you're holding back is the best news ever. No offense, but it's stupid not to tell him." Motherhood has really worn down Michelle's patience, because she wastes no time dancing around feelings.

Maybe she's right. I should just open up to him and see if he'll do the same. It's not like I'm sharing any deep, dark secrets that would change the course of our relationship.

"Fine. I'll tell him when I get a chance."

"Good. Because I'd hate for things to go south with Hunky McHunkerson. That man is a fine piece of—"

"Rene." I pinch my temples, trying to squeeze that name from my mind. "How's number eighty-eight?"

"Ooooh, girl. Let me tell you..."

My trick works, and for the next forty-five minutes, I paint, drink wine, and listen to Rene tell us about his latest SportsCenter highlights, his press conferences, and social media. She's activated full stalker mode, and I'm not convinced she wouldn't be an asset to the CIA if she was motivated enough. Need to track down one of America's most wanted?

Just tell her he's "hot as all get-out" and wearing tight pants. She'll track him down.

By the time she runs out of things to say, our paintings are done, dry, and we're ready to go.

Michelle climbs into a ride-share to get home to her rambunctious three-year-old girl, while I climb into Rene's car to hitch a ride. She didn't drink because she has to work tomorrow—boring—but at least I don't have to walk home in the freezing cold.

We pull up in front of my building and my best friend reaches over to grab my hand before I jump out.

"I'll never tell you to dismiss your instincts, but don't forget to live a little too."

It might be a common saying, but I can't help but think about Archie saying the same thing before our ride in the *Centennial Wheel*. And maybe it's time I throw caution to the wind.

29

TIED UP

Six days since I last spoke to Georgia, and I'm lost in a sea of confusion. Sanders is now my full-time partner, rather than just a floating backup for whoever needed him, but I can't talk to him about all the elements of this case. Sure, I can discuss the things I've written in my reports and analyze evidence, but if I confessed anything else, I'd have to excuse myself. And I'd likely end up on probation.

I'm less concerned about what that means for my career at this point and more worried about what that would mean for Georgia if another agent follows the same trail I did.

This latest heist at *Smith Goldstein & Co.* resulted in one of their mainstays being stolen. This time, it wasn't even replaced with a forgery. That's how the story broke so quickly. With the other thefts, we've managed to keep things quiet and out of the news.

The security service the gallery employs has two guards on a rotating schedule between three other neighboring businesses. One guard on duty ate some bad seafood and spent half of his shift in the bathroom at the art gallery. When I initially interviewed him, he said—and I quote—"I thought I was going to melt the paint off of every piece of art in the place." Charming fellow. While he was in the midst of his extreme intestinal distress, the thieves broke into the gallery. At first, the guard, Casper, thought it was his co-worker, so after a few minutes he shouted out to him to ask for some Pepto-Bismol. Luckily for Casper, he had locked the bathroom door, which we assume the criminals didn't want to waste time on, so they cut and run. Literally cutting the painting from the frame and took off before the man could call for backup.

What was even weirder, though, is how Georgia received notification of the theft before I did. She also seemed bothered by the situation. Whether that's because of her love for art or because she knew what they were aiming for and fell short, I can't be sure. I want to be confident that she's not involved, but these seeds of doubt keep planting themselves, and now they've taken over more than my houseplants.

"The curator at the gallery called. They confirmed that they only lost the one painting, but we should go back down there and call the appraiser to be sure." Sanders drops into a vacant chair beside my desk and wheels it closer. "Any luck on your end?"

"Not really. The guard has recovered from his bout of food poisoning, so I'm going to talk to him again shortly. And I hope I can connect with my CI to see if he has any new leads."

"Need me to come with?"

I smile at my eager partner, grateful to have him on my team—even if I am keeping things from him. Seems that's a reality with a few people in my life. "Nah, I'm good, thanks. My CI is skittish."

"Understood. I'll keep rolling through the rest of the footage we didn't send to the AV lab and let you know if I come up with anything useful." With that, he stands and walks back to his cubicle thirty feet away.

The second I get a response from Casper that he's available to talk, I inform Sanders I'm leaving, grab my coat, and head to a cafe near the gallery.

Casper is waiting in a booth, looking every bit the friendly ghost his name implies. He's pale and looks like he's just come back to life. He waves me over like we're long-lost friends.

"Mr. Gibson, thanks for meeting me," I state, dropping into the booth opposite him.

"Yeah, sure. Whatever I can do to help. I feel awful about the whole thing."

It's funny, because his near interaction with the thieves is the closest anyone has come to them for months. If only he wasn't confined to the toilet at the time.

"These things happen. Now it's just my job to make sure it doesn't happen again. What can you tell me about your regular routine?"

"We rotate through the gallery, the plastic surgeon's office, and two realtor offices opposite each other. No place is left unchecked for more than ten minutes. But we alternate checking inside and outside with each pass. I had just come out of the doctor's office and was making my way to the gallery to restart my loop when... well, you know." He grimaces, fiddling with a crumpled up paper napkin.

"Unfortunately, yes. So you went into the gallery. Did anything appear off when you entered?" I know I've already asked this, but sometimes witnesses recall new information after a few days. Especially since our initial interview took place with Casper on the other side of a bathroom stall and me struggling to talk without breathing.

"Now that I think of it, I didn't have to shut off the alarm."

Interesting.

"What time was this at?"

He tenses his face as if thinking is really uncomfortable for him. "I guess around midnight? My shift started at ten and I had done three loops. About 10 minutes at each stop. Forty minutes per loop. Two hours total."

"That's helpful; thank you."

He smiles and releases the napkin, letting it drop on the ignored menu. A server comes over to ask us for our orders. I request a coffee, but Casper understandably asks for ginger ale.

"So you didn't turn off the alarm. Did you unlock the door?"

"That's the weird thing. You saw the bars on the doors and windows. Those were all locked. How did these guys get in?"

"How do you think? Any vulnerable spots that would give easier access?"

Casper's thinking face returns for long enough, our server brings our drinks. "No. That place is sealed up tight."

I force my posture to stay rigid so I don't let on how disappointing that is. We talk for a few more minutes, downing our drinks, and discussing the finer points of Casper's job. By the end of our conversation, I've got no more helpful information.

Still, I thank him for his time, pay for our drinks, and walk toward the door. Before I exit the building, I get a text.

Sanders: *Techs found video of black BMW in parking garage nearby. No plates. Going to comb footage and hope we can find it again.*

Of course they'd choose the most common, generic car in the downtown area. Every banker, realtor, and doctor has a black BMW of some sort. Still, it's a better lead than I generated from my chat with Casper.

Prewitt: *Good work. Going to meet CI now. Casper didn't have much to add.*

I feel defeated as I drive south on La Salle, toward where I'm supposed to meet Bobby. This case doesn't seem to be coming together. At all. I'm not sure if it's the sophistication of the criminals, my ineptitude, or my distraction. I want answers.

But now, not to prove myself to my superiors and launch myself into a promotion. I want them so I can confess to Georgia who I am. So I can clear her name.

Hopefully, the answers I find ensure that happens.

As per usual, I park and watch the entrance to the alleyway where I'm supposed to meet Bobby for thirty minutes before he appears. He's wearing a new designer coat and a shiny watch peeking from his sleeve. I have my doubts he's obtained either from a regular nine-to-five.

I step out of my SUV and stroll past the alley opening in one last scan of the area. The fact my three-hundred pound neighbor snuck up on me last week has made me extra paranoid.

"Bobby."

The smarmy swindler raises his hands and steps forward. "Prewitt."

"I need answers, Bobby. You've been giving me nothing for months, and I'm fed up."

"Ha! Good one. *Fed* up." Bobby smirks, and I can't help but think that's the kind of thing Georgia would laugh at too.

My glare in response rids Bobby of any hint of a smile.

"Tough crowd. I've been giving you all I've got. People don't trust me with their secrets."

Gee, I wonder why. "No kidding. You're such an upstanding citizen. I can't imagine why they'd hesitate."

"See, now you're just being hurtful for no reason. I've put my neck on the line and done what you asked."

I almost feel sorry for the guy for a second. But everything he's given me has been useless or something I already knew because it was after the fact. The one promising lead he gave me hasn't resulted in anything but a stress-induced ulcer and pain in my chest.

"What have you learned since we last spoke?"

He rolls his eyes and huffs a breath that consumes his face in a fog. "There's chatter about paintings being shipped out. Whoever has them won't sell them in the city, so they need the resources to transport them. Not just any old shipping container will do. They need proper temperature and humidity controls. So look into people who have access to that sort of thing."

"Any names? Someone you'd suggest?"

"Prewitt, I'm your informant. I *inform* you of what I know. It's not my job to do yours."

I'm starting to feel like Bobby is more trouble than he's worth. If I'm not getting a new name, I might as well ask about an old one. "How did Georgia Dewan's name come up?"

"Come on, man." Bobby tucks his hands in the pockets of his bright blue Burberry coat. "We've been over this. Some of my contacts said she was the most talented artist in the city who didn't have any gallery exhibits. Plus, she's versatile... and easy on the eyes, if you catch my drift."

I lurch forward, losing all control for a split second. For Bobby's sake, he's lucky I find it quickly.

"Ahh, so that's what this is about. Got a thing for a con, Archie?" His amused expression returns, and this time, I have a distinct urge to strangle it off. "Don't let a pretty face fool you. Look at me. No one ever suspects the pretty ones." His infuriating smirk grows into a wide grin, testing my resolve.

I turn to walk away before I leave myself any more exposed. If Bobby knows how I feel about Georgia, there's no stopping him from exploiting that—which he will if it benefits him.

"You have three days to find me some answers, Bobby," I holler back at him from the mouth of the alley. "Something concrete. Your current deal only covers previous crimes, so don't think for one second I won't find something else to use against you."

He doesn't reply as I merge into the foot traffic along the sidewalk and walk away. Still without any answers to most of the questions consuming my life.

But I have settled one. It's time for me to come clean.

Georgia

30

JUST ICE

Finally, after six days of radio silence, Archie shows up at my apartment. I pull the door open a crack to keep my work hidden. Now, the secrecy is for no one else's benefit but my own. I know I told my friends I'd try, but after his disappearing act, I'm not sure where we stand.

"Hi."

He exhales, letting his shoulders droop. "Hi. Are you busy?"

I hold up my smudged hand. "Kind of. I'd invite you in, but my stuff is all over."

Unlike other times, he doesn't try to peek inside. "Uh… can you come to my place?"

I study Archie's face, noting the down-turned lips, dull eyes, and relaxed jaw. The epitome of defeat. It leaves me with an uneasy feeling. "Sure." I pull the door open, realizing I'm in a plain white tank top and yoga shorts—which barely qualify as shorts.

Archie's eyes bulge wide and he blows out another breath. "Peaches."

"One second." I close the door, ignoring the way he uttered my nickname, and reach over to grab a sweater from my closet. At least that will conceal the fact I'm not wearing a bra.

He's waiting in the hallway when I exit. His hair is a disaster, like he's been tugging on it and the hair gel has given up. His stubble is longer than I've ever seen it. But, more than that, he just seems uneasy.

"What's wrong?" I ask, trying to refocus his attention away from the ceiling.

It works. His eyes land on me, and he takes two long strides before placing one hand on either side of my face and planting a searing kiss on my lips. "I'm sorry."

That leaves me with more questions than answers. "For what?" Is he sorry for kissing me? Disappearing for days? His weird behavior? Or something else entirely?

He takes my hand and leads me to his door, which he unlocks, telling me he stopped at my apartment before going to his own. "I need you to come in and sit."

"Archie, what's going on?" I plead as he closes the door behind me.

Again, he repeats his move from the hallway, taking my face in his hands and my lips against his. This time, it's not a quick kiss. He expertly sweeps his tongue across my begging lips, so I open them, desperate for more. He backs me down his short hallway until my legs hit the edge of his bed. Despite my head screaming at me that I shouldn't move from this position, I lean back and pull him with me. He catches himself on his elbows so he's not crushing me, but I want him to squash all the insecurities and doubts flooding my mind. I just want to feel reconnected to this man whose reception is as reliable as an analogue antenna in a Chicago snowstorm. Having him in my grasp, I realize how much I missed not seeing him for the past few days.

"Peaches," he whispers, moving his mouth to my neck.

"Archie," I hiss, arching myself against him.

He growls and grazes his teeth along my collarbone. "You're perfect." He pulls his head away, propping himself up on straight arms. "I need you to know that. I think you're perfect, and I'm sorry I haven't been."

I mimic his earlier gesture, placing one hand on his bearded cheek. "You don't have to be perfect; I just need you to open up to me." I say that knowing I owe him the same courtesy. Before I can open my mouth again to tell him about my exhibit, he pushes himself to stand and walks the few steps to his kitchen. I lift myself up on my elbows to watch him as he looks up at the ceiling and scrubs his hands over his face, then comes to a stop in front of his plants.

The distress he's showing chases away any reckless lust I was feeling sixty seconds ago. That allows for my jelly legs to solidify again and carry me to the kitchen.

I stand beside him but keep my hands to myself, because I don't want him to shut down on me again. "What happened with Penny?"

"Huh?" He tilts his head to look at me from the corner of his eyes.

"Your sister… When you left the other night. Is everything okay?"

He straightens and squares his shoulders to me. If Sandra was looking for more depressing drawings, Archie's eyes would be a perfect subject. "It's a mess, Peaches. Everything is a mess."

That propels me forward until I can't stop myself from grabbing onto his forearm to prevent him from running it through his hair again. "Oh no. What happened?"

"Penny is fine." His eyes scan his living area before landing back on me. Only now his expression says something completely different.

That look—the one he's giving me now—I recognize it. It's the same one I've searched for on faces for half of my life, trying to capture it on paper. The one that encapsulates feelings that are hard to put a name to. A look that is so intense and vulnerable, its meaning is obvious without words.

Finally, I blink away, taking a deep breath to gain control of my pounding heart.

"Peaches?"

I don't look up. "Mm-hmm?"

"I need to tell you something." The strain in his voice increases the intensity of my beating heart.

We barely know each other. I'm not ready for this bombshell confession I'm sure he's going to drop on me. It's foolish and impulsive, and I'm neither of those things. I'm eccentric and creative, but even those are traits used with great care and consideration. From what I've learned about Archie, he's not impulsive or foolish, either. He's measured, assured, and confident. Albeit, mysteriously so.

That fear makes me do the only reasonable thing I can think of. "Oh no! I forgot I have to meet Rene. I promised her I'd be there at"—I glance at my wrist, even though I've never worn a watch in my life—"fifteen minutes from now." I avoid looking at him, so I don't have to know if any hurt registers on his face. That might be my undoing right now, because I don't actually have a reason to meet Rene. I'm not even wearing pants. As I move toward the door, I add, "I better go get dressed."

"Can I give you a ride? Then we can talk on the way?" Archie asks from behind me with the same strained voice.

"No, no. It's fine. We'll talk later." I'm about to run out the door when I realize how dismissive I'm being. I'm not running away because I'm afraid he loves me or, at the very least, he's falling; I'm running because I'm afraid I love him—already fallen. Before I leave, I turn back and give him a peck on the cheek. "We'll talk later, okay? Promise."

He nods, but doesn't reply. That look he had moments earlier is gone. Now he wears the expression I imagine he had when he found out he was allergic to cats.

I rush out into the hall and tuck back inside my apartment, locking the door behind me. I fumble in the pocket of my sweater for my phone and pull it out to dial Rene. No answer. I try Michelle with the same result. Without friends to confide in, I do the next best thing and stand in front of my easel set up by my windows.

For several hours, I shade and shape my current piece to suit my vision. I get so caught up in creating, I tune out the noise in my head. That is, until I finish my portrait and the person staring back at me is the same one I ran out on earlier. One with the same look in his eyes that terrified me.

For almost two months, I've been frustrated with his hot and cold demeanor and his unreadable expressions. With his mysteriousness and the feeling he wasn't being honest with me. But the minute he gave me a *very* readable expression and tried to open up, I ran.

I can only imagine what Michelle would tell me if I explained to her what happened. She'd demand I march back over there and speak to Archie like a mature adult, because if I can't handle that, I have no business even thinking about a relationship. Well, she'd be nicer about it, but that would be the gist of it. And she would be right.

Rene would tell me that Hunky McHunkerson deserves better from me because he was just trying to do what I've been waiting for all along. She'd also say I need to pull myself together and not be such a coward. She'd wrap all of that up in a sports metaphor like *there is no 'I' in 'team', but there is in Archie, so go give him your all.* That was terrible. I'm better at puns.

Imaginary Michelle's and Rene's advice are on point, so I walk out my front door and knock on Archie's. But my streak continues, and he doesn't answer either, leaving me standing in the hallway, wondering how I can make this right.

Georgia: What did the cookie say to the milk?

I walk back to my condo and take a seat in front of my most recent work, admiring the realism. The raw emotion I've captured. One I've waited my entire adult life to see looking at me. So why did it scare me so much?

Archie: ?

That's a disappointing guess. One that says he doesn't want to talk to me now and I've screwed up my opportunity to get him to open up.

Georgia: I'm sorry for being so crumb-y.

I wait for twenty minutes without so much as an emoji in reply.

So I do what I always do, and I go back to putting emotions on paper since I'm so terrible at handling them in real life.

31

FRAMED

My eight-week window is over in five days. I've spent fifty-five days in this apartment and have nothing concrete to show for it. And I squandered the opportunity I had to confess to Georgia when I ignored her knocking at my door last night. I knew if I answered, she'd want me to explain what I was trying to tell her earlier, but I lost every bit of nerve I had built up. The way she ran out on me yesterday made me reconsider whether telling her was the right thing to do after all.

When my phone rings while I'm on my way to the office, my stomach churns at the name that pops up.

"SA Prewitt."

"I need to see you in my office the second you get here. Don't keep me waiting." Lancaster, who isn't known for her drawn out conversations, is especially short on this occasion. The phone clicks, and that's the end of it.

For the rest of the short drive, I analyze potential pleas I can use to encourage her to keep me on this case. I know, in her mind, the art thefts are secondary to the few assaults that happened, which are the police department's territory. To Lancaster, this looks like a matter for CPD and not one to waste federal resources on. To me, I'm not ready to give up because I need answers.

I park my Jeep and enter the building, scanning my security pass and going through the mandatory metal detectors. By the time I reach the fourth floor, my heart is pounding, and it's not because I took the stairs. I knock at Lancaster's door, and she waves me inside.

"Prewitt, have a seat."

This is it. This is the moment I get pulled from the case, and it will be the first case I haven't found a resolution to since I started working in this department. That's not why I feel sick about it, though.

"I got a call from the Buffalo field office this morning."

My mind drifts back to my brief conversation with Kensington weeks ago, but nothing has come up on my end regarding Buffalo or money laundering, so I haven't given him much thought since.

"They made a bust overnight. A massive one."

"Always good to hear. Do you need me to assist with something?" I'm confused about what this has to do with me.

"Your artist"—she looks down at her paperwork—"Georgia; a piece of her artwork was seized in the bust."

My stomach sinks. "What kind of art?"

"A family portrait, from what I gather."

I feel a little levity in my gut, hearing that. Kensington mentioned Georgia speaking to his target's wife.

That reprieve is undone when Lancaster continues, "It was in an ornate gold frame, like they'd use in a gallery, and when scene techs pulled off the back, there was over a hundred thousand dollars in counterfeit bills inside."

My brain's processing speed works at half-capacity while I try to understand what this means. For more than half a year, I just wanted to find the guilty parties responsible for these art thefts. For the past two months, I've flip-flopped between wanting to solve the case and wanting to sweep it under a rug. For almost three weeks, I've been convinced she had nothing to do with the heists, even if she is being secretive about her work. This changes everything. My instincts are unreliable.

Every part of me wishes I could give her a cushy deal like Bobby, but it's unlikely any prosecutor or judge will go easy on someone involved in a cross-border operation to defraud the US government.

"What does this mean for my case?" I finally ask.

"It's time to bring her in. What we have might be as solid as soup right now, but hopefully she'll give us something we can go on when we make her sweat. Take Sanders and go pick her up. I want something to report back to the Buffalo office by end of day." And with the flick of her wrist, she dismisses me.

I place both hands on the armrests of the upholstered armchair, raise myself on my shaky legs, and make my way out of her office. The noises around me buzz about, but I can't decipher anything on account of the blood thumping in my ears.

During my training, I've been part of intense raids and tactical drills that have made grown men wet their pants. I'm not a coward. Yet, knowing I have to expose who I really am to Georgia when I never got the chance to tell her the truth makes me more scared than I've ever been.

Twenty-five minutes later, Sanders drops an arrest warrant on my desk, clamps a hand on my shoulder, and asks if I'm ready to go. This isn't something I could ever be ready for.

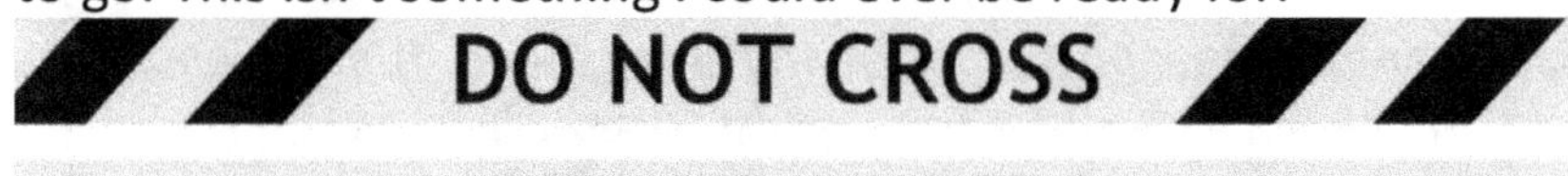

The elevator dings on the fifth floor, and Sanders steps out first. He walks to Georgia's door and stands to the side with his back to the wall. I should be doing the same, but I'm stopped in front of the charcoal gray door with the number 502 etched on a gold plate below the peephole, thinking about all the times I've knocked and she's answered before. From her little dinosaur pajamas to her stunning black dress, I've seen her at both ends of the spectrum. I've seen her when she was expecting me or when I dropped by to surprise her. Somewhere along the line, it became less of an effort to catch her in the act of doing something illegal and more because I just wanted to see her.

My hands are shaking as I lift my fist to knock. I can hear her inside, listening to Charlie Puth—one of her more modern singer-songwriter choices. I hate that I know that about her. That I know her music preferences and favorite sports teams. Hate that I know what she'd choose for takeout and her favorite type of cocktail. Mostly, I hate that I know how her lips taste and how her skin feels.

"Earth to Prewitt. You good, man?" Sanders eyes me with one hand on his service weapon.

I wave off his concern and finally knock on the door. The volume decreases on the upbeat pop ballad drifting into the hallway. Footsteps near the door, and after a brief pause, the chain lock and deadbolt disengage and the door opens enough for Georgia to greet me with a smile.

"Hey. I didn't know you were home to—" She stops speaking when Sanders moves to stand beside me, looking every bit the mountainous federal agent he is. "Oh, sorry. I didn't know you brought a friend."

"Peach—" I stop myself before I utter her nickname and give Sanders reason to doubt my headspace. It's a mess, yes, but he doesn't need to know that. "Georgia, we need you to come with us."

Sanders narrows his eyebrows. "Miss Dewan?"

Georgia mimics Sanders' gesture, but directed at me. "Yes?"

He pulls out his badge and flashes it at her. "I'm Special Agent Sanders and this is Special Agent Prewitt. We've got a warrant for your arrest. You'll need to come with us." Sanders slips his badge back into his jacket, exposing the pistol in his holster.

I'm afraid to make eye contact with Georgia, so I stare at Sanders, getting irrationally angry with each movement he makes.

"What are you talking about? Special agent? I don't understand." She opens her door wide, exposing her black-smudged overalls, her easel set up near the window, and drawing supplies sprawled across her kitchen island. "Archie? What is he talking about?" she shouts.

"I promise I'll explain everything. We just need you to come with us."

"Archie! He just said he had an arrest warrant! What the hell for? I'm not going anywhere until you tell me what's going on."

At that moment, two of our neighbors open their doors to peek their heads out. Meredith with the slew of cats in 504, and Mrs. Nitske in 510. Sanders turns and tells them to stay inside, leaving me facing off with Georgia. If looks could kill, she'd also be adding murder of a federal agent to her list of charges.

"Please, Peaches," I whisper while Sanders is out of earshot. "I'll explain everything shortly."

She doesn't speak. She doesn't move. The only indication she's a living person and not a statue is the tear running down her cheek. One that I'm afraid is the precursor to many.

"Come with us, ma'am." Sanders reaches around his back to grab handcuffs.

I hold my hand out to stop him. "Those won't be necessary. Right, Georgia?"

"Miss Dewan. Only people I can trust call me Georgia." She grabs a jacket and her keys from the hook by the door and shoves them in my hand. "Lock up for me, will you, *Special Agent Prewitt?*" She spits my name like it's the most vulgar curse word a person could utter. In the three minutes from when she opened the door with a smile until now, it's clear her feelings toward me have changed drastically.

Not that I can blame her. I should have told her the truth before now. Before this all blew up, just like Nate predicted. Now I not only have to contend with her potential criminal charges, but with her hating me for being a hypocritical liar.

Georgia walks with Sanders, allowing him to loop his arm through hers. She stands as far as possible from me in the elevator. Sanders opens the rear door of the SUV and slides in the back with Georgia. Our suspect.

The ride is silent, except for the persistent sniffles coming from the back seat. Each one tears me open a little more.

We lead her into the basement interrogation room at headquarters, sitting her in an uncomfortable metal chair that is bolted to the floor. Protocol is to leave the suspect for a period of time and study their behavior. When I step into the room on the other side of the two-way mirror, she looks like a person who has been crushed. Her shoulders are slumped, her face is streaked with tears, and her eyes are red. There's not a hint of defensiveness in her posture or guilt in her eyes. Only heartbreak.

"I'm going to handle the interrogation, Prewitt. You're too close to this," SA Hopper says from behind me.

I don't argue. I am too close to this and I know I'm not the best person for this job. Not for Georgia, and not for the bureau. My allegiances are divided, and one team has a larger portion than the other.

Still, I stand and watch. Hopper enters the interrogation room, and Georgia doesn't even look up. She just stares at nothing, blinking out one tear after another.

"Georgia Dewan, I'm Special Agent Hopper. Can I get you anything before we start?"

Finally, Georgia's eyes flick to Hopper. "I'd like some answers."

"We'll get to those. First, I need you to tell me why you think you're here," Hopper instructs as he takes his seat.

"I. Don't. Know. That's why I'm asking." She narrows her eyes and tenses her jaw. "If I thought I had a reason to be here, I wouldn't be so confused right now."

"Okay." Hopper slaps down a folder on the table, opens it, and slides a photo out. "Tell me what this is."

"It's a commission I finished a few weeks ago. How did you get this?"

"I'll ask the questions. What was your customer's name?"

She hesitates to respond. "If you've seen this, I'm sure you know the answer."

"Listen, Miss Dewan. This will go a lot easier if you answer the questions as I present them. The more you cooperate, the more likely you are to get a deal."

Again, she pauses. She doesn't appear to be nervous about answering, just refusing to. "Let me ask you, Agent Hopper; have you ever pretended you cared about someone, weaseled your way into their house—into their heart—then dragged them out of their home for no apparent reason and refused to answer their questions?"

That summary of my actions—the accurate summary—is enough to cause a fist to clench around my heart and two more to twist my stomach in opposite directions.

"No, ma'am. I'm not a field agent."

"Well, then I guess there's no reason I can't be honest with you." Georgia looks straight at the two-way mirror, right where I'm standing.

There are two things I'm uncertain about. One, that this piece of glass is, in fact, a mirror on the opposite side. Two, that I'll ever recover from the hatred in her eyes.

KEY WITNESS

I have no idea what's going on right now. This Hopper guy seems to think he can make me confess to some crime I've committed without telling me what I'm actually here for. Joke's on him, though. I don't even jaywalk. We can sit here all day, and the best he'll get from me is that I once almost stole a grape at the grocery store, but I felt bad, so I put it back. That was also twenty years ago.

But I'm a lot less upset about being in this room than I am about the person who brought me here. The man who made me fall in love with him, only for me to find out it was all a lie. That he's not a fire inspector. That he didn't just show up in my life in some kind of funny meet-cute. That the feelings I have—had—for him are not reciprocated. Everything was an act. And I still don't even know why.

"Honesty is the best policy here, Miss Dewan," Hopper states. "If you answer my questions, then this will be a lot easier for everyone."

"My customer's name is Isabella Russo."

He writes something down, then refocuses his eyes on me. "And how did you meet Mrs. Russo?"

I note the use of 'Mrs.', which implies he knows she's married. This obviously has something to do with her or her husband. "I didn't. She heard of me from a friend, then contacted me from my social media page. We've never met."

He studies my face for a few more seconds, so I lift an eyebrow that I hope portrays I'd like to move on.

"What was the friend's name?"

"Caroline something. I don't know her either. We only ran into each other about two months ago. I drew a picture of her family, so I gave it to them. Oh, Brown. Caroline Brown."

Hopper continues to ask me about my interaction with Caroline, where we were and what exactly was said. He asks how she contacted me afterward. I show him the messages on my phone, as well as the initial call log from Isabella. I never thought having a diary of messages and phone calls would come in handy, but I also never thought I'd have to prove my innocence for a crime I'm in the dark about. Then I also explain about Isabella's request to sign the legal document, insisting I not share their photos or videos.

"Those are all being brought into evidence now. What else can you tell me—"

"What do you mean their photos are being brought into evidence?"

"I'm not sure if you realize this, Miss Dewan, but our warrant includes seizing anything in your apartment we deem helpful for our case."

That freezes me in a panic. All of my drawings for the exhibit are packaged for transport and tucked under my bed frame. If any of them get ruined or brought into evidence, it would be nearly impossible to re-create them all in less than three weeks. Nor do I *want* to re-create some of them. After a few seconds, I plead again, "Just tell me what this is about, please. I'm not a criminal."

"We'll get to that part. What can you tell me about the art thefts in Chicago?"

Thefts? There have been multiple? "Agent Hopper, we seem to be on completely different channels. You're talking to me like I know what you're saying, but I don't. I know of a theft from *Smith Goldstein & Co.* because I have news alerts set for that gallery on my phone. Other than that, I haven't heard of anything."

He furiously writes down something else before looking at me from a pair of non-expressive eyes. That must be a class at Quantico. "Why do you have alerts set?"

I take a deep breath, folding my hands together on the table in front of me. "I'm supposed to have my first exhibit there in a few weeks. Ever since I finished the drawing for Isabella, I've been working on pieces for that. I set alerts to see when the official press release went out so I could share it with people I care about." Again, I look at the stupid window that every person who's ever watched a TV show knows is a two-way mirror. I'd be willing to bet Archie is on the other side.

"So you haven't heard about the other thefts in the area?"

This guy is dense. Is it an interrogation technique to repeat every question and hope I'll give a different answer? If it is, it's stupid.

"No, I haven't."

"Have you ever painted a replica of a famous work, Georgia?"

I guess now we've established enough rapport, he thinks he can use my first name. "Yes."

His eyes shoot wide for a split second, but he schools his expression like a good little agent. "Care to elaborate on that?"

"I went to art school, Agent Hopper. Replicating famous works is a good way to hone your skills and train your eye to notice the smallest details. Not to mention, I've done at least twenty paint and wine nights with my friends. I don't know how many versions I have of Starry Night, all in different stages of drunkenness. I can gift you one if you're interested."

He bites his bottom lip, but I don't miss the near smile. "Have you ever sold a forgery to anyone else?"

"Woah. Slow down there. There's a big difference between painting a replica and creating a forgery, Agent Hopper. The paintings I've made have been either for educational purposes or for entertainment. I'd never *forge* another artist's work." Even the implication I'd do something that atrocious makes me furious. "Art has been my life for as long as I can remember. And not in the way most people see it. I feel art. It's like oxygen to me. That might sound crazy or stupid, but it touches me on an emotional level. What any famous work represents is that artist's ability to touch people's hearts with the stroke of a brush or curve of stone. I wouldn't sell a forgery to save my soul."

This guy studies me again, like I'm an SAT prep course. He's put more effort into getting something out of me than I did in high school biology. "That's a passionate speech."

"If that's what we're calling the truth these days, then sure. Though, it seems people in your office have a hard time with truth called any name." I glance up at the mirror again, but it gives away nothing. No shadows or movement to indicate someone else is there.

Hopper leans forward, resting his elbows on the table. "Do you know anyone who would create a forgery?"

If someone is out there forging art that not only means something to me, but to thousands of people, darn right I'm going to try to help. My heartbreak has to have a reason. "You need to give me more to go on here, Hopper. What kind of forging are you asking about? I'm assuming paintings, since that's what you asked about, but are we talking realism? Pop art? Abstract? Impressionism? What time period? Modern? Renaissance? What medium? Watercolor? Oil?"

He glances down at his notes, grabbing a few papers and adjusting them on the table to straighten them. "A little bit of everything."

"Then you're not looking for one person. You're looking for multiple artists." I lean back in my chair, now studying Hopper with the same intensity he gave me.

He raises one eyebrow as he asks, "What makes you say that?"

"Because there's a big difference between forging an oil portrait from the renaissance and a watercolor landscape from the forties. No one is that good at everything that they could pass them off for the originals."

He scribbles down some more notes, then pushes his chair out to stand. How nice his isn't bolted to the floor. Mine is secured at a distance better suited for someone six feet tall.

"I'll be right back." With that, he walks out the door, leaving me alone with my thoughts.

Georgia

33

FED EX

After all this time, I still don't know why I'm here. Archie promised he'd explain everything to me, but he's either been ordered not to speak to me or he's a coward. Whatever his reason, I'm not sure I'm ready to hear it. Everything was a lie. Not everything. The times he looked like he was at war with himself, those were no doubt real. The times I felt like he was hiding something, they were definitely real. His cat allergy appeared real; I don't know about the shellfish. But the care and concern, the interest he pretended to show in my work, it was all a lie.

In a stunning turn of events, the door opens after several minutes and in walks Archie. Looking every bit the six-foot-tall chastised child he deserves to feel like. "Georg—"

"Miss Dewan."

He heaves a sigh as he drops into the chair across from me. "I turned the cameras off. Everyone else is off discussing everything you told Hopper."

I clench my jaw, wanting to say so much and nothing all at the same time. I settle on, "I'd rather be in a room full of shedding Siamese cats."

"Peach—"

"Don't. Call me that," I grit out, now hating the nickname I used to love. It's the same kind of polarizing feeling I have about the man across from me. "You owe me the truth, Archie, if you're capable of it."

"I was doing my job, Pe—" He cuts himself off this time.

"Is that what it was? Every time you held my hand and traced circles on my skin with your thumb? Each time you pulled me close to whisper in my ear? Every time you kissed me, Archie? That was just doing your job, right?"

He looks ill again. The same look he had when he came to my door a few hours ago. He scrubs his hands over his face, dropping them into his lap. He proceeds to tell me about the art theft ring operating in the city. How an artist is providing forgeries, and the crew is executing heists with expert precision. The interesting part is when he tells me someone gave him *my* name, which is what started Archie on my trail. And, apparently, my portrait for the Russo family was seized at the Canadian border with counterfeit money in the frame.

Like somehow any of this information is supposed to justify the lies he told me.

"I shipped that drawing in a mailer tube, Archie. I still have the receipt for the shipment."

"Okay. The team processing your apartment will find it."

I forgot about that part. "Will they unwrap my other art? Ruin any of it?"

He dismisses my question and asks one of his own. "Why didn't you tell me about the exhibit at the gallery?"

"Really? You're going to ask me about why I kept a secret?" I cut off his attempt to speak and continue my fury-fueled rant. "I didn't tell you because I'm sick of disappointing people. Tired of being the girl who doesn't have other skills beyond drawing, but can't seem to use that to function like an adult. For once, I wanted people I *cared* about to be proud of me. So I was waiting for the gallery to make an official announcement before I went bragging about it. Plus, I didn't want anyone getting in my head and derailing my process."

He nods, looking more defeated than I feel. "I texted the lead agent in your apartment. They'll be careful with your art."

I almost thank him, but he's the reason I'm in this position, so I stay quiet.

"Who would do something like this? Help us solve the case and everything that has added up against you won't matter." Archie's expression is pleading. If his hunched posture and down-turned mouth are any indication, he has regrets.

But none of that makes me feel sorry for him. Not when I'm the one on the suspect side of an FBI interrogation table, facing off against the man I thought I loved.

"There can't be anything against me because I haven't done anything wrong." My voice gets louder than I intended, but *I* don't regret it. "But far too often, when priceless works of art are stolen, they end up destroyed, damaged, or never found. I don't want that to happen."

"So, what can you tell me?"

I think of every possibility, now knowing the works that have been stolen. Art sales have never been my strong suit, or I would have been more successful by now, but I know it's a huge industry. Black market art sales are not uncommon, but it never seems to go well for the more famous works. They're too hot. People notice them, and no one wants to steal them, just to have to store them properly for years until that heat dies down. Art requires proper conditions to maintain its integrity and value. I'm sure he knows all of this.

"My best guess is it's a private collector. Someone who has the means to protect it, but at little risk of anyone seeing them."

Archie pulls out a notepad and starts writing, just as Hopper did. The sight of him sliding into his role here makes the heartache flood through me in a deluge all over again. But I won't let him see that anymore. He's seen me cry enough already.

"So you think it's someone who wants to build up their own collection? Not someone trying to sell them for a profit?"

I swallow down my emotions to answer. "It wouldn't be a collector who is doing well for themselves. They put a lot of time, effort, and money into their personal collections." I lean back in the uncomfortable metal chair, trying to create distance between us. "Maybe someone who is having money troubles. I don't know, Archie. I'm not a part of that world—though you seem to think otherwise."

He continues writing, then after an enthusiastic dot, looks up at me. "What's the deal with Bernard Shaw? What were you meeting him for?"

My jaw almost drops of its own volition, but I clamp it shut. "How do you even know about him?"

"It was my job to look into every aspect of your life, Geor— Miss Dewan. Part of that was looking into associates too."

My jaw and eyes clench simultaneously. I can't look at him. I shake my head, pulling in a deep breath and commit to spilling my guts so I can get out of here. "Bernard was a security guard at *Adler Planetarium*." I open my eyes to glare at Archie. "Though I'm sure you know that. He claimed he fell in love and was moving to a hundred acre coffee plantation in Costa Rica with this person, but he wanted to capture the beauty of the skyline he had come to love. So he hired me to create it for him."

"How did he hear about you?" he asks, still writing copious notes.

"I didn't ask."

He drops his arms to his side and leans back, locking his eyes on me. I don't flinch; instead, returning his sorrowful expression with a furious one.

"What about your income? How did you afford your apartment and living expenses? Your tax returns show you barely made enough to cover rent over the last two years."

Is this guy serious right now? How is it that I wrongfully get suspected of a crime, and now I have to lose every shred of dignity and open myself up like a supermarket tabloid to share every aspect of my life? "You want to know the truth? Since there's no limit to your deceitfulness, I'll share some honesty. My parents supplement my income. Not a lot now because I manage to keep my own lights on, but when I need it, they send me some money. That's part of the reason I'm such a perpetual disappointment. They hate that I've chosen this path and can't support myself, so they give me financial support instead of any other kind." I stand from my chair and lean over the table. "Are you happy now? To know what a failure I am? Does it help *your* career at all to know that mine is so pathetic?"

Hopper returns to the room before Archie is able to answer my rhetorical question and gives both of us a questioning glare. Archie stands to whisper something in Hopper's ear, then both men return to sit across from me. Like a suspect trying to earn points for good behavior, I sit back down.

Any sorrow I'm feeling makes way for more fury, leaving me so angry, I have spots in my vision. My blood is thumping through my body with such force, I'll be surprised if my heartbeat isn't audible to the two men in the room. One of whom I have a new hatred for, even though a large part of me is clinging to the hope this is all a misunderstanding. That he actually cared and wasn't just manipulating me to solve a case.

They continue to ask me more questions, which makes me more angry by the second. If any of them had asked me the same things, viewing me as a law-abiding citizen, I would have been happy to answer. I would have been thrilled to take down people who are destroying things that are important to me and hurting people in the process. But being dragged in here, embarrassed in front of my neighbors, and treated like a criminal, that's a different scenario. There's not an ounce of happiness left in me.

A few more hours pass. Both Hopper and Archie are in and out of the room, but one of them is with me the entire time.

Finally, I work up the courage to ask, "So, am I going to need a lawyer, or am I free to go? I've answered all of your questions, and you've scoured every inch of my private life. Have you clued into the fact I'm not a criminal yet?" I'm praying they don't tell me I need a lawyer, because my bank account won't allow for that.

"Just sit tight a little while longer," Hopper replies.

Both men exit the room, leaving me alone for the first time since before Archie entered earlier. Alone time doesn't bring me any kind of peace like it normally does. My world feels like it has imploded, and this scenario will linger in my mind every day for the rest of my life. It will make me question every person's motives and every kind word. Is it genuine, or is it a tactic designed to get something out of me? I hate Archie for doing this to me.

But he returns about twenty minutes later and tells me I'm clear to leave, and that resolute hatred I had minutes earlier is overshadowed by the way his presence made my heart soar mere hours earlier.

I stand and exit the interrogation room, squinting at the bright lights in the hallway.

Archie points me toward the exit. "At least let me give you a ride home."

If this man thinks I'm ever going anywhere with him, he's mistaken. A mistake I won't let him make again.

"Is Nate even your real brother?"

Again, he stares at his feet. "Yes. Everything I told you about me was real… except my job."

"You know what? I think that might be even worse. The fact you claim you were ever honest with me when everything was built on a lie. And the fact you'd use your brother as a pawn. For what purpose, Archie? In hopes I'd meet your family and spill my guts about some supposed criminal life I was keeping secret?" My volume has reached new heights as tears begin streaming down my cheeks again. I'm not sure if it's the betrayal or heartache that hurts the most, but together, it's debilitating.

Archie takes a deep swallow and tucks his hands in his pants pockets. His defeated body language almost makes me feel bad for him. A few hours ago, if I had seen him with slumped shoulders and sad eyes, I would have comforted him. I'd have done anything I could to make him happy again. But he lost that level of concern the minute his lies were exposed.

I step toward him and lower my voice so we don't attract any more attention. "Stay away from me. Don't text me. Don't show up at my door. From this day forward, pretend you never knew me. That's one thing that will be easy for me, because it turns out, I never knew you." I turn to walk down the hall, refusing to look back or give him another minute of my attention.

Right now, I need my friends. People who I can actually trust.

Archie

34

PRIME CRIME

Georgia walking away stings. No, sting isn't the right word. It feels like a hot lance piercing my heart that sends a flood of ice water through my veins until I am incapacitated. I want to explain myself. I want to beg and plead for her forgiveness and hope she'll understand I was just doing my job. Or tell her I tried to confess before things came to this. But if the roles were reversed, I don't think I could forgive someone who betrayed me the way I did her.

Nate was right. I ruined my chances with the best thing to happen to me.

Bruce was right. There's so much more to life than a career.

Georgia was right. Nothing good comes from a relentless pursuit of vengeance.

So now this has to be worth something. I need to have given up the perfect woman for what I thought I wanted all along. A promotion. Career advancement and policy change. Retribution for Nate.

I settle back into my desk and read through the reports Kensington sent detailing Georgia's involvement in the Russo's money laundering sham. How did Lancaster justify bringing Georgia in when it's so obvious she just drew the picture? There is nothing concrete linking her to the actual crime other than her work of art. They couldn't arrest Ikea if Mr. Russo had chosen a mass-produced painting to ship counterfeit bills across the border.

A large part of me wants to be angry with my superior, but the logical part sees my anger for what it is: displacement. I want someone else to blame for things going south with Georgia. I don't want to admit that I screwed up—job or not. She didn't deserve any of it.

I continue distracting myself by combing through the non-redacted parts of the reports until I spot a familiar name. Tom Conti. One of the city's art collectors is an associate of the Russo family. Those old country connections run deep. Caroline and Steve Brown also stayed with Mr. Conti when they visited the city two months ago. A deeper dive into Tom's business financials shows that it's struggling. After the theft of his art, we didn't have justification to look into his business. His old-school warehouse where he sells custom Italian furniture is not faring well, but it is an excellent way to launder money and ship items without suspicion like Bobby suggested.

Was the answer in front of me all along? If I had asked Georgia for her input a month ago, could I have stopped the robberies that happened in the meantime? I'll never know.

No matter how much I try to tell myself I was just doing my job, it all still feels wrong. I was so blinded by Georgia, I missed the red flags around the people likely responsible.

It's time I set this all right.

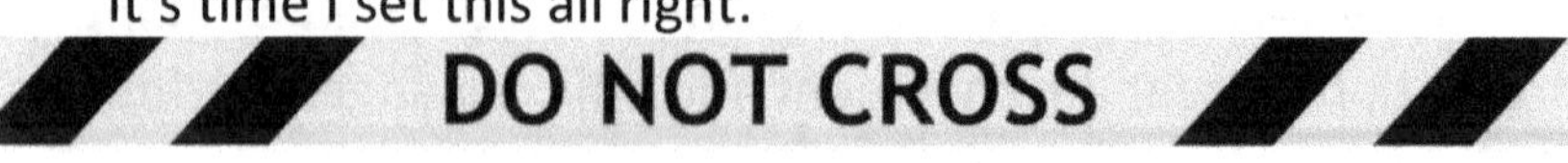

I return to the bureau in the morning and spend the next several hours scouring the client records of the galleries that have been targeted. Tom Conti's name shows up on each one as a prospective buyer or as a potential donor.

Before I get ahead of myself, I take the information to Lancaster to see if I have enough to go speak with Mr. Conti again. I assure her I'll insist we're doing a follow-up regarding his recently stolen artwork, and we just have a few more questions. Reluctantly, she agrees.

Sanders tags along, so I fill him in on the drive to Conti's home address. It's after business hours, but if we can catch him by surprise, that's even better.

We stand at the front gate, which is only twenty feet from the front door, but it serves the purpose of keeping us out. I use the buzzer, which Mr. Conti answers himself. Times must be tough, because I can imagine he had staff to do that for him once upon a time.

"Mr. Conti, this is Special Agent Prewitt of the FBI. My partner and I would like to ask a few follow-up questions regarding the theft of your art."

This guy responds like he expects us to have this discussion through his gate intercom. Sanders interrupts and convinces him to let us in, so we're not sharing sensitive information with pedestrians and neighbors.

When Tom Conti answers the door—probably another mundane task he used to have hired help for—he's sweating. Not like he just got out of his $20,000 home gym kind of sweat, but like he's about to be baking under the terrible lighting of an interrogation room. His perspiration rate rivals naked Bruce.

I try my hardest to sound like a polite law enforcement professional attempting to help a person who has been victimized. It's hard. Especially since the efforts I put into acting with Georgia have backfired spectacularly. I wish I could just be a straight shooter, ask direct questions, and get direct answers.

But Sanders and I play Mr. Conti like we're the Steelers and he's the Super Bowl.

Within twenty minutes, he has not only denied ever visiting the list of art galleries, but claims to not even know they exist. He acts surprised by the rash of thefts across the city. However, he's not a convincing actor.

I want to be careful not to jump to conclusions again and end up wasting more time investigating a dead end, so Sanders and I wrap up our conversation and head back to the bureau.

"What do you think?" he asks as I pull up to a red light.

"He has the means, motive, and opportunity. We just need to figure out who he's working with, because I will not give him a chance to get off easy by rolling on his crew."

Sanders stays silent until the light turns green and we speed southbound on Halsted Street. "We don't know he's guilty, Prewitt. We have to follow the evidence."

I swallow down the embarrassment that causes. Sanders is too nice to say it, but he must know Georgia was more than a suspect. He's alluded to that several times, but never called me out.

"Then we need to find the evidence, man. We need to put this case to bed and stop these guys. At this point, I don't care what it takes."

"That's half of your problem right now."

I can't bring myself to look at Sanders. Even though I'm one hundred percent sure what he's referring to, I play dumb and pretend I don't know. "What are you talking about?"

We round the corner onto Roosevelt before Sanders replies, "Anyone with half a brain can see you're cutting corners and blurring lines on this case. Trust me, I've been on the giving end of some questionable choices before because sometimes the situation calls for it, but I've never compromised a case."

"I didn't—"

"What if she *was* guilty, Prewitt? Then what? You're so in love with that girl, you can't see straight."

His words cause me to jerk the steering wheel to the right, nearly hitting a small hatchback traveling beside us.

"See. You're so blinded by your feelings for this girl, you can't even drive."

I have nothing to say to that. It can't be possible to be in love with someone after two months. Falling, yes. But all the way there? I don't think so. Especially not when those two months consisted of me lying and pretending. There were so many secrets piled up between us, there's no way. But then, how else do I explain the pit in my stomach that feels a lot like an ulcer? The one that is only second place on the pain scale next to the hole I have in my chest. I'd rather take a bullet than feel this way... and I would take a bullet for Georgia. Without question.

"What do I do now?" I ask, staring straight ahead.

Sanders reaches his meaty hand over and places it on my shoulder. "We catch these guys, find the answers we're looking for, then you make things right."

I gulp down the ball of compounding emotions and finally turn to look at my partner when we roll to a stop. "Let's get to work, then."

 DO NOT CROSS 

● JUST KIDDING ● KEEP GOING, YOU REBEL ●

"Jared Duffy is Jerry Adkins." Sanders slaps down an employee file on my desk with a photo and resume of Mr. Jared Duffy. The partner of one Casper Gibson, who happened to be working the night of the *Smith Goldstein & Co.* robbery.

"Are you kidding me?" I rifle through the pages, comparing the information on the employee file from Tom Conti's former security team. "So this guy worked for Conti, then changed his name to apply for a new job? Sanders, they're the crew. They have to be." I jump up from my chair and start rummaging through my files.

"Archie," Sanders interrupts, once again placing his hand on my shoulder that feels a lot like having a ham hock resting there. "We just talked about this, man. We're not jumping to conclusions."

I take a deep breath and stand, pulling a file from my drawer. "I'm not looking for more circumstantial evidence that fits some narrative in my head, Sanders. Promise. This time, I'm following the facts."

"Good man. Let's find some answers, then."

Sanders and I stick around the office until there's no more than a skeleton crew left. By the time we're finished, we've sent off requests to different departments to help us track down our remaining two former employees of Mr. Conti—one woman, one man—and submitted Mr. Choi's, Mr. Conti's, and Mr. Duffy/Adkins' financials to our forensic accounting division. The surface level search I did is nothing compared to the deep dive they'll do. It's like the difference between going for an eye exam or going for a colonoscopy. Hopefully, they can find something that will bring these guys down.

Mr. Conti's trade routes and services he uses to ship his expensive furniture worldwide would also make a perfect cover to ship stolen art. All that's left is to prove it.

For now, we're at an impasse and have to wait for the other departments to get back to us with new information.

For the first time in two months, I might get a real day off, and with that, real answers. No more pretending to be Archie Prewitt, fire investigator. No more hiding my real life from the one person I wanted to share it with. Just me, alone with my thoughts. And I can already predict that I'll be thinking about how to fix this colossal mistake.

35

FELON LOVE

"**Y**ou were right," I admit to my brother.

He stares back at me, no hint of triumph or anger on his face. It appears he's as gutted as I am over the situation I'm in. One I can't think of a way to correct.

"So why did you do it?" he asks, adjusting his recliner so he can intimidate me a little better.

I'd rather be on the opposite side of an FBI interrogation table, to be honest. "My job?" I ask, needing some clarification which faux pas he's referring to.

Nate shakes his head and, for the first time, his expression changes from neutral to one of pity. Somehow that's the worst one to be on the receiving end of. "This wasn't about your job, Archie. This was you, trying to get vengeance for something I never asked you to get vengeance for."

That statement churns my stomach. Why didn't I listen? I prioritized my own feelings about it instead of respecting his, just like Georgia said. "I'm sorry. Really, I am."

"You don't have to be sorry, Arch. I told you that already. But at the end of the day, no matter how high you climb on the ladder, you'll never rid the world of bad people. I appreciate that you wanted to go to bat for me and for anyone else whose life has been changed by greedy people, but I don't want that at the expense of your own life. Throwing your happiness away doesn't fix anything."

Janine walks in the front door after returning from wherever she was and immediately runs over to Nate. She doesn't even see me—or if she does, she doesn't care—as she jumps into his lap and wraps her arms around his neck and greets him with a kiss.

He clears his throat and directs her attention to me near the front window.

"Oh, Archie. Hi!" Her eyes bounce around like I've just busted her in the commission of a crime. "Where did you park?"

If I were in a laughing mood, I'd chuckle at that question. "Hi, J. Down the street." When I arrived, I needed a few minutes to compose myself before facing my brother, so I parked half a block away.

She climbs off of her husband's lap and walks over to give me a hug. It's far less enthusiastic than the greeting Nate got. Somehow, that serves to remind me how I destroyed my chance at ever having that with Georgia.

"I'll let you guys chat," she says once I fill her in on my dilemma.

Then Nate and I are left alone again. Right now, looking at my big brother, he seems to be a world ahead of me in every aspect. He was forced into a career change that he's thriving in. He has a wife who looks at him like he hung the moon. His smiles are genuine. He never needed me to come to his rescue.

After several seconds of silence, Nate demands, "Go fix this, Archie. You'll never forgive yourself if you don't. It's obvious how you feel about her. I knew that from day one. That's not something you throw away."

"How?" I run my hands through my hair and drop onto the end of the sofa farthest from Nate. "How can I possibly fix this? She hates me."

"No, she's hurt. And she's justified in that, but it's not impossible to heal. You're a persistent bugger, Archibald Prewitt. Prove it."

I sit with my thoughts for a few seconds, wracking my brain over potential solutions. This is so far beyond flowers and chocolates, I'm not sure where to even start.

Janine pokes her head back in the living room to ask, "Sorry to interrupt again. Can I get you guys anything?"

I smile at her and stand, not wanting to bother them any longer with my drama. "No thanks, J. I've got to get back to work, anyway."

"I admire your perseverance, Archie. But don't get so caught up in making a living, you neglect to have a life."

That one statement sparks so many trains of thought in my head, it's rivaling Union Station.

"Thanks, J." I send her a tight smile, then give my brother a fist bump as I swipe my jacket from the coffee table and run for the door. Before I run outside, I shout back, "Congratulations!"

Their faces are priceless.

I run down the sidewalk, dialing the number I hate calling most.

"Archie, what can I do for you?"

"We're going to have words, Bobby, but I don't have time for that today. I need you to do me a favor."

Bobby reluctantly agrees and says he'll call me back within the hour.

Sure enough, before I reach the city limits, he returns my call and arranges a place to meet. He may be a devious dimwit who gave me Georgia's name in the first place, but hopefully this time, he actually comes through.

Thirty minutes after our second phone call, I'm standing at the edge of a downtown park, trying to figure out what to say. I'm not sure how to approach this without sounding like the kidnapper Georgia accused me of being.

Bobby disappears into the shadows after I inform him he is doing this favor out of the little goodness of his heart he possesses and he will not be getting paid for it. This is not bureau sanctioned.

"Excuse me," I say as I approach a woman and her young daughter.

They're both bundled in a thread-bare sleeping bag that looks like it might have a thermal rating of forty-five degrees at best. It's hovering around thirty. Yet, they both greet me with smiles.

"Yes?" the mother replies.

I hand them the hot drinks and sandwiches I grabbed at the cafe around the corner and take a seat on the cold ground across from them. "I'm Archie Prewitt."

"Theresa. This is Xena. Thank you for this, Archie." She holds up the tea before taking a sip.

"My pleasure, Theresa. Actually, I have something else for you, and I know it might come across as a little strange, but I promise my intentions are good." I pull my badge from my pocket to prove who I am. "My house in Oak Park is sitting empty at the moment, and since it's getting colder out, I was wondering if you wouldn't mind house-sitting for me."

Xena's little cherubic face lights up, but Theresa is understandably skeptical, studying me with her head tilted.

"Why would you offer that? I could be a criminal."

I give her a reassuring smile, trying to ease her concerns. "I don't think you are. Seems to me you're someone trying to do right by your daughter. Plus, in my experience, crime pays, so if you were involved in anything shady, you wouldn't be here."

She takes another sip of her drink, which she's also using to warm her bare hands. "My husband, Xena's father, is not a nice man. I knew if we didn't get out, we never would, but I'm afraid he'll look in the shelters for us, so we just keep moving from place to place."

While Theresa speaks, Xena stares up at her with such adoration in her eyes. This young girl, who can't be more than seven, doesn't seem to hold a hint of resentment for their situation. It's obvious she's had to grow up faster than she should have.

"I'm sorry, Theresa. If you don't mind me asking, do you have any work experience you can fall back on if you get settled somewhere?"

She releases a short laugh. "Believe it or not, I was a hairdresser. I'd love to get back into it, but people don't want you doing their hair when you look like... this." She gestures to her ratty clothes and tangled black hair tucked under a knitted cap.

"Well, I think it's time things turned around for you. What do you say? I can take you to look at the house first, if you'd like."

Unsurprisingly, she doesn't reply right away. "I'm still confused *why* you would offer. It... doesn't make sense. You don't know me. Why us?"

"No, I don't, and you don't know me either, so I get why you're hesitant. If I'm being honest, I'm afraid karma is keeping a tally, and I'm in the red."

Theresa asks what that means, so I give her surface-level details without compromising my case. She asks a lot about the logistics, like if I'm expecting her to pay rent, where I'll live in the meantime, how long they can stay, basic ground rules, and so on. I even warn her about Bruce's habits and insist I'll buy some blinds. They've been through enough.

We continue to speak until my backside is frozen and I can no longer sit on the concrete.

"I'll come back tomorrow to see what you've decided. If you decide no, I'll take that with no hard feelings, but I do hope you'll give it a chance."

"Archie," Theresa asks, rising to stand. "I don't want to be some charity case used to win back a woman you've wronged."

I glance up at the graying sky, feeling even more guilty she felt that was my reasoning. "I'm not using you as a ploy, Theresa. She'll never know about this. She… uh… doesn't even know I own a house." That makes me realize just how big some of the lies and omissions between me and Georgia really are. She knows me better than anyone ever has outside of my own family, yet she doesn't know me at all.

Theresa nods. "I'll think about it."

With a final round of goodbyes, I take my leave and head back to my house to spend the evening installing blinds and packing up any valuables. I might be feeling generous, but I'm not reckless. Though, what I value most isn't *in* my home. She *is* home, and it's me who is homeless.

DO NOT CROSS

● JUST KIDDING ● KEEP GOING, YOU REBEL ●

I couldn't sleep last night. Anticipation over the case. Over Theresa. Mostly over Georgia. I don't know if I can ever make things right again. This is such a mess.

The blinds in my window are a nice addition to block Bruce's naked parades, but it limits the light in the living room. I walk to the large, uncovered window to look out as the sun rises and discover we got several inches of snow overnight. My immediate thought is the inconvenience of having to brush the snow off of my car before heading to headquarters. That is quickly squashed by the realization Theresa and Xena spent the night in a tent with a worn-out sleeping bag.

Rather than taking my time to get ready and prepare for my day, I rush to get dressed, clear the snow off of my Jeep, then head into the heart of the city. I stop at a coffee shop on my way to grab some hot drinks and arrive where I left Theresa and Xena yesterday.

I approach their small tent in the corner of the park. "Theresa? It's Archie. Are you guys okay?"

No response. For a brief second, I hope they were able to get into a shelter last night, but that hope is dashed when I hear rustling from inside and see shadows moving inside the snow-covered tent.

"Theresa?"

"We're here, Archie." She unzips a small section of the door and peeks through the opening. Her bare hands are glowing red. "I don't want to let out what little heat we have."

"Here." I pass her the tray of warm drinks, a few packages of disposable hand warmers, and a pair of gloves I had in my car. "Is Xena okay?"

"She's managing. This was our first snowfall, and it was a lot worse than either of us expected."

I don't want to guilt or pressure her into accepting my offer, but I am worried about them both. "It's going to get a lot worse." It's an unnecessary statement. Anyone who has lived in Chicago through one winter knows what to expect.

"Yeah, I know." She unzips the doorway enough to step out and closes it behind her. "But I thought about your offer."

I breathe out a sigh that clouds the surrounding air with a fog. "And?"

"We've been through a lot, Archie. You seem like a nice guy and I appreciate this, but I'm nervous about counting on someone else. Especially someone who, until yesterday, I didn't know."

"I get that. Really, I do. If someone came up to me and said they had an answer to one of my problems with no strings attached, I'd be skeptical too. At least let me take you back to the house and you can stay there for the day. If you decide by the time I'm done work that you don't want to accept my offer, so be it. But at least you'll be warm."

Xena's head pops out of the tent door. "Yes. Please." Her wide eyes plead with her mother, and that's all Theresa needs to concede.

I drive them the twenty minutes back home just as the sun fully rises. We park in the driveway of my modest house and I warn them not to look to their right as we climb out of the Jeep and go inside.

"Archie, this is beautiful!" Theresa exclaims as she enters the kitchen.

"It's simple, but you should have everything you need. Make yourselves at home. There's food in the fridge, blankets and towels in the closet, and I'm sure Xena can figure out the TV. My number is beside the phone if you need to get a hold of me."

Theresa's hesitant expression is offset by Xena's excited one.

Before she can second-guess my intentions any more, I utter a final farewell, and walk out the door, careful to shield my eyes.

I may have lost my feeling of home, but I hope I can give it to someone else.

Georgia

36

HARD TIME

"**Y**ou always were one to jump into things with your heart instead of your head, Georgie. This could be a good lesson for you," my mother says while lifting a cat off of the kitchen counter, but I'm so hopped up on antihistamines, I could be hallucinating.

In the heat of the moment, after leaving the FBI headquarters six days ago, I wanted to get out of the city. More importantly, I wanted to get out of my building because I couldn't face Archie if he came back. I'm not opposed to locking myself inside my condo, but too much reminded me of him.

"Lesson learned, Mom. Thanks."

"I'm not trying to be harsh, but you always did live in La-La-Land. Something like this was bound to happen."

It took me five days of moping in a motel room before I confessed what happened with Archie to my mom. For the past twenty-four hours, she's been taking every opportunity to tell me it's my fault. The comfort I was seeking when I begged Rene to drive me home is nowhere to be found. I'm still Georgia the letdown. Not only that, but I've only seen Leah for a total of twenty minutes in the past six days. Casey allegedly had plans to go stay with her parents in Jonestown, so she and Leah left the day after I arrived.

My phone dings on the table beside me. If I wasn't in the midst of an uncomfortable—unwanted—conversation with my mother, I'd ignore it, but I need an excuse to cut this short. Though, to my surprise, it's not a text message or an email. It's an alert for *Smith Goldstein & Co.* They've posted their latest round of press releases for my exhibit announcement amongst a few others scheduled for December.

"Don't tell me it's him making your face look like that."

I lift my eyes to look at my mother, who is standing a few feet away with one hand on her hip. "No. It's the announcement for my exhibit at a prestigious art gallery in two weeks."

"Oh." That's all she says. Not a word of congratulations. Nothing to hint that she's proud of me. No excitement what-soever.

It shouldn't surprise me. She's always seen me as the kid with her head in the clouds. The one with big dreams and unrealistic expectations. This is why I thought my full name was 'Oh, that Georgie,' until I was about eight years old. I've never met her expectations and slinking home after an epic failure of my love life hasn't helped her perception of me.

"I'm going to head back *home* today." Without waiting for a response or any questions about the sudden decision, I stand from my chair and walk over to give my mom a hug. "Thanks for giving me the push I needed."

She looks confused as I pull away and walk to the door. Her dismissiveness reminded me that I've got work to do, and I'm doing this for myself. Not for anyone else's approval. If I'm not enough for the people in my life as I am, so be it. If other people don't get my passion or appreciate me for who I am, then that's not my problem.

 DO NOT CROSS 

Four hours later, I'm walking into my building, towing my suitcase and some groceries I picked up, keeping my eyes to the floor. I don't know what Archie's living arrangements are after the fact, but I'm terrified of running into him. Not because I'm scared, but because I don't trust myself to stay mad at him. And I am. Furious, in fact.

I take a deep breath as the elevator passes the fourth floor, trying to strengthen my resolve. When the doors open, I step out into the hallway, and my heart is momentarily stalled.

There lies a pile of belongings outside of an open door. Recognizable things. Namely, Christofern and Vincent van Grow. Archie's beloved houseplants that he cared for like they were set to inherit his estate and have authority over his care home location someday.

The building superintendent steps out of the apartment with another armful of items and tosses it on top of an open box.

"What are you doing with this stuff?" I ask.

"Donate what I can, but I'll probably just toss most of it in the dumpster." Without waiting for a response, he walks back into the apartment.

My head says don't do it. Don't pick up the plants. Don't touch the red hockey jersey. Definitely don't touch the gray CFD T-shirt I vividly recall clutching onto while Archie kissed me senseless. That senselessness must remain, even after all this time, because I pick up the two articles of clothing and both potted plants. Much like Archie did upon his arrival, I struggle to carry the plants, suitcase, and groceries. The difference is, he's not here to offer me help, and I don't think he ever intended to.

These plants look a little worse for the wear, and given how much Archie babied them, I bet they'd stick him in a bottom-tier care facility that serves microwave TV dinners and has no hot water for abandoning them. I can't say I disagree with that decision.

I scroll through internet articles about care for zebra plants and Boston ferns, trying to determine the best course of action for them. They don't deserve to wither away and die just because my relationship with Archie did.

It's stupid, but it gives me a small piece of him to hang on to, because I'm not quite ready to let go. I guess that's also why I'm now wearing his T-shirt.

Instead of pushing him out of my head, he's back, fully consuming me. I putter around, watering both plants a bit at a time, watching them like they're going to spring back to life the second their soil is hydrated. They're much like my own broken heart, though. There's still a little life left, but it won't be a quick process to recover.

"We'll get there together, Christofern. Vincent, you've got to be the strong one. Show us the way." Since the zebra plant is holding up a little better, we'll have to look for him to take the lead.

Unsurprisingly, they don't have any solutions. I think they probably hold some love for him too, even though he abandoned them. It's the time he spent caring for them that sticks with them the most. At least, that's the impression I get from Christofern. Vincent is a little more mysterious.

Archie told me it was scientifically proven that plants thrive when they're spoken to. While my friends are great listeners, they have a habit of trying to offer solutions, when what I want is just to unload how I'm feeling and get it off my chest. Normally I turn to art for that, but my inspiration has been lacking, and Sandra doesn't want any more depressing work.

So I pull out the rest of my vodka, pour myself a healthy glass that would be more suitable for juice than alcohol, and spill my guts to my wordless companions.

"I hate him, Christofern. You probably do too because he left you there, helpless, without a second thought. Well, that's not true. He really cared about you guys, so I bet he thinks about you. I wonder if he thinks about me too."

The vodka is taking effect already. Likely on account of my empty stomach because I haven't had an appetite for the last week. To help it along, I take another swig. Sadly—perhaps unsurprisingly—it doesn't fill the hole in my heart.

"Now, looking back, his actions and reactions make so much sense. His weird lines of questioning and the changes in his mood. That's why he was awkward every time he started talking about the CFD. I knew he was hiding something, and I fell for him, anyway. What a fool, huh? That's what I get for ignoring my instincts."

Neither plant looks like they're even listening at this point, so I'm not sure if my talking is helping or making them wish they had been left to their demise. It isn't helping me.

"Why do I love him? I hate him and love him at the same time. How is that possible?"

It's safe to say the vodka has well and truly broken through the blood-brain barrier, but it's not doing its job. Maybe it's confused because last time I got stupid drunk, Archie came in the next day, then he apologized and we picked up where we left off. Or maybe I'm not drunk enough.

That's probably it.

"Vincent, I don't want to love him." I take another gulp of the alcohol, allowing it to burn my throat. "How do I make it stop?" I climb into my bed, pulling the covers over me with my glass still in my left hand. "He never cared about me. I wasn't enough for him, either."

Archie

37

Give The Slip

Our forensic accountants struck gold with their search into Tom Conti's financials and his former security staff. Enough so, we were able to secure a warrant for their arrests, and have six people in custody. We still don't know the artists who were creating the forgeries, but after her hours of interrogation, Lancaster is confident Georgia was not one of them. I didn't need hours of interrogation to prove that.

From what we've gathered so far, Conti originally approached his appraiser, Guillaume, because he wanted to sell a few paintings. He was on the verge of bankruptcy and at risk of losing his eight-million-dollar home.

Guillaume was the puppeteer and has operations running in New York, Los Angeles, and London. He's what you call "a big fish." The conniving Frenchman convinced Conti to fund the operation by selling one of his less expensive pieces. That allowed them to pay for new identities and equipment they needed and gave his former employees incentive to go along with the plan.

With a team on board with security knowledge, they positioned themselves in new security gigs at different locations. Conti cased the places, pretending to be interested in buying pieces from galleries or donating to museums. Guillaume used his contacts to learn about which pieces gave them the best chances at a payday, and the rest of them put their skills to use, making it appear as if they were never there.

Apparently, their paydays weren't as much as they were expecting and they got greedy, so they "stole" Conti's paintings to collect the insurance money. He needed to infuse some legitimate cash into his business, and that was the quickest way to do it.

As one would expect with criminals, there's no loyalty. They roll on each other faster than a ground ball up center field at Wrigley.

The only thing missing is the artwork. When our team raided Conti's shipping containers in a New York port, they only recovered four—and two were paintings we didn't know they had stolen.

I know it won't mean much, but I want to find them for Georgia. To preserve the art that she loves and protect that bit of history she's convinced holds the power to change people. It's the least I can do, even if I'll never tell her about that either.

"We did it." Sanders walks up next to me behind the two-way mirror, places his arm around my shoulders, and squeezes the breath out of me.

"Almost," I cough out, trying to hint at him to relax.

Mercifully, he does. "What's left? You want to find the artists?"

"No. I want to find the art."

My friend and new roommate seems to understand what I'm getting at. "Why don't you go talk to her?"

I scoff. "Would you forgive me?"

"If I loved you as much as you love her, probably. Once I understood how it all went down." He drops his arm, then spins around to lean on the glass overlooking the empty interrogation room. "You didn't set out trying to deceive her. Talk to her and she'll understand."

I smile at the big oaf who has been letting me crash on his couch for over a week. "How 'bout we find that missing art first, hmm?"

"Give Conti's sweaty hide one day in jail and he'll be dishing his deepest secrets. We'll find it." He pushes off from the window and walks to the door, stopping a few feet shy. "But we've had a long day. Drinks are on me."

DO NOT CROSS

● JUST KIDDING ● KEEP GOING, YOU REBEL ●

Just as Sanders predicted, three days later, Conti gave up every last piece of art his crew was part of. As a bonus, to earn himself some favor and a cushy white-collar prison sentence, he even gave us a few names to look into in the three other cities Guillaume operated in. That's beyond our scope, though. As far as we're concerned, the Chicago case is closed.

Tactical teams raided the warehouses where Conti had the artwork stored in a synchronized bust yesterday. Now everything is secured in an FBI evidence locker until it can be processed, logged, then returned to its rightful owners.

Sanders and I have the privilege of touring the city to inform the galleries and museums that their art has been recovered and give them an estimated timeline for its return. The only decent thing Conti has done is confess to everything, so it will spare the taxpayers a long legal battle and ensure the return of the art a lot sooner.

We've been to five stops already, and now we're pulling into the parking garage for *Smith Goldstein & Co.* Knowing that Georgia is supposed to have an exhibit here is making me nervous about going inside. She could be here. Or at the very least, her art might be.

My partner and I walk into the gallery, and I scan the room for anything that screams Georgia. I can't see any of her art, but my eyes stop their survey of the space once they land on a copy of the press release announcing her exhibit one week from today. I read the official announcement twice before I'm interrupted by a clearing throat.

Sanders pulls my attention just as a familiar woman approaches.

"Hello, gentleman. How can I help you?"

"G'day, Sephora. Is Mrs. Robbins in?" Sanders asks.

Sephora gives Sanders a broad smile. "She's stepped out, but she should be back in about ten minutes. Can I interest you in a tour while you wait? I know last time you were here, you didn't get a chance to experience the artwork."

Her phrasing *experience the artwork* reminds me of Georgia. It's also an incentive to get a tour of the gallery to see if her work is already here.

"We'd love that. Thanks."

She tours us through the various displays, which are sectioned off into curated exhibits. There is a variety of different work, but none of it appeals to me more than something nice to look at. It doesn't evoke the same emotions as *The Captive Slave* or the few pieces of Georgia's art I've seen.

"What do you think? Anything stand out to you?" Sephora asks, wrapping up our brief tour.

I'm not sure how to answer without being rude. Thankfully, Sanders goes off on a tangent about a sculpture we saw in the far corner, so he occupies his time speaking to Sephora about it.

That leaves me to stare at Georgia's press release photo and read the information they've shared about her education, her talent, and her promising future. A future I likely have no place in.

"We're very excited to be hosting Miss Dewan next week," a voice says behind me.

I spin around to find Sandra Robbins removing her heavy winter coat. I feel like I've been caught red-handed, so I attempt to sidestep her comment. "Happy to hear your business hasn't been too heavily impacted by recent events. That's actually why we're here."

Sanders and Sephora walk over to join us, but neither of them speak.

"Oh, with good news, I hope." Sandra's face eases into a terse smile.

"Good news indeed. We've recovered your painting." Again, I look over at Georgia's photo, because I wish I could see her face when she finds out the artwork is all safe and being returned to where it belongs. That knowledge would make her smile, and for the hundredth time in the fourteen days since I've seen it, I realize how much I miss it. I miss seeing her in any way. Her ridiculous puns. Her goofy pajamas. Her non-stop rambling about sports and art.

"SA Prewitt?" Sanders' voice cuts my thoughts short.

I look at Sandra and Sephora's expectant faces, alight with excitement. "Right, sorry. We have a few pieces of paperwork for you to sign, if you don't mind."

"Absolutely. Come to my office." Mrs. Robbins waves at me to follow her.

Sanders stays in place to speak with Sephora, but doesn't neglect to give me a knowing look that tells me I need to keep my head on straight.

"Thank you for finding this piece, Agent Prewitt. You can't imagine the embarrassment over the situation. I spent three days on the phone with artists—who are very protective of their work—assuring them their art was safe. I had two clients cancel upcoming exhibits. It has been such a mess, so I thank you for your diligence." Sandra rounds her ornate stainless steel and glass desk, dropping into a chair that looks like it was designed for style, not comfort.

I want to tell her that it was really Georgia who set us on the right path that resulted in answers. She was the real hero in this. But I can't admit that and risk exposing her as someone involved in the case. If word got out she was seen as a suspect, it could have catastrophic effects on her career. So I accept the praise I don't deserve myself. "Just doing our job, ma'am."

Sandra signs the paperwork that she'll need to have the artwork returned once it's processed, and slides it across her spotless desktop toward me. "Thanks again, Agent Prewitt. If there's ever anything I can do to repay the favor, just say the word."

Under normal circumstances, I'd never consider accepting that offer. But my predicament with Georgia isn't normal circumstances. "Actually, there is something you can do for me."

 DO NOT CROSS 

● JUST KIDDING ● KEEP GOING, YOU REBEL ●

Sanders and I return to the office after our tour of the city's victimized galleries and find Lancaster smiling at my desk. It's concerning.

"You know, I didn't think you could do it, Prewitt. You've got real promise."

Again, I don't feel like that praise is mine to accept. At least with Lancaster, I can be honest. "It wasn't my doing, ma'am. Miss Dewan was the one who set us in the right direction."

"Don't be ridiculous. She was a suspect. If you hadn't played her the way you did, she wouldn't have given us anything."

My stomach turns at the truth in that phrase. I did play her, and it makes me sick.

"I'd say your days in an undercover capacity are over, though. You're being asked to hold a press conference tomorrow."

"A press conference?"

"Don't tell me you can take down a criminal enterprise, but you can't understand a simple sentence, Prewitt. Yes, a press conference." Lancaster stands from my chair, never breaking eye contact. "Tomorrow, 1p.m. in the media room. I expect you both to be there." With no further discussion, she walks away.

I guess tomorrow afternoon is when the rest of my life starts.

Georgia

38

STOLE HER HEART

"Turn on the news right now," Rene shouts into the phone the second I answer.

"Well, hello to you too. Which news? SportsCenter?" I ask, grabbing my remote, assuming she has some exciting news about number eighty-eight.

"Girl, the real news. Channel six."

I grumble but don't argue. "Give me a second."

All it takes is that second for me to realize why she's so adamant. There, on my small TV screen, is the man I gave my heart to.

"What is he…? Why is…?" I can't form a logical sentence. I have so many questions as I read the news ticker at the bottom of the screen. *FBI identifies people responsible for Chicago art thefts.* "They caught them?"

Rene doesn't reply. The woman who was speaking introduces Archie as the lead on the case and credits him with bringing down the criminals involved. My heart and stomach plummet as he steps up to the podium. He looks tired. Not like he's not sleeping, but his soul looks tired.

I wait with bated breath as he adjusts the microphone to his height and clears his throat.

"Thank you, SSA Lancaster, for your guidance and support on this case. I... uh... I'm actually not the person responsible for the resolution. Unfortunately, for that person's safety, I can't share their name, but I can say their knowledge of the art industry and passion for protecting Chicago's reputation as one of the premiere art destinations in the world proved invaluable. I wouldn't have been able to solve this case without them, and these thieves would have continued to torment art collectors and galleries city wide."

"I think he just gave you credit for the bust," Rene whispers.

"Shh."

"The investigation proved even more lucrative than we initially thought, with art thefts occurring across the United States and into Europe. In a joint task force with Scotland Yard, we have been able to return forty-seven works of art to their rightful owners. Unfortunately, six pieces are unaccounted for, but everything that was stolen in Chicago has been recovered."

"Did you hear that, girl? Almost everything recovered because of your help," Rene whispers again.

"It would have been nice if they just asked me for help in the first place," I snap.

Rene sighs into the phone. "He couldn't have known, Georgia. Yeah, I'm mad at him for lying to you too, but it wasn't without his reasons. He doesn't seem like the type to lie just for the sake of being dishonest."

Before I can reply, the clamoring of the press conference dies down and Archie continues speaking.

"With this case closed, I'm resigning from my position with the FBI, effective immediately."

Reporters in the crowd begin shouting, and cameras flash in the background. The woman Archie referred to as SSA Lancaster steps up to him and whispers something in his ear.

He doesn't acknowledge her and continues his speech. "This case took me in a direction no investigation ever has before. That turned me into a person I didn't recognize and one I'm not proud of. I was so hungry to solve this case, I lost who I was as a person. I hurt someone I love, and I never want to be in that position again. As much as I've appreciated my time at the FBI, and have deep respect for my fellow agents, I can no longer serve in the capacity needed of me.

"I wanted to enact change because someone very close to me had his life changed by people whose punishment did not fit their crimes. But that person recently taught me that change doesn't mean ruin. Different doesn't mean bad. You can still get to your destination when you veer off course, or maybe you were never meant for that destination in the first place. So after today, I'm taking a different path." Then, without turning to speak to the shocked faces of his co-workers or the angry face of Lancaster, Archie exits the camera's view.

Silence. I'm sure there is some sound coming from my TV and my phone, but I can't process any of it. What does he mean that he turned into a person he didn't recognize? What does he mean he's taking a different path? Suddenly, I'm terrified that could mean he's leaving Chicago and I'll never see him again. So I guess my biggest question is why that even matters. He betrayed me. Lied. Manipulated.

"Did that man just admit on national television that he loves you?" Rene interrupts my panic.

"What?"

"He said he hurt someone he loves. Oh, my heart can't take it. He loves you. He done told the whole world he loves you, Boo. You need to go talk to your man."

The irony here is that Rene is usually the one out of the three of us who can hold a grudge the longest. I'm always the first to offer forgiveness and try to smooth things over. That's probably why my family dismisses me and disregards my feelings, because I don't make an issue of it. Now, with the roles reversed and Rene trying to encourage a resolution, it feels backwards.

"He's not my man. He never was. The one I knew doesn't exist. So even if he thinks he loves me, the man I love is only as real as a painting. He was something to look at that evoked deep emotions within me, but he's a forgery."

"Girl, you know I love you, and I wouldn't say this if I didn't think it was what you needed to hear. Every famous artist has had to live through a little tragedy before they have their triumph. You've suffered your tragedy. Don't miss out on the good part."

With that bit of expert advice thrown at me, Rene tells me she'll see me on Friday, and ends the call.

But now Friday isn't the number one thing on my mind.

Today marks the big break I've been waiting for since I graduated. I've never been so nervous. It's possible I'll show up and no one else will. Or worse, a huge crowd of people turns out and I still don't sell anything. Actually, I don't know which one is worse out of those two options.

I'm no stranger to having my work critiqued, because that's a huge part of art school, but something about putting it out into the public eye and opening myself up to judgment makes me feel more vulnerable than ever. More vulnerable than sitting on the wrong side of an FBI interrogation table, and I'm certain not a lot of artists can say that.

Ready or not, here I go.

I arrive at *Smith Goldstein & Co.* three hours before my exhibit is supposed to start. I was here for a few hours yesterday, working on finalizing pricing, and making last-minute lighting adjustments. Today, I'm giving myself extra time to calm my nerves. Though I may need a sedative.

"Georgia, darling. Are you ready for your big night?" Sandra asks when I enter.

"I'm not sure if ready is the right word, but I'm here."

"Oh, pish posh. Every artist says the same thing, but I'll tell you the same thing I tell them: No one has ever walked out of here with every piece they brought in. I've already had some interested buyers call to inquire about your work."

I freeze, tugging off my jacket. "How is that possible?" From the press release? Or my friends? It's not like I have a huge fan base.

"Word has gotten around about your remarkable talent." She sends me a brief smile before she spins toward her office. "I've got some work to finish, but Sephora is buzzing about if you have any other questions. Take a breath, Georgia. This is your night."

I'm at a loss for words as I stare at Sandra's retreating back. Maybe things will work out and my tragedy will be worth it.

DO NOT CROSS

● JUST KIDDING ● KEEP GOING, YOU REBEL ●

I sold out. Every piece I created has a sold label on the nameplate. The first one to sell was the drawing of the couple crying in the cemetery, titled *Longing*, and once that one sold, the rest quickly followed. There was a crowd surrounding my work the entire night. I nearly broke down in tears when I watched their faces transform as they moved from one piece to the next. As if everyone was reflecting the emotions I captured.

Amazement, when they looked at the child and the police officer.

Adoration, looking at Nate express his love for Janine, only using his eyes.

Loyalty, studying the soaring eagles performing their intimate mid-air dance.

Betrayal, scrutinizing Archie's face from the day before things ended between us. That one in particular was the most difficult, because when I look at it, I don't *see* betrayal, but I know it's there.

Big feelings in small moments. Ones that can easily be invisible to the human eye when we aren't looking for them, but they paint a bigger picture than words alone ever can. I'm humbled that people walked in here and recognized that in what I created.

The crowd has dwindled, leaving me, Sandra, and Sephora.

Sandra walks toward me after locking the front door. "Congratulations!"

"Thank you. This wouldn't have been possible without you. Thank you seems so inadequate. I'm still at a loss for words."

"It was our pleasure. I hope you're already planning your next exhibit, because we'd love to have you back again."

"Wow. I'm flattered. Of course, I'd love to."

"That's assuming you don't end up with commissions piling up when everyone hears about how amazing you are. One of your purchasers was a very influential art collector. He was very impressed by your oeuvre." Sandra winks at me, and it's the most relaxed I've ever seen her.

I can't say the same for myself. "Influential art collector? Is that who made purchases over the phone?"

Sandra's relaxation all disappears. Her shoulders tense and her eyes widen. "Uh, no." She draws out that last syllable. "That was a new client who... saw your press release and wanted to grab some of your art before you became so well known, he couldn't afford it."

Sephora is standing across the room, smiling with her lips pinched together. I get the impression they're both keeping something from me.

It couldn't be him, could it?

"Which ones did this mystery person buy?" I ask.

Sephora reaches behind her to grab a file folder with my name written in bold letters across it. "*Betrayal, Loyalty, Perseverance,* and *Adoration.*"

I blink at her, struggling to form words. That's not a coincidence. Three of those four works are related to Archie in some way and were all purchased by some mystery person. I don't need to be an FBI agent to connect the dots of this case. But instead of feeling proud of selling out my first exhibit, now it feels pathetic. Like he's trying to pay me off, so I won't hate him anymore.

I wish I could hate him. Only hate him. But even seeing him on the TV caused my heart to react the same way it did when I'd see him leaning in his doorway, or when he'd kiss me until I forgot the rest of the world existed. As hard as I try, I still love him.

Few things are as tragic as unrequited love. But maybe Rene is right. This is my tragedy.

Now, all I can do is wait for my triumph.

Archie

39

A BRIEF CASE

Sandra Robbins called this morning to inform me my purchase has been packaged and is ready for pickup. I'm filled with conflicting emotions over it. While I'm happy to have Georgia's work in my possession, knowing she titled a drawing of me *Betrayal* hurts. A title I earned, but that doesn't mean I like it.

I leave Sanders' house well after he's left for work, and drive to the gallery. The closer I get, the sweatier my palms are, and I'm not sure why. I turn down the heat in my old car, hoping that will help, but I seem to have the same affliction as Bruce at the moment.

My heart starts pounding as I pull into the parking garage behind the gallery. Maybe on account of the huge chunk of my savings I dropped on these pieces of art? I'm not sure what the reason is, but I don't like it, either.

I swipe my palms on my jeans as I walk around the front of the building, and the second I enter, my pounding heart makes sense.

She's here. Looking every bit the stunning angel she always has. Her hair is tied back, which I haven't seen before, even when she was painting. It exposes her delicate neck that I miss kissing, and her angry eyes that I so deserve.

"I knew it was you." Georgia glares at me from fifteen feet away. She looks as conflicted as I feel. "If you think this makes things right, that you can just pay me off, you're wrong."

Clearly, we're skipping right over any casual greetings or pleasantries.

I'm not really sure what to say. "Peaches."

"Are you that self-absorbed, you want a portrait of yourself?" she asks, stepping closer.

Now I know the right answer. The truth. "No. I bought it because I wanted a reminder of when I was happy."

She stops short of reaching me and takes a deep swallow.

"And I wanted to rename it."

She scoffs. "You can't rename an artist's work."

"What were you going to name it? Before everything."

"Before I found out what a massive liar you are? Before I realized you never cared about me and played me for a fool? You mean then?" Her eyes glass over, and I can only hope she doesn't shed another tear over me. "It took every ounce of self-preservation I have not to light them on fire. But a fire inspector I once knew taught me that would be a hazard."

Now I gulp down the lump in my throat and step forward, hoping she won't retreat. "Do you want to know what I'd title it?" I ask, hoping she'll let me finish. I remember her telling me the first time I saw her art in her apartment, that she titles work after the dominant emotion she experiences. This time, I'm hoping she'll let me name it after mine. "Love. I'd call it love."

Now tears trickle down her cheeks. "You can't say that."

"It's true, Peaches." I know she asked me not to call her that, but she didn't correct me last time, so I'm hoping she'll let it slide again. "I'm so in love with you," I choke out, trying to keep control of my emotions. But it's hard with her so close, yet so far.

She shakes her head and covers her face with her hands. "You broke me, Archie. You've made me not able to trust myself anymore. I don't trust other people. I question every person's intentions when they so much as look at me. What you did, it's changed me in a fundamental way I can't change back."

I step forward to wrap her in my arms. I know it's a risk and there's a great possibility I'll witness some of her alleged jiu-jitsu moves, but I take the chance, anyway. She doesn't push me away. Instead, she collapses against me.

"That day you left to go out with Rene, when I said I had something to tell you, I was going to confess everything. Who I was and why we met. How I felt. All of it. I wanted to be honest with you so long before that, but it was more than just my job on the line. People were being hurt, and I was supposed to stop the criminals responsible. Please understand that I never set out to hurt you, Peaches. I never set out to fall in love with you either, but I did. And I may not deserve you loving me back, but I'll do anything to earn your trust again."

She sniffles against my chest and that sound alone crushes me. "I don't know if I can trust you again, Archie. Or myself. I knew something was off, but I gave you my heart, anyway. How am I supposed to recover from that? I understand you were doing your job, but that doesn't make it hurt less."

"I'm so sorry, Peaches. Truly. I quit my job, so I have nothing to offer you. I'm an ex-federal agent with a mortgage and a collection of house plants. Hardly a glowing resume. But my heart is yours."

She lifts her eyes to meet mine and staring into those baby blues feels more like coming home than walking through my front door ever has. "I have Christofern and Vincent van Grow. They're very needy, FYI. And I think they're a little upset with you too."

Before I can ask how she ended up with my plants, she stands upright and pulls herself away.

"What do you mean, you have a mortgage?"

This is one of the many truths I have to share with her. "I own a house in Oak Park, but I'm not living there."

"Why not? Where are you living?"

I sigh because I don't want to explain who is living in my house. I promised Theresa I wouldn't use her situation as a ploy to win Georgia back, and I meant it. "Currently, I'm staying on Sanders' couch in his one-bedroom apartment that makes your condo seem spacious."

She narrows her eyes at me, seemingly unbothered by the other people in the gallery who are studying us as they pass by. "Why aren't you living in your house?"

"Because someone else is renting it right now. Didn't make sense to leave it empty." I know that's a half-truth, which is the opposite of what she needs from me right now. But I'm caught in a catch twenty-two scenario.

"Show me." Georgia places one hand on her hip, all signs of upset long gone.

My heart picks up its pace. "Show you… the house?"

"Yes."

"Peaches, someone else is living there. I can't—"

"You said you'd do anything to gain my trust back. I want to see your house. Just the outside."

That's an unexpected demand, and I'm not sure how it helps regain her trust. I try to come up with an alternative and pull out my phone. "I can show you some pictures."

"Archie, it's a simple ask. I've met your brother and sister-in-law, who went along with your lie. The home you welcomed me into wasn't yours at all. You lied about your job and I don't know what else. You could show me any photos and I wouldn't know the difference. A house is something that doesn't lie." Her determination that this is an important step is hard to ignore.

Especially when I'm desperate to regain her trust.

"Okay. Let me grab my purchases and we can do a drive-by." I swallow down the lump in my throat, yet again. I can give Georgia the glimpse into my life she's looking for without compromising Theresa's privacy.

"You can't pay for these, Archie," Georgia replies. "I can't take your money."

I step forward, closing the gap she created moments ago. "It's not up for debate, Peaches. I'm not buying them to bribe you. I'm buying them because I love them and someday, when I'm back living in my own house, I want them on the walls."

"I don't want your money," she whispers.

"Well, I already signed the sales contract." I turn to Sephora, who has appeared with my bundle of four canvases. "Do you need any help here? Or do you want me to come back later?" I ask Georgia.

She glances at Sephora, who gives a nod. "No, you're the last one to pick anything up. I was just here to get my check."

"Okay." I hoist my new artwork carefully after a thank you to Sephora for her help.

Georgia shrugs on her coat, then walks to the door to hold it open for me.

Of all the times she followed me without asking questions, I owe her the same courtesy. If seeing the outside of my house will help earn her trust back, I'll risk the sight of Bruce's pasty cheeks to make that happen.

Georgia

40

federal man date

"This is your car?" I ask as Archie approaches an old cherry red Mustang.

"Well, I didn't leave my job at the FBI to pursue a career in car theft, if that's what you're asking. Can you grab the keys? They're in my pocket." His arms are full, but reaching into his pocket is a level of intimacy I wasn't prepared for.

Granted, I wasn't prepared for him to walk into the gallery in the ten-minute window I was there, either. If Sephora hadn't held me up taking her time to get my check, I would have missed him. Maybe it was intentional on her part. I could be mad, but I'm not.

Truth be told, I'm happy to see him again. Not on the TV, but in person. Close enough, I can smell his body wash as I reach into his pocket to pull out his keys.

He sucks in a breath when I tug them from his jeans. "Peaches."

It's a good thing he's holding a bundle of artwork in front of him, or a combination of his earlier declaration and his presence would be enough for me to kiss him. But all is not forgiven. I'm not sure what seeing his house actually accomplishes, but part of me just wants to know that is true. That he shared a real part of his life with me. Something more tangible than photos or documents with a fake address.

I turn away from him to open the trunk of his car, then he slides the artwork inside.

Once his hands are free, he steps closer and takes my hand. "I hope you know how sorry I am, and how much I mean what I said. I love you."

The words want to spill out, but I've made enough concessions already. I may have asked him to show me his house, but during our last interaction, I swore I'd never get in a car with him again. One thing at a time.

"I haven't been to Oak Park since I did a gallery tour there a couple years ago."

Archie blows out a breath and drops my hand. "Okay, let's go." He walks to the passenger door, unlocks it, and opens it for me. "Your chariot awaits."

I climb in and wait for him to get in the driver's seat, then we sit in silence as he navigates his way out of the parking garage and onto Michigan Avenue. I can't help but watch him from the corner of my eye as he shifts gears and weaves through the downtown streets. He looks nervous, and this time, I'm not going to ignore my instincts.

"What's wrong? Why do you look like you'd rather be doing anything else right now?"

He glances at me before he returns his eyes to the road. "No, I'm… It's surreal, having you beside me right now. I just don't want to surprise my tenants by showing up unannounced. That's all. Honest."

I can't decide if that's a partial truth or he's just distracted by driving. "You said you'd do anything to regain my trust,

Archie. I'm not asking you to take me inside and give me a tour. I just want to know that it's true."

"It is true, and I'll show you. No more secrets, Peaches. Ask me anything, and I'll tell you."

One thing in particular has been on my mind the last few weeks. "Did Nate and Janine know what you suspected me of?" I ask, my throat going dry. I may have only met them once, but for some reason, their opinion of me matters.

"They knew you were a suspect, yes, but not what for. And if it's any consolation, Nate knew from day one that you weren't guilty of anything. It was my stupid obsession with my job that stopped me from seeing it too." Judging by the guilt on his face, that's true.

"When did you decide I was innocent? During the interrogation or before that?"

"Before. When we went to *Navy Pier*. That night, I was convinced you had nothing to do with it." He flicks his signal to merge onto the Kansas City Expressway, looking over his left shoulder.

Once he's looking straight again, I ask, "Why didn't you come clean then?"

"It's not that simple." He checks his blind spot again so he can speed past a slower minivan in the right lane. "I regret how I handled everything, and most of all, I regret that I hurt you," he says with a strained voice, "but at the time, I was torn between my feelings for you and the oath I took to protect our country."

That statement makes goosebumps erupt down my arms. I finally understand the immensity of the conflict he was feeling. "I'm sorry, Archie."

He reaches over to place his hand over mine, now that he doesn't need to shift gears as we coast along the expressway. "You have nothing to be sorry for. I just hope I can make it up to you."

We travel the next few minutes in silence, with Archie holding my hand and me not resisting. He requires his hand back to downshift when we exit the highway and continue west on Garfield Street.

"Why Oak Park?"

He flashes me a soft smile as he turns onto another street. "It was far enough from work to have a little separation."

That makes sense. If it was my job to infiltrate criminal organizations, I wouldn't want to live anywhere near them, either.

"How long have your tenants lived here?"

"Uh, just a few weeks."

That *doesn't* make sense. That was around the time he left the condo.

I don't get to ask him before we pull up along the curb about halfway down the block. I look to my right, but Archie draws my attention the other way.

"This one. That's home. Or, at least, the one I own. Minus what I owe the bank." He points to a brick bungalow with a large oak tree in the front yard and a big picture window. It also has a ramp built onto the side of the house, which is another hint that he's telling the truth.

"It's cute. Has great curb appeal."

Archie turns to me and smiles wide, like that is the best compliment he's ever received. I almost get lost in his eyes, but I'm distracted by the appearance of a woman and child walking out the side door. They both have long dark hair, tucked inside knitted caps, and thick coats on.

"Are those your tenants?"

He spins around so fast, he releases his foot from the brake and the car lurches forward a few feet. Luckily, there's nothing in front of us, but it does draw the attention of the woman and child.

As soon as the little girl spots the car, she starts flailing her arms and shouting, "Hi, Archie!"

He yanks up the parking brake and exhales through his protruding bottom lip, blowing his breath upward. "I should go say hi. I'll be right back." He leaves me with a tight smile and a gust of cold air as he opens the door to step out.

I watch the interaction as the young girl and woman greet him with smiles and hugs. It's the friendliest landlord and tenant interaction I've ever seen. But as they stand there talking, I can't help but feel like this woman looks familiar. I can't place her, until I look at the little girl, who is looking up at Archie with the same look she had for a piece of white bread many months ago.

That's the woman and daughter from the alley. Why are they in Archie's house? I'm suffering from some sort of out-of-body experience as I open the door and cross the street without even looking for traffic. My eyes are locked on the little girl as I step over the small snowbank. The crunching snow pulls the trio's attention my way.

"Georgia," Archie stammers. "I'll be back in a second. Just making sure everything is okay here." He looks frazzled. Conflicted. Just like he has so many times before.

"This is Georgia?" the young girl asks.

I look down at her, surprised she's familiar with my name. "I am. What's your name?"

"Xena. Like the warrior princess."

"Nice to meet you, Xena." I give her a smile and look up at her mom, who is staring at me with a wide grin.

"Do you guys want to come in for a minute? You can check on your plants, Archie," the mom offers. "Oh, I'm sorry. I'm Theresa." She reaches out her hand to shake mine, which touches a piece of my heart every time.

"Nice to meet you too, Theresa." I look over at Archie, who looks very uncomfortable. "We didn't mean to interrupt. We were just driving by."

Archie's eyes bounce between me and Theresa. "Actually, if you have a minute, I'd like to show you something," he says to Theresa.

"Of course. Let's get inside before Bruce makes an appearance." She chuckles and heads for the door.

I look at Archie as if I'm asking for permission.

"Go ahead. I'll be right in." Then, like it's the most natural thing in the world, he leans down to kiss my temple, above my glasses.

The contact sends the same pulse of electricity through me that it did before he shattered my heart. But I realized today that mine isn't the only one that shattered.

He walks past me, grazing my hand, and grasping it for a split second before he lets go.

The feelings I contended with for the last three weeks are not at war anymore.

"Come inside, Georgia. I can show you my room." Xena grabs a hold of the hand Archie just released and pulls me to the door. She's so excited, it's hard not to absorb some of it.

We walk inside, and the space is spotless. There's a huge collection of plants spread in between the living room and dining area. The walls are bare, painted a plain white and there's not a single thing left out on the kitchen counters. It looks like a very tidy bachelor pad.

I remove my coat and step into the dining room right as Archie returns with a piece of my art. Specifically, *Perseverance.* It's still wrapped, but it was the only one that size I had at the exhibit, so it's not hard to tell.

He smiles at me as he walks over to set it on the table, then proceeds to peel off the protective layers. Xena and Theresa watch closely as he does. My favorite part is watching people's faces transform when they look at my art, so I keep my eyes on them.

Once the plastic and thin foam layers are removed, Theresa gasps. "You… you drew this? It looks like a photo."

"I told you she was amazing." Archie's eyes lock on mine when I look up. "So this is my house, but right now, it's Theresa and Xena's home. I didn't think you'd ever speak to me again, and honestly didn't think I deserved it, but I remembered the woman and child you drew and what they meant to you on that day."

Very few times have the subjects of my work come back into my life to see it. The Brown family, which didn't work out well, and I guess Archie. Now, Theresa and Xena.

"I used my resources to track them down and asked them to stay here until they can get back on their feet, however long that might be. You told me 'you're never truly down and out until you give up on yourself.' I'd like to think that applies to us too, because I'm not giving up on us, Georgia." He steps closer to me, stopping inches away. "Can we start over?"

I try to ignore the other two people in the room, who are unwillingly a part of this conversation, and just focus on Archie. The fact he gave his home to this little family who were without one speaks to his character. And given how nervous he was to bring me here, I know he didn't do it to win me over.

So I reach down to take hold of his hands. "I'd rather we just pick up where we left off."

Theresa releases a squeal behind me, but then tells Xena to follow her to her bedroom to give us some privacy. I listen to their retreating footsteps as Xena asks her mom questions, much like Savannah does. The whole time, I'm watching Archie, whose face is lit up in a bright smile. The kind of relaxed, genuine smile I'd draw if I was trying to capture pure happiness.

I tug him closer and lift my arms to wrap around the back of his neck. "But no more secrets. Ever, okay?"

Archie's lips press against mine with a new understanding between us. A new depth of emotions. Love.

The trust I lost won't be repaired overnight, but I believe he didn't set out to hurt me. That's a start.

He pulls me tight against him and caresses my lips with his. Our kiss doesn't get too heated, because we're still standing in the dining room that belongs to someone else at the moment.

When we break apart, he whispers, "No more secrets. I promise."

I smile up at him. "Actually, I have one I need to tell you. I love you too."

Georgia

Epilogue

GOT THE GUY

"What's this?" Archie asks as I drop a piece of paper in front of him.

"You promised me a date, and I didn't forget."

He picks up the single sheet and reads the details. "Beach volleyball tickets?"

"Time for you to see what all the fuss is about, Prewitt. Grab your shorts and a hat. It'll be more fun if you go topless." I wink at him and duck into the bathroom.

"I could say the same for you," he shouts as I close the door.

That makes me laugh. I walked right into that one. "The last thing I need is for another highlight of me to end up on SportsCenter, thank you. Get yourself ready. We leave in thirty."

It's a complicated dance, both getting ready in my tiny apartment, but we manage.

Archie let Theresa and Xena stay in his house for a few extra months, but they're finally moving into their own apartment in the same neighborhood next week. Archie has been staying with me for a few months, after he felt he had more than worn out his welcome on Sanders' sofa, so it will be weird when I have the place to myself again.

Twenty-eight minutes later, we're both ready. As requested, Archie is wearing shorts and a whole lot of sunscreen. I'm wearing my favorite denim cut-offs and a tank top, despite Archie's request we wear matching outfits.

We opt to take the subway to Oak Street Beach, and it feels so nostalgic, considering this is where we first met. I don't think either of us would have predicted we'd be here under these circumstances nine months later.

There's a small crowd gathering at the beach when we arrive, but we're here a little early. I wanted to make sure we got good seats to enjoy the action. It doesn't take long for us to walk past a few women who are well over six feet tall for Archie to give me a look that says *wow, you were right.* He watches in awe as these impressive athletes get themselves prepared for their matches. Finally, I drag him toward the bleachers that have been set up, and we get situated to the left of the net, three rows up from the sand.

"The water is calm today," Archie notes, looking out at Lake Michigan.

"Those are *micro-waves.* Get it?" I laugh at my own joke, which prompts Archie's too.

"That was *o-fish-ally* your worst one yet, Peaches."

I bump him with my shoulder, still laughing. "Rude. No need to be *salty.*"

He grumbles, but leans in to give me a quick kiss.

The first match is a perfect demonstration of what I was trying to explain to Archie all those months ago. He's enthralled by the rallying and intensity. Seeing how fast the athletes react and their well-practiced moves is amazing.

"I have to hand it to you; this is pretty cool." He smiles at me and, like every time he does, it makes my stomach flutter.

The Archie I first met was so conflicted and withdrawn, but I still saw glimmers of who he really is. Given the situation he was in and what he suspected me of, his behavior made sense, but now, getting to see him thrive as his true self makes me fall more in love with him every day.

He reaches over to squeeze my hand. "What's on your mind?"

I doubt my sunhat and sunglasses hide the blush that engulfs my cheeks like a burning flame. "It will be weird."

He raises an eyebrow, which peeks out the top of his own aviator glasses. "What will?"

"Not waking up with you every day."

His head drops to look down, but before he can speak, his phone rings. He pulls it from his pocket and turns the screen to show me. "It's Nate."

"Answer!" I demand.

"Hey, bro." He stops for a second to listen, then shouts, "What? Now?" Another pause. "Okay, we're on our way."

I'm bouncing in my seat by the time he hangs up, hoping what I think is happening is *actually* happening. "Is it time?"

"Yeah, J is at the hospital now. Come on. Baby's coming with or without us."

He doesn't need to tell me twice. I hop up and grab his hand, dragging him through the bleachers to the exit. I'm full of so much excitement, I could probably run home, but I'm wearing flip-flops, so we opt to take the subway. It's a short trip and a quick walk back to our building. We don't even stop to change; we just go straight to the parking garage to get in Archie's old Mustang.

DO NOT CROSS

● JUST KIDDING ● KEEP GOING, YOU REBEL ●

We arrive at the hospital a little over ninety minutes after Nate called. The woman at the nursing station says we can't go into the room while Janine is in active labor, but we can sit in the waiting room and she'll let them know we're here. Archie texts Nate to tell him as we walk down the hall to the waiting room.

Surprising us both, his sisters and parents are in the waiting room already. Penny and Elle jump up to hug us. I've only met them twice, but they're both really sweet. Archie's father, David, offers handshakes and his mom, Angelina, squeezes us together in a joint hug.

"Any news?" Archie asks once all the greetings are out of the way.

"Well, you know Janine is a tough cookie. She didn't want to labor in the hospital because they've spent so much time here over the years. By the time she got here, she was eight centimeters dilated. Shouldn't be too long now," Penny answers. "What's with the outfit, Arch?"

Total detour of the conversation, but we both still look ready for the beach. Thankfully, Archie had a clean T-shirt in his car, so he's not still topless. He explains where we were when Nate called, which seems to satisfy everyone.

We occupy the next thirty minutes with updates on what's happening in each other's lives. Archie mentions he's moving back into his house soon, which forms a pit in my stomach again. All of his family members are looking at me, though, so I try my best to keep my expression neutral.

Nate bursts in the room seconds after Archie's comments, averting everyone's eyes. "He's here. Oakley David Prewitt." His eyes are glowing with pride. So much so, my happy tears burst from their dams.

The entire family gathers around to ask questions and arrange amongst themselves to go see the new baby. Graciously, his family members insist Archie and I go first since we have a long drive back to the city. I feel a little out-of-place meeting their grandson before Angelina and David do, but they tell us they'll have plenty more time with baby Oakley in the future. It's a stark contrast from my family and the arrival of baby Leah—whom I have still only seen three times.

Nate leads us into the delivery room where Janine is holding Oakley on a propped up hospital bed. Archie quietly walks toward her, stopping at the far side of the bed. His smile is wide and unreserved. A facial expression I've seen a lot over the past few months, and it's always easy to read.

"Hey, Momma. How are you feeling?" He leans down to kiss Janine's cheek, then reaches his hand out to touch the cute cotton hat on Oakley's head.

"I'm fine. This little guy was in such a hurry, he didn't torment me for too long."

"Taking care of his mom already. Good man, Oakley."

Janine offers for Archie to hold him, so I sneak in and position myself on the opposite side of the bed. Once Archie is staring down at his new nephew, I lean down to give Janine a hug.

"Congratulations, J. He's beautiful."

We both stare at Archie as he does the same to Oakley, all while shifting from one foot to the other to rock him.

"Why Oakley?" he asks out of nowhere.

Janine and Nate exchange a look that tells me there's a funny story behind the name.

"Uh…" Nate holds onto the single syllable for several seconds. "We named him after where he was conceived."

"Oakley? When did you go to California?"

Nate pinches his lips together to suppress a smile. "Not California. Oak Park… Specifically, South Oak Park Avenue."

Now I understand what's so funny. Janine chuckles, but grimaces, which stops her laughter. Nate rushes forward to ask if she's okay. Archie is still processing Nate's comments.

"But I live on Oak Park Avenue…" Finally, recognition sparks in his eyes. "Oh. Oh! You guys! I let you stay in my house and you… You know what? I'm not even mad. I'm burning the mattress, but I'm not mad." He looks back down at his new nephew. "Welcome to the world, little Oakley."

Finally, it's my turn to hold the baby.

Archie places him in my arms and takes a step back. "Looks good on you, Peaches." He winks at me, and I swear my ovaries just about reach out to grab onto him as he walks the few feet to where Nate is situated.

I stare down at the new little bundle, taking stock of his dark eyes, tan skin, light downy hair covering his exposed skin, and the cutest button nose I've ever seen. The number of times I've tried to capture pure joy and love in an expression, I think this is the epitome of both. A perfect moment I can't wait to re-create.

Minutes later, I realize I've been so caught up in studying Oakley's features, I tuned out the ongoing conversation around me.

Nate is staring at Janine, speaking to Archie. "All the hours and weeks spent in this hospital, I've never felt happiness inside these walls before. But watching the woman I love give birth to our child, Arch, all of those old memories are eclipsed by that moment."

Archie lifts his eyes to look at me, but addresses his brother. "I'm happy for you, man. Really. He's beautiful."

"Promise me something," Nate requests, turning to face Archie. "Learn to let things go or they'll only bring you down. You can spend your life dwelling on everything that went wrong, or you can hold on to the moments when things went right. Only one way will make you happy."

Archie doesn't hesitate, still looking at me, he replies, "I promise. I know where my focus needs to be now."

Nate claps him on the back, his massive smile growing impossibly wider. "Good."

We stay in the room with the happy couple and their new gorgeous baby boy for about twenty more minutes before the nurses come in to transfer Janine and Oakley to the maternity ward. We congratulate them one last time and say our goodbyes with promises to come back within the next week to visit once they're settled at home.

Penny and Elle are missing when we return to the waiting room and update Angelina and David on the room switch. David takes the opportunity to ask Archie about his new job. The pride in his dad's eyes is obvious when Archie talks about his switch to private security consultant. He drones on about how the world is relying so much on technology, which, with the right skill-set, is easy to override, so his focus is on old-school methods in conjunction with technology to protect homes and businesses. He finally looks excited to talk about his work.

Angelina strikes up conversation with me to ask about what I'm working on and admits she tried out a paint night—without wine—with Janine, but discovered they're both terrible artists. She shows me pictures of their paintings and if that's how good Janine's karaoke skills are, I'd be afraid for my ears. We have a good laugh over what is supposed to be a city skyline, but looks more like a mutant frog. That in itself is a remarkable talent.

A nurse returns to let the Prewitts know they can go meet their grandson, so Archie and I say our goodbyes as they head out.

Instead of leaving, Archie pauses by the windows, staring out over the parking lot.

"Do you want to wait for your sisters before we head out? Your mom said they're in the gift shop."

He spins around to face me. His movements are rigid and slow. "Move in with me? I don't want to wake up without you."

All the air escapes my lungs. Archie has told me he loves me every day since he first uttered those words, but this confession feels like taking our relationship to another level.

"I'll turn the spare room into your studio. There are a few windows, so you'll still have good lighting. Bruce will provide plenty of inspiration. Whatever you need, we'll make it work. I just... you make me happy, Georgia, and I like to think that I have the same effect on you."

I nod. "You do."

He clasps both of my hands and pulls me against him, then wraps his arms around me. "One day soon, I'm going to ask you to marry me, but I don't want to go backwards. I love you, Peaches."

My heart skips a beat, leaving me with stalling lungs and a faulty cardiac rhythm. But I've never doubted that my heart beats for this man holding me upright. "Okay. Yeah. Let's do it."

He loosens his grip on me, only to place one hand on each of my cheeks, tilting my head to look at him. "Yeah?"

"I don't want to wake up without you, either. But you could have left a little mystery about proposing." I laugh to stem the happy tears from starting again.

"No more secrets, remember?"

Thank you, dear reader, for joining me on Archie and Georgia's journey. This story wouldn't exist without the encouragement of my dear friend and talented author, Elena. Initially, she encouraged me to write and submit a story for an open call for clean romance novels. If it were up to me, I never would have found the confidence to do something that bold, but her faith in me pushed me to give it a go. However, the publishing company ran into some issues and folded before the submission deadline. That worked out fine, though, because it gave me full creative control of the story. So, I'll forever be indebted to Elena for giving me that vote of confidence and allowing me to immerse myself in Georgia and Archie's world.

Also, thank you to Sarah, Rebecca, and Harriet for your feedback on this story. You all have helped me become a more confident writer and storyteller.

To my childhood friend, Kenny, thank you for showing me that no matter the obstacles in a person's way, they can overcome them all with love and determination. You're never truly down and out until you give up on yourself. Thank you for teaching me that.

Finally, while this book has no affiliation with The Art Institute of Chicago, I felt inclined to share a link to "Georgia's" favorite painting for anyone interested in viewing it for themselves. It is a stunning portrait, and though I'm not an art expert in the least, it spoke to my heart, which is why I chose it.

You can view it online here: https://www.artic.edu/artworks/193664/the-captive-slave-ira-aldridge.

Also By This Author

You Are Enough Series:

<u>We're All a Little Broken</u>: Book 1 (Zara's story)

<u>We're All a Little Overwhelmed</u>: Book 1.5 (Zara's extended epilogue)

<u>We're All a Little Guarded</u>: Book 2 (Chelsea's story)

<u>We're All a Little Tired</u>: Book 2.5 (Chelsea's extended epilogue)

<u>We're All a Little Scared</u>: Book 3 (Isla's story)

<u>We're All a Little Determined</u>: Short Story Collection (Available free on my website)

This women's fiction series focuses on various aspects of mental health and overcoming trauma. It addresses anxiety, depression, panic disorders, miscarriage, adoption, grief and loss, racism, discrimination, and more, but in a light hearted way that will also make you laugh. The entire series is set in Muskoka/Bracebridge, Ontario.

<u>Dear Sister, Never Again</u>: Available free on my website as an eBook, or through Amazon as a paperback. This women's fiction novella explores the concept that DNA is not the only factor to determine family.

Suburban Watchdogs: This silly PG-13 crime comedy features four dads, three idiotic criminals, one slobbery dog, a determined cop, and a nosey nonagenarian neighbour. It's full of vigilante nonsense, terrible dad jokes, and a pursuit for justice.

Set in a small town north of the big city, these dads are not going to let criminals waltz into their neighbourhood without resistance.

A New Leash on Life Series:
This series will consist of twenty interconnected standalone romance novels.
Total Bull (Angel and Damian)
Ay Chihuahua (Dina and Holden)
Tell-Tail Sign (Sophie and Boyd)
The Pugly Truth (Hannah and Caleb) Coming 2023
Pitty Party (Oscar and Frankie) Coming 2023
Chemistry Lab (Hollis and Myer) Coming 2023

Trip and Fall: This standalone road trip romance follows two twenty-somethings who each have a different reason for wanting to leave town and explore the countryside. One out of a sense of wonder; the other, a sense of desperation. Will they find more than the adventure they were looking for? Coming 2023

Sign up for my newsletter, access my website, or follow me on social media to keep up to date with new releases and sneak peeks.
Linktr.ee/TiffanyAndrea

www.ingramcontent.com/pod-product-compliance
Lightning Source LLC
Chambersburg PA
CBHW060908210726
48293CB00006B/2015